DEATH AT THE THREE SISTERS

JO ALLEN

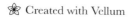

AUTHOR'S NOTE

All of the characters in this book are figments of my imagination and bear no resemblance to anyone alive or dead.

The same can't be said for the locations. Many are real but others are not. As always, I've taken several liberties with geography, mainly because I have a superstitious dread of setting a murder in a real building without the express permission of the homeowner, but also because I didn't want to accidentally refer to a real character in a real place or property. So, for example, although you might take a reasonable guess at where the Three Sisters, the Ullswater Falls and the Walsh sisters' cottage *might* be, you won't be able to place them exactly on the map.

Although I've taken these liberties with the details I've tried to remain true to the overwhelming and inspiring beauty of the Cumbrian landscape. I hope the many fans of the Lake District will understand, and can find it in their hearts to forgive me for these deliberate mistakes.

ONE

'It's a Christmas present,' said Kirsty, to the slightly harassed-looking woman who had emerged from the tiny room on the far side of the treatment pod. 'And I'm so looking forward to it. January gets you down, doesn't it?' Especially when you had a toddler who'd just experienced her first meaningful Christmas, a magic couple of weeks accompanied by a full symphony of magic, sugar and temper tantrums.

'Oh God, yes.' The woman rolled her eyes — more, thought Kirsty, in self-mockery than anything else — and laughed. 'I know just how it must be. It's always a quiet month for us, though.' She shot a look past Kirsty towards the empty reception area. 'Is it just you? The booking is for two of you.'

'My sister was supposed to be coming but she had to cancel. She said she'd called last night.'

'I expect she left a message. Maybe Hazel picked it up and didn't tell me,' said the woman, with another, reassuring, laugh. 'No problem. In fact, it's a bit of a blessing if I'm honest. One of our girls hasn't managed to make it in today.' A furrow of irritation appeared briefly on her immaculately made-up face and was gone within a second. 'I'm Suzanne, by the way.'

There were three sisters who, appropriately enough, ran the Three Sisters Spa and Kirsty, who had been a regular visitor before she'd married and a baby had called a halt to everything she considered a luxury, knew all of them. But it had been a while since she'd been so it wasn't unreasonable for her name to slip Suzanne's mind.

'I'm Kirsty.' She yanked the belt of her towelling robe, unable to decide whether wandering about in little more than her underwear at ten in the morning made her feel like a slob or a film star.

'It's a shame your sister had to cancel.' Suzanne ushered her into a small, peculiarly boat-shaped area and whisked the curtains around the huge glass windows which encompassed half of the wall space, before moving swiftly to touch a long taper to some scented candles. That done, she moved towards the door. 'Never mind. We'll try and make it a special treat for you anyway. Just slip out of your robe, Kirsty, and lie down on the couch and I'll tap on the door in a couple of minutes and we can do your massage. Back, neck and shoulder, was it? Hot stones?'

When Suzanne had left the room, Kirsty did as she was told, hanging her robe on the back of the door and settling down on the couch, designed with a hole so that clients could lie face down without discomfort. The Three Sisters' unique selling point was its three pods that jutted out into Ullswater, with glass panels set in the floor. Kirsty had always loved them, loved the way they seemed to offer an opt-out from the mad world as she looked down at the rippling water. Sometimes, if you were lucky and the light was right, you could catch a glimpse of fish twitching lazily in its depths.

The light wasn't right today. On a cold January morning the water was high and the low sun didn't reach it; it looked murky and mysterious, with a frill of ice. Occasionally something — the wash from one of the steamers, probably — sent a tiny wave splashing up against the thick glass floor. And even in summer there were downsides, when the lake level dropped dramatically and there was nothing to see but parched, cracked mud.

What a place the Three Sisters had been in its day, mused Kirsty as she waited for Suzanne to come back, but even as she thought it she wondered if her memories were playing her false. It had seemed the height of sophistication when she had been a teenager but maybe it had always been slightly tired, its paint always peeling. Maybe Suzanne Walsh had always looked a little too tight-lipped to be enjoying herself, and her smile had always been forced.

'Okay, Kirsty?'

On the affirmative reply, Suzanne bustled in and began moving around the pod, her sparkly flip-flops treading a well-worn path and her shadow reaching over Kirsty and jumping nervously as the candle flames guttered in the draught. Music started up from speakers above them, some strange cross between pan pipes and whale music, low and calming.

'You know the drill,' said Suzanne, who must have taken the opportunity to check the client histories and realised that Kirsty had once been a regular. 'It's straightforward. You don't need to do anything except relax.'

She slid a hand, glistening with drops of essential oils, under the gap in the couch and a strong scent of tea tree and lavender drifted up to assault Kirsty's nostrils.

'Mm…' In a second Kirsty felt alive. 'Oh, that's gorgeous.'

'It'll relax you now and revive you later. That's the idea, at least. I did tell your sister when she booked that she's to make sure you don't do anything for the rest of the day. You don't want to fritter away the benefits of the treatment.'

'My husband's got the day off to look after our toddler. That's part of the deal.' Kirsty grinned. Becca, who was exceptionally organised, had taken care of everything except the one thing she had no control over. *Goddam it*, she'd said, in a most un-Becca-like way when she'd called to apologise the night before. *Four cases of winter vomiting on the team. I can't do tomorrow morning. I'm going to have to go in and do the essential visits, but that's all I'm doing. We won't cancel your treat.* 'And my sister's coming around this afternoon to ply me with treats and we're going to watch Hallmark movies until wine o'clock.'

'Exactly what I'd recommend.' Warm essential oils pooled over Kirsty's back with a delicious, unexpected thrill and Suzanne's skilful fingers slid over them in an initial reconnaissance. 'Goodness me, those shoulders! I can feel the knots in your muscles. Don't worry, I'll get to work and we'll soon have you sorted out.'

Kirsty yawned. The scent of the oils and the candles was almost overpowering. 'I'm sure I'll fall asleep.'

'Go right ahead.'

She didn't sleep. It was impossible, with Suzanne's fingers isolating every knot in her shoulder muscles and wrestling with them until she felt them ease, but she closed her eyes and let the music, the oils, the sweeping pressure of the hot stones on her back lull her into some kind of half-doze. It was an absolute treat to have a morning with no risk whatsoever of being disturbed. No phone, no Rosie whining for a snack, no Calum calling to say he'd be late, no well-meaning neighbour keen to chat at exactly the wrong time.

It was a shame Becca couldn't be there. Half the fun was the gossip, the herbal tea — or hot chocolate — afterwards in the reception area with its stunning view along the lake. As Kirsty dozed it struck her as odd, that remark Suzanne had made about being short-staffed. Becca's absence was an appointment that hadn't needed to be done so a missing staff member was hardly the end of the world. It wasn't as if the place was mobbed, either. When Kirsty had arrived there had been only one other customer, an elderly lady sitting in the adjacent pod getting her nails done in a startling shade of light blue.

Yes, such a pity about Becca. Under the influence of the oils and the accumulated tiredness of motherhood, Kirsty grew melancholy. Becca worked even harder than she did, a whole-hearted commitment to any and every local cause or needy person. You didn't have to be a psychologist to see that was displacement, an attempt to fill the gap left in her life by the absence of the family life and children she'd so desperately wanted and which had somehow escaped her.

The room was warm. Her brain flickered into blissful somnolence under the weight of the oils and the relentless pummelling of Suzanne's forearms. God, what strength the woman had. And how strange that anyone could take pleasure from this and yet…

Hot stones, smooth as sin on her back. Thick air. Heat on a cold day. She opened her eyes and looked down at the hypnotic flicker of the dark, oily ripples so close to the glass floor.

And a hand. A human hand, white like that of a Hallowe'en ghost, its palm upwards in the water, its fingers curled, its nails long and dark and desperate.

A massage was meant to relax you, not disturb you. The thick fog of essential oils must have done something to her head. She stared at it, willing herself to wake up.

But she wasn't asleep. Suzanne's hands were still holding her hard down on the couch and she looked downwards through the couch, through the glass floor.

A wave came, and another, the wash from the passing of a lake steamer. The hand bobbed up and its scarlet fingernails tapped on the underside of the glass like a trapped soul.

Kirsty jumped off the couch in a shower of hot, oiled stones and screamed and screamed and screamed.

TWO

Jude Satterthwaite took a long deep breath, picked up his coffee (miraculously still warm) and prepared to enjoy a moment which, if not quiet, was nevertheless one he could afford to enjoy. The cold easterly wind that swept through Cumbria from the Pennines, across the Eden Valley and into the fells and dales of the Lake District, brought with it a bite of ice and a glaze of frost, a blessing for a few in his profession just as it was a curse for most others. Winter's fiercest bite always caused a sudden rise in workload for those of his fellow police officers who dealt with incidents and accidents, who traced lost walkers and retrieved vehicles skidding off icy roads and into ditches, but for him and his CID colleagues it was a relatively quiet period. Once the flush of drunken assaults that too often came with the festive season had died down, the cold kept a fair number of the local criminals inside and out of the way.

The work didn't ease up. There was always plenty to do, plenty of paperwork, plenty of head-scratching over how to allocate resources to the cases in hand — and there were enough of those backed up to fill several weeks — but at least at this time of year Jude sometimes found himself with the luxury of drinking his coffee before it got cold and a fighting chance of getting home at a reasonable hour of the day.

'Keeping busy, Doddsy?' he asked his office mate, who was yawning over his desk. 'Or is that just a monumental hangover?'

Doddsy, who didn't drink, laughed. 'It's old age, creeping up on me. It'll get you too, son, before you know it. Just you wait. You won't be laughing then.'

Jude grinned and swung his chair around to look out of the window. From his office there was a glimpse of light where the weak sunlight shone on the River Eden but even as he watched the sun faded and the bright water dimmed to a dull, gunmetal grey. The sky lost any liveliness and hardened to a cold, bleak, mass. It could have been the last, lingering minutes before dark rather than half past eleven in the morning, though in these short midwinter days there was little noticeable difference between the two.

His phone rang. He spun the chair back round and looked at it.

'Earth to DCI Satterthwaite,' said Doddsy when Jude made no move to answer. 'That's your phone. You're supposed to answer it. No coffee breaks for the senior ranks.'

'It's Ashleigh.' Jude let the phone ring once more while he drank the last of his coffee. Ashleigh O'Halloran was his on-off partner as well as his colleague but as both of them were resolutely and vainly in love with other, former, partners even their close friendship was sometimes strained. Nevertheless, he didn't usually find himself so reluctant to answer.

If he'd thought it was a personal call he would have left

it, but it wouldn't be. He put the cup down and answered the phone. 'Ash. Hi. Are you bored?'

'No,' she said, sounding businesslike, 'but I thought you might be so I've decided to give you something else to think about.'

'Is that right?' He laughed. 'Let me just check my to do list and my diary and see how much time I can spare you. Thirty seconds, maybe.'

'Thirty seconds might be all it needs. It's probably something just as straightforward as it seems,' she went on, without laughing at the joke, 'and yes, it is one of those that looks nasty but not criminal.'

'What normal folk call an accident, you mean,' he said. He knew Ashleigh very well indeed and she normally came to the point much more quickly than that. The fact that she was rambling on without producing the facts up front — *one, two, three, go!* — immediately made him raise an eyebrow.

'Yes, but—'

'What's happened?'

'I've just had a call that they've found a body in Ullswater. At the Pooley Bridge end. A young woman. Charlie Fry is down there right now doing all the basic stuff but he didn't like the look of it so he called for a detective to come and give the place a once-over. I'm heading down shortly to see what's going on.'

He shook his head. PC Charlie Fry was an old head on old shoulders, a man who'd seen many an accidental death, many a suicide, way too many homicides. If Charlie thought he needed help something was up. 'Right. Any suspicious circumstances?'

'Nothing obvious. As in, who knows? I was a bit surprised to be asked about something like this, if I'm honest, but I trust Charlie.'

'Where was the body?'

'Just at the edge of the water, fully clothed. Charlie reckons it looks as if she's been there some hours, and there are no obvious signs of violence. She hadn't been reported missing.'

'We know who she is, then?'

'Yes. Her name is Sophie Hayes. She's twenty-three and works at the Three Sisters Spa. That's where she was found. You know it?'

'I can't say I'm a regular,' he said, and laughed. 'I know of it. It used to be quite the place, I believe, but it was always a bit limited in terms of facilities — no pool, for example — and there are other places much more trendy, now. According to my mum, that is. She knows more about these things than I do.'

'I always have this idea that I'm going to find the time to get acquainted with the local spa scene,' she said, rather fractiously, 'but somehow it never seems to happen, so I'll defer to your mum. Anyway, there you have it. If you need me at any point in the rest of the morning you'll find me freezing to death down by the lake.'

There was nothing unusual in a close examination of a suspicious death, a matter that would more usually be dealt with by someone a rank lower than Jude, who was a chief inspector. 'Okay. And you're calling me because?'

'You know why I'm calling you. It's because sometimes you look at these things and they don't seem quite right. Charlie thinks it's odd. It costs me nothing to put in a call. If it turns out to be nothing it doesn't matter and if it is something you can give me a gold star and then take on the glory of solving the case.'

Something was bothering her. 'What else? Why me, rather than Doddsy,'

'You can always tell, can't you? Right. You know the person who found the body. It's Kirsty McKellen.'

Becca Reid's sister. Complicated. Jude and Becca went back a long way, a relationship which stubbornly refused either to die or to revive but just sat in the back of his head — and Becca's, he suspected — as a matter unresolved, a failure neither of them could forgive themselves for. Kirsty, who had once been part of his social circle, had embraced her sister's side of the fallout so wholeheartedly he thought even Becca was sometimes embarrassed about it, and wouldn't give him the time of day when their paths crossed. 'Is she okay?'

'I think so. Well, no. She didn't actually find the body, but she was the one who saw it floating in the water. She was at the Three Sisters for a massage, I think, and she saw it from one of those pod things they have. Anyway, she screamed the place down and the people who run the place went out and managed to haul the body in, and called 999. Poor Kirsty just about managed to tell Charlie what she'd seen and then collapsed into a heap and had to be taken off and given strong sweet tea and all the stuff. The people who own the place told us who the girl was. Sophie was a beauty therapist there, and she'd been the last one to leave the place last night. They left her to lock up. And now of course they're beating themselves up for being put out when she didn't turn up this morning.'

'So she might have been there all night.' Jude cast his mind back to the Three Sisters. It was about half a mile out of Pooley Bridge, a conversion of an old stone boathouse on a promontory jutting out into Ullswater, whose waters ebbed and flowed beneath it with the seasons. It was located at a point where the Ullswater Way met a badly-tarmacked track that had once connected the boathouse with the house to which it had belonged and which now functioned as a farm track. The boathouse was shielded from the near-constant stream of fair-weather walkers by a thick hedge of holly. 'It's quite secluded from that side. From the other side it's a bit of a landmark, but nobody would have seen her in the water even if it hadn't been dark.' Sophie, like most of the rest of them, would have arrived at work and left it in the smothering secrecy of night. January was no friend to anyone. 'Who was there when you arrived?'

'Two of the Walsh sisters, Suzanne and Hazel. The third one arrived later. Tessa.'

For a while, when the spa had passed from the ownership of a mother to her three daughters, it had been something of a joke. The three sisters running the Three Sisters. 'What time would Sophie normally have left work last night?'

'The last booking they had finished at eight. Suzanne — she's the oldest of the sisters who own it, jointly — says they occasionally get walk-ins from the campsite or the village but only in summer, so it wouldn't have been much later than that that Sophie would have gone. She'd have had to sweep up, wipe down the room she'd used and lock up. Apparently that's standard practice.'

'How did she get to and from work?'

'Walked from Pooley Bridge, I think. Charlie said something about her car being left on the street there. I'll check that when I get down there.'

'There's a car park, isn't there?' Or a bit of hard standing, at least. It couldn't have taken more than three vehicles. There were double doors into a space under the building, if he remembered correctly, but it was surely too small and the roof too low for a garage.

'Yes, but they try and leave that for customers, and if not the Walsh sisters have priority over it.'

'Okay. So from what you say, apart from wondering what the hell she was doing in the water, it does scream *accident.*'

'Yes, I know. It's all pretty counter-intuitive. Charlie's all for telling me the lass slipped, it gets bad down there by the water if you don't know what you're at.' She made a passable attempt at mimicking solid old PC Charlie Fry, and Jude barely suppressed a chuckle. 'He still asked for us to come down there, though. It was a foul night last night but there's the path to Pooley Bridge and if she didn't fancy that in the dark, there's the road.'

'Okay,' he said, thinking about it. 'You'd better get down there and have a look. Maybe take Aditi with you, if she's not too busy. And keep me updated.'

'I will. And I expect I'll see you later on anyway. Unless something comes up,' she added, gloomily.

'I expect so.' He hung up and turned to Doddsy, who had been unashamedly listening in.

'That doesn't sound good,' said Doddsy, with a frown.

Jude shook his head. 'No.' He turned back to his laptop and the list of all the things he had to do, and tried not to think too hard about the death of a young woman on his patch, and about the curse of coincidence that meant Kirsty had been there, and how Becca, who always seemed to seek a grievance against him even as she couldn't seem to leave him be, would somehow find a way to blame him for everything that went wrong.

THREE

It was close to midday and the sun was at its height, or would have been if it had been able to struggle free from the thick grey mass of angry cloud, when Ashleigh and her colleague Aditi Desai arrived at the Three Sisters Spa. The last part of the road — a not-too-well-kept track of broken tarmac and icy puddles — was clogged with emergency vehicles so Ashleigh manoeuvred her Ford Focus into a gateway and she and Aditi made their way to the spa on foot. At the point where the track intersected with the lakeside path a thick hedge, some seven feet high, formed a barrier shielding the spa from public view. As they stepped beyond it, a man escorted a woman from the building, an arm around her. They passed the two detectives without acknowledging them, though the man had paused to thank Charlie Fry who was stationed at the bottom of the steps and even the woman, who was pale and had obviously been crying, managed a watery smile for him.

'That must be Kirsty McKellen,' said Aditi, when the

couple had passed them and were heading along the track. 'What a hell of a shock she must have had.'

'Not exactly the relaxing morning she'd have been hoping for,' agreed Ashleigh, sparing the two of them a second look. Kirsty had a look of her sister, Becca, about her, an aura of exhausted common sense. She looked utterly shattered. 'It's just as well we didn't have to talk to her. It would probably have been more than she could take.'

'Charlie's nice and friendly.' Aditi waved to him and received a wave in reply, as if to prove the point. 'She'll have been all right with him.'

Charlie Fry had, indeed, seen the McKellens off in a particularly jovial manner as if by so doing he could somehow put everything right, but when they'd gone his expression immediately became more sombre as he turned to the newcomers.

'Hi Charlie,' said Ashleigh, briskly. 'Nasty business.' As was almost always the case when their two branches of the force, the uniformed and the CID, came into contact.

'Aye. Poor lass,' he said, jerking his head back towards the building. 'Looks like she must have slipped on her way home.'

'And you called us?'

'I'm getting soft in my old age,' he said, ruefully. 'The lass has a look of my youngest about her. But the CSI folk are having a look just now, so we'll see if I was right.'

Charlie was talking himself down, no doubt reluctant to admit to anything other than hard fact, but as a copper you had to trust your gut and there was a niggling doubt in Ashleigh's mind, too. How had Sophie Hayes come to be in the water? Keeping a safe distance, she left Aditi to hear the details and peered around the side of the building towards the lake. The car park, all but a pathway into and out of the building, and a large chunk of the shore beyond it had been cordoned off. A long shape covered in tarpaulin lay by the water, where a figure in a white forensic suit was busy photographing the surroundings.

'Tammy?' called Ashleigh.

The figure turned, stuck up an affirmatory thumb and then made her cautious way up to the edge of the tape. 'You clodhoppers mind and keep off my turf!' she said, and laughed.

'We wouldn't dare.' Ashleigh took a step back in mock fear, then got back to business. 'Any joy?'

'Joy isn't the word. Poor kid.' Tammy Garner shook her head. 'But on a first look I can't see anything out of the ordinary. Her phone was by the water.' It lay near the body. 'Dropped it, maybe. Stumbled picking it up, hit her head. I don't know. That's for you to work out.'

Pebbles were unforgiving terrain. They might trap the odd clue, a cigarette end or a lost coin, but they never held a footmark, not even one to show that Sophie might have entered the water there. And it had rained heavily the previous night so if there had been anything to see the chances were it had been washed away.

'Do you reckon the body had been there long?' asked Aditi.

'I wouldn't want to say how long, what with the water and it being so cold. That's a question that'll get answered at the lab. But yes.' Tammy shrugged. 'I'd say overnight. I can't see how she'd have got there if she hadn't had a fall or a faint, but folk don't always read the lake well. I'll have a look around up on that little bluff in a bit.'

Ashleigh surveyed the situation in more detail. The spa was a split-level building, its original stone core extending both outwards over the lake and back inland with extensions to the side and rear and an enclosed storage space beneath. On a normal day it stood four feet or more above the lake but in winter it was much less. The path back to Pooley Bridge split into two; the low-level route along the shore was presently under water and the drier alternative was pinched between a thick hawthorn hedge and a steep bank that dropped a good ten feet into the water. 'She could have fallen from there, I suppose?'

'It was dark, and it was miserable. Windy, too. So yes, she could.'

But that didn't make sense either. There was a tangle of trees along the bank, more than enough to break a fall or at the very least to give someone something to grasp at, or to haul their way out, and the water at that point was only a few inches deep. Even in the dark it would have been impossible to stray away from safety without realising. On the Pooley Bridge side of the spa there was a lump of ground ragged with scrubby bushes and sodden grass, but the path skirted it on the inland side and even there it was a drop of only a couple of feet; the water below it was shallow, though possibly cold enough to incapacitate her. The post-mortem and toxicology tests would look for drink and drugs, but Sophie had been coming from work, not a wild party.

'Or there,' said Ashleigh, pointing to it. 'But why would she be up there?'

'That bit's your job.' From behind the mask Ashleigh sensed a grin. Tammy was as light-hearted as it was possible to be under the circumstances, and there was no offence intended. 'I'd best get on. Poor kid. The sooner we sort this out, the sooner her family can put her to rest.'

Ashleigh turned back to Charlie. 'I think we'll go in and have a chat with the owners, now. I take it you've got everything covered here?' An unnecessary question. Charlie would have everything covered. He always did.

'Aye, I have. I spoke to the woman in charge. Suzanne Walsh, her name is. She went into the water to try and get Sophie out. Not that there was a chance the lass would be alive, but she wasn't to know that.'

Ashleigh headed up the three broad wooden steps with Aditi behind her. A neatly-lettered sign fixed to the stone wall (gold on pink, a nightmare for the colour blind) welcomed them to *The Three Sisters' Beauty Suite*. Glass doors opened onto a small lobby with a board on the wall. Under the heading *Our Staff* (still in that almost illegible colour scheme) photographs of four women smiled out, all in dusky pink tunics, all perfectly coiffed and made up, all smiling at the camera.

Ashleigh read the labels. *Suzanne, Hazel, Tessa, Sophie.* She gave the last photo a long look, but it gave away nothing of the character behind, just a blank mask, an image of a pretty young woman putting on a face for her employers.

'Okay?' said Aditi, and turned to a second set of glass doors that led them to a spacious reception area whose picture windows on the left looked out over the choppy grey waters of the lake. On a better day there would have been breathtaking views of the western shore, over towards Gowbarrow Fell with maybe even a tantalising glimpse of Helvellyn or Catstycam on a good day, but today the cloud was clamping ever harder on top of the higher fells and it was impossible to see anything much beyond the far side of the lake.

The reception area was clean and bright, with comfortable chairs arranged around three low tables on which were bowls of apples and bananas. On a sideboard near the door there was a jug of water with slices of lemon and cucumber and a coffee machine, with a pot next to it containing sachets of herbal teas and hot chocolate powder. At one of the tables three women, two in those trademark pink tunics and the third in a pink towelling robe, sat in a grim silence around a portable gas heater. All three looked up as the door opened.

The three sisters. They couldn't be anything else, their faces much more similar in distress than they'd looked under the forced smiles of their corporate photographs, though one looked substantially younger than the other two and another, in natural light, had the startling colouring of a natural redhead. She was the one who jumped to her feet when the two detectives arrived, with the others following suit.

'You're the police?' she asked, with an anxious look at her sisters.

'Yes. Detective Sergeant Ashleigh O'Halloran and Detective Constable Aditi Desai.'

'I'm Hazel Walsh,' said the redhead, and turned to introduce the other two who had got to their feet rather more slowly. 'My oldest sister, Suzanne.' She gestured at the woman in the robe. 'And this is Tessa, the youngest.'

Ashleigh smiled at them and they stared back in silence. Some people approached the police like that — with suspicion. Sometimes it was a guilty conscience, more often a concern based in ignorance. She hastened to reassure them. 'It's a routine visit. We're here to establish the circumstances surrounding Sophie's death. That's all. So what we'd like to do is have a chat with the three of you individually, about Sophie and what her routine was, and what her normal working life was like and so on.'

'Poor Sophie. I had such hopes for her. She was such a good worker.' Suzanne shivered, pulled her robe more tightly around herself and shuffled back to the warmth of the heater. 'Shall I go first? I'd like to get home and get some dry clothes on.'

'Sue went into the water when we found Sophie,' said Hazel, protectively. She squeezed her sister's arm. 'What an idiot you are. But such a sweetheart. You did the right thing, of course. But goodness me, going in to the lake when it's that cold…you know the shock can be fatal.'

There was a small pause, in which all five of them must surely have thought about Sophie, blundering into the icy water in the dark, and Ashleigh remembered an incident of her own, a foray into icy water in an attempt to save a life — an attempt in vain, just as Suzanne Walsh's had been. 'Are you sure you're all right, Ms Walsh?'

'Quite sure.' Suzanne pulled herself together. 'Yes, it was cold, but I had a hot shower and we do have these lovely warm robes, and Hazel fixed me up with a hot chocolate. When we're done here I can go home and get sorted out. Your man out there — PC Fry, was it? — did say I could go straight home and speak to you later but I wanted to stay and get it all over with so I can try and forget about it.' Her face set into a grim expression. She wouldn't forget what she'd seen, or done, or the grim futility of that plunge into the water, and she almost certainly knew it.

'If you're quite happy to do that,' said Ashleigh, struck by something she couldn't quite define about Suzanne Walsh, whose expression carried ingrained defiance and who was somehow much more interesting than either of her sisters. 'Perhaps if I speak to you and Aditi can speak to—'

'Me,' said Hazel, promptly, and Tessa nodded assent as if there was a natural order of things and she knew her place, always at the back of the queue.

'I wasn't here,' explained Tessa, as though to justify her absence. 'I came along later. You probably don't need to talk to me.'

There was no surer way to pique Ashleigh's interest. 'It's routine, as I said, but yes. I think I would like to talk to you. Is there an office, perhaps?'

'I'll take you through to the pods,' said Suzanne, setting her jaw even more than before. 'That's where I was when we saw her.'

'Sue,' said Hazel, anxiously, 'surely you could take the sergeant somewhere else—'

'DS O'Halloran will want to see it.' Suzanne brushed Hazel's arm from her sleeve abruptly. 'And I'm going to have to go back in there some time. Anyway, it's warmer in there.'

'This way, sergeant.' They might be three sisters, but one of them was definitely in charge. Suzanne flip-flopped her way ahead of Ashleigh across the room, her bare feet encased in white towelling slippers, to a door marked *Treatment Rooms*. She hesitated slightly before opening it, then seemed to gather herself and force herself onwards. 'Through here. this is what we call the pods. What makes the Three Sisters so unique. What makes this place — and us — what we are.'

FOUR

The pods were, thought Suzanne as she led the senior of the two detectives from the reception to the treatment area, in their context quite remarkable. The reception was in the newer part of the building but the door through which they passed was set into the rough stone of the original building. As she closed the door behind Ashleigh O'Halloran she kept half an eye on the sergeant and was immediately gratified at the startled look — maybe even awe — that crossed her face.

So many people reacted like that.

'This was the boathouse,' said Suzanne, flicking a switch and adding soft lighting to the harsh greyness of the day, showing off the space to its advantage. 'It's pretty big, as you see. My father was an architect and my mother was a beautician. Twenty-five years or so ago he bought the place and converted it as an anniversary present for her. She was coming to the end of her working career by then, but she'd always been an employee. It was a gift for her — her own business, at last.' And, as a result, her mother had stayed on long after she should have retired, probably at risk to her health. The most thoughtful of gifts could have unintended consequences.

She waved a hand at the three pods extending out over the water. The central one had two chairs, one large and comfortable, and the two on either side held beauticians' couches. Tessa had made a hurried attempt at clearing up the carnage Kirsty McKellen had left behind her but she'd fallen well short of Suzanne's exacting standards.

'Are the pods on stilts?' asked the woman, looking at them. 'I couldn't see from outside. Because of the...'

'The tape,' said Suzanne, evenly. 'Yes, they are on stilts, but pretty solid. These two, on either side, can be screened off. See? Clever.' She demonstrated, pulling out a folding screen that isolated the left-hand pod from the others and made it into a small cubicle compete with sink and a separate walk-in cupboard, whose door stood open to reveal a pile of towels and beauty supplies. 'We just use the middle one for manicures and pedicures. We can't close it off because of the way it's designed, but people do like to sit and look out over the water when it's a nice day.'

'Yes, I see that. All part of the Three Sisters experience.'

Suzanne gave her sideways look. 'You've spotted the obvious flaw, I can see.'

Ashleigh O'Halloran walked to the window of the enclosed pod, which jutted out a good six feet over the lake, and looked down at the heavy perspex panel in the floor. 'It does seem a bit exposed.'

'Exactly. Dad adored Mum and was so taken up with his wonderful idea and so insistent it should be a surprise that he didn't think to ask what she'd like.' Her father hadn't been that sort of man. Nor, on reflection, had he been that good an architect. The door to the pods opened outwards when it would have been more convenient for it to open inwards, the space underneath was intended for storage but was inaccessible from inside the building and therefore impractical, and there were endless corners that had no real function. 'When he proudly presented her with this I think she was a bit taken aback. Dad was thinking of the views, of course. It never occurred to him that if you're looking out on the lake then people on the lake can see in, and even if it had done I don't think he would have thought that women in a state of undress having massages or intimate waxing don't really want paddle boarders goggling at them or swimmers popping up like seals to give them a cheery wave.' He'd been quite crestfallen when her mother had tactfully pointed that out. 'Curtains solved that. Mum decided there was no need to cover the panels in the floor, but after having seen the state poor Mrs McKellen got herself into I really wish we had.' Even at this point, Suzanne kept her voice firm. 'Come and sit down. I'll talk you through what happened.'

'It was this pod?'

'Yes.' The air in the room was heavy with warmth and lavender and the place was in some disarray. Suzanne bent down and picked up a towel from the floor, tossing it onto the couch and resisted the instinct to turn on the whale music and light some candles. 'Have a seat.'

There were two chairs in the pod, one of which doubled as a table and she removed the pile of clean towels from it and placed them on the couch, waving the woman, who had already produced a notebook and pen, to the more comfortable of the two and then sitting down.

'Poor Mrs McKellen,' she said. 'It was a Christmas treat for her but the person she was supposed to be coming with couldn't make it, so she decided to come on her own as she had the babysitter all sorted. It was a back and shoulder massage. Obviously we had the curtains closed.'

They were open now. She looked out and saw a shaft of sunlight break through unexpectedly and flash a dazzling stripe of light across the lake.

'You must have been moving around.' The detective jotted something down. 'You didn't see anything?'

'Through the floor? No.' Suzanne shrugged. There was a stone from the ruined massage loose on the floor and she leaned over to pick it up. It was cool and oily under her fingers. 'To tell you the truth I don't really like looking down on the water. It never used to bother me but as I get older it starts to make me a bit uncomfortable. It must be the sense that everything under my feet isn't stable. So I tend to keep my feet on solid ground as much as I can and try not to look down when I have to be at that end of the pod.' Age had nothing to be said for it. She thought about that a lot these days. 'I was at that end at the beginning of the treatment. The client lies with her face in this hole so she can breathe, you see, and I always like to give an aromatherapy massage a bit of a kick start by wafting something under the table so it drifts upwards.'

'Okay.' The detective leaned forward in her seat and took a quick look round. 'Talk me through what happened.'

With the curtains closed and the candles lit the room was relaxing and even inviting, but in the cold light of day its shortcoming showed. There was a crack in the glass at the top of the pod, and an attendant draught. The paint was faded and peeling and the apple green of the wall was marked with the soot from too many candles. There were signs of damp on the join between floor and walls. Seeing all of these things as if through the detective's eyes, Suzanne cringed inwardly with embarrassment on behalf of her beloved Three Sisters.

'Mrs McKellen was in for an aromatherapy massage,

booked in for ten o'clock.' She inspected her fingernails, which were perfectly polished, evenly shaped and finished with white tips. Tessa had done them for her the previous day. 'We went through the usual procedures. I was in here first thing to set up, close the curtains and so on, but I didn't notice anything unusual. I do always take a moment to stand and look.' Though she never looked down and never dwelt too long on the spa's shortcomings. 'The view is beautiful in every weather.'

On cue, the sun slipped out to tease them and slipped back again almost immediately. The brown slopes of the lower fells opposite turned briefly gold, the steamer forging its way back from Howtown to Pooley Bridge flashed bright and then faded into the dark grey of the water.

'Did you look down?' asked the sergeant.

'No.' Suzanne got up and retraced her steps. 'I stood here for maybe two minutes, closed the curtains, set the place up. Hazel was on the desk and I could hear her dealing with my client, telling her where to get ready and so on. There was another lady in getting her nails done and that would ordinarily have been something Sophie would have done before going on to do the massage for Mrs McKellen's sister, but she'd cancelled. So all in all it was a bit chaotic, and Hazel was having to do the front desk and the manicure. I was in here for about five minutes setting up and then my client came along and I got her all settled.'

'But again,' came the question again, 'you didn't look down.'

Suzanne's sigh was fractious this time. The woman's disbelief was polite, but it was disbelief nonetheless, and reeked of suspicion. How soul-destroying it must be to be a police officer and have to question everyone and every-thing that crossed your path. How did you ever trust? 'The novelty of walking on water wears off after twenty years, I can tell you. So no. As I say, I was up at the top end of the couch at the beginning of the treatment and I must have been standing on the glass panel, but after that I was working at the side of the couch.'

'How long is a massage?'

'As long as you want, but this one was thirty minutes. I aim to be calming so I don't chat unless the client wants to, but they rarely do. So many of them just want a little time to themselves.' She moved away from the window and sat down, pulling her towelling robe more tightly around herself. The pod was cosy but the draught, now she'd noticed it, was penetrating. 'I keep an eye on the clock, of course, and I was just a little more than twenty minutes in when she suddenly screamed and jumped up and ran out of the room. Of course I went straight out after her, with a robe — I mean, with all those windows. Hazel's client had just left so she grabbed a robe too and took Mrs McKellen away to reception to calm her down and I went back into the pod to see what was going on.'

She stopped again, got up, took a few tentative steps and stood on the glass panel, facing her fears. 'I looked down. It was Sophie. I couldn't see her face but I recognised the nails. I did them myself — a very strong colour, Blood Fantasy, one of her favourites. For a second I stood there in complete shock and then I realised. She might have fallen in on her way to work. So I ran right out of the building and down onto the shore and I waded in. She was trapped under the building. I managed to grab her and pull her towards me but her coat was caught in something and she was all twisted.' The wash of the waves whipped up by a strong wind, must have pushed Sophie's body under the pod and trapped it there. 'It wasn't deep, barely chest high. I pulled it free and then I managed to get her out from under the pod and get her onto the shore and as soon as I did that I could see I was too late.'

'And then?

'Tess came out. She'd just arrived. Hazel had called her when Sophie hadn't turned up because we knew we were going to need her, although it should be her day off.' Tessa had had plans, she knew, but too bad. When you ran a business you had to make sacrifices for it. 'She took me back into the spa and made me go and get dry and she called the police. Hazel was dealing with Mrs McKellen, calling her husband to bring her home and then calling all the day's clients to cancel.' A wry smile. 'Not that there were many on a day like this, with the party season over. But we have our regulars.'

The detective, nodding, allowed Suzanne a moment for quiet reflection which she took and for which she was grateful. She must look a sight, those immaculate nails tap-tapping on the cushioned arm of her chair, the mascara-streaked eyes staring out through the windows of the pod. The weather had closed in again. It was one of those days, brief glimpses of spring promise rapidly over-run by the anger of winter.

'Tell me about Sophie,' invited Ashleigh O'Halloran, when she must have decided Suzanne had long enough to think.

'Must I?' Still Suzanne stared out, but this time her eyes flicked down briefly to that all-revealing glass panel in the floor. Grey, flecked with white like the spittle of a madman, the water slap-slapped at the panel as if it were trying to get in. With so many cracks and creaks and so little in the budget to spare for repairs it was only a matter of time before it succeeded.

'In any case of unexplained death we need to find out

everything we can about the victim,' said the woman, gently.

'Yes, I know.' Suzanne, looking at her, concluded she disliked Ashleigh O'Halloran. She was young and though not beautiful was nevertheless strikingly and unjustly attractive. She was the sort of woman men looked at twice, and then looked back at their wives and their girlfriends and found them wanting by comparison. There were few enough women like her, but they did enough damage. 'But it was an accident. Wasn't it?'

'As yet we don't know. And, as I say, even in the case of an accident we need to do everything we can to find out what happened and why.'

Fair enough. People's actions weren't always sensible but they were often characteristic. Impulsive people could make fatal mistakes, and Sophie had been impulsive in many ways though not, as far as Suzanne was aware, with regard to her personal safety.

'I suppose so.' She sighed, reached up to tuck a strand of hair behind her ear. First thing that morning it had been as immaculate as Hazel's but her unscheduled dip in the lake had rendered it lank and unruly. 'I don't want you to think I'm being obstructive. Anything but. But I was very fond of Sophie and it was such a shock.'

'I can imagine. But it would be very helpful if you could tell me about her.'

'All right.' Suzanne shivered in frustration. There should be so much to say about Sophie, even if it was just to accentuate how normal she was, but all she could think about was her white, bloated face. 'Sophie has been — had been — with us for a few years now. I think it was five years back that she came. No, that's not right. She was a Saturday girl for us for the year before that. She did all the rubbish jobs — the cleaning up, mainly, and a bit of taking the bookings and so on. But she was smart and keen, and most of all she was motivated. When she left school she did a course at the college and came to work here. Part-time only.' If they'd had enough work for another full-time post she'd have taken Sophie on full-time like a shot, regardless of what her sisters thought. 'She was terrific with the clients, especially the younger ones. Sometimes I think I'm a bit out of touch. I can't chat about YouTube and Insta-gram and so on, and when they ask for the latest trend in their nails or the makeup we three oldies are at a loss.' She caught the woman's appraising look and challenged it. 'I'll be sixty next year.'

'You're the oldest?'

'Yes. Hazel's three years younger than I am and Tessa's rather younger. My parents were prudent and had children when they could afford them.' She managed a wry smile.

'No thoughts of retiring?'

'Yes, of course. It's hard work at the best of times, fighting people's knotted muscles for hours every day. I'm feeling aches and pains of my own, and I've already cut back on the massages I do. These days I do more facials and manicures and leave the harder physical work to the others. So yes, I can see where this is going. I saw myself stepping back from the business and letting Sophie step in.'

'The three of you own it jointly, is that right?'

'Yes. We don't always agree about what to do with it in the long term — none of us have children and with Tess being so much younger she'll be working here long after I've shaken the dust of the place from my flip-flops. I know the others have been a bit concerned about what will happen when I've had enough. And so it did seem eminently sensible to me to do some succession planning.'

'You all got on fine with Sophie?'

'Oh yes. I mean, she was a really wonderful young

person and a very hard worker. I said she only worked part-time here, and I think she did shifts in one of the pubs in Penrith the rest of the time, but I always thought her heart was here. The clients all adore her and she's got a bit of a head on her in terms of business, too.'

The detective made a note. 'And what about her working patterns?'

'She worked a full day and a couple of half days every week, depending on her availability and how busy she was elsewhere. She was here last night. She used to leave her car up at Pooley Bridge, because although we do have a car park it's small, as you'll have seen, and we used to leave it for the clients and for my sisters and myself. Tess and Hazel share a cottage about half a mile yards up the lane towards Howtown and they usually walk. I live in Pooley Bridge and it isn't far, so I often walk too in the summer.' At her age the damp whispered weakness to her bones; she was on her feet all day and didn't need the extra effort even of a short walk home. She was making excuses, justifying her actions to herself. The sergeant would know it. 'When it came to the car park I'm afraid I pulled rank. I bitterly regret that.'

'It's not a difficult walk from Pooley Bridge, though is it? I'm not a local but this bit of the Ullswater Way was one of the first places I visited, and I keep coming back.'

'It's not difficult at all.' The path was usually bustling with kids and older people, dogs and young couples too busy looking into one another's eyes to look down and see where they were going. The fact that it was busy had always meant, in Suzanne's view, that it was safe. 'One of us usually offers to run her down there if we aren't too busy but she always says no.'

'Did you see her go?'

'I'd left by then, or I would certainly have given her a

31

lift. Now I wish I'd waited.' She reached for a box of tissues and dabbed discreetly at her eyes. A smudge of mascara came away on the tissue.

'And do you know which way she went?'

'I assumed she'd go along the path, but I can't say, in all honesty. Sometimes she might go along the road if it was muddy like last night.'

'The path is quite busy, isn't it?'

'It is further along. I mean, you get people who stay at the campsite walking to the pub and so on.'

'Are there many at this time of year?'

'Not many, but there are always some. We have a booking for tomorrow in fact, a lady who's camping up here for her fortieth. Not my idea of a treat, I have to say. And there are the ones who stay self-catering and we have some regulars who have second homes up here and don't mind about the weather but come up whenever they can. But I've never thought of it as dangerous. And I did have a thought.'

'Oh?'

'Yes. It's difficult to process. It's so awful.' Sophie had laughed at everything. She had been young enough for fun and optimism to flow without fear of consequences; like all young people, she had thought herself invincible. *Nothing will happen. I'll be fine*, she'd say when Suzanne offered her a lift. 'When I was getting changed all I could think of was how she got there and I wondered if she might have gone into the water to help someone. Or more likely something.'

'Is that the sort of thing she'd have done?'

'Oh God, yes. She was a real animal lover. She used to feed the ducks down here when she first came, but we had to put a stop to that. Rats, you know. She wanted us to have a tank of goldfish or a Three Sisters cat.' Appalled, Susanne felt her eyes filling with tears again and reached for another tissue. More mascara came away. It would be all over her face; she must look as if she'd been in a fight. 'She was always out making a fuss of people's dogs when she was on a break during the summer. And Hazel had given me a row — out of shock I suppose — shouting at me and telling me what a stupid fool I'd been to go into the water and I said to her. That's exactly what Sophie would have done, if there had been an animal in trouble in the water, or even if there wasn't. She would have gone straight in there. Tripped, maybe. Gone under. Hit her head. I don't know. But yes. When I was getting changed I could see exactly how it might have happened.'

FIVE

'I mean,' said Hazel Walsh to the young police constable who was now sitting in the right hand pod and gazing out down the lake as if she'd never seen it before, 'it's a shock. Such a shock. It really is.'

She picked at a piece of mud on the front of her usually pristine tunic. That had happened when she'd had to rescue Suzanne from the results of her own precipitateness. 'I've never seen a dead body and poor Sophie...well. It wasn't very nice.'

'No,' agreed the woman. 'It wouldn't be.'

Of course; she would see things like this all the time. Feeling foolish, Hazel picked at the tunic again, rubbing it with her forefinger and succeeding only in making the mark worse. Damn; it had been fresh on and now it would need to go in the wash, and not even Sophie there to do it. She was a fastidious woman, almost obsessively so, and in this moment of shock the muddy stain distressed her more than anything else. She looked at the policewoman again, more covertly this time.

'Why don't you tell me what happened?' suggested Aditi Desai.

It was right outside her comfort zone, that was the problem. Part of the job of a beauty therapist was to listen, and Suzanne had always been very big on this. *They aren't here to listen to you rambling on about your trials and tribulations. They're here to talk about their own. Your job is to listen.* Under these circumstances, sitting in her own space where she was normally the questioner, Hazel didn't know how to start telling her own story. 'I did speak to your policeman out there about it.'

'Charlie's great,' said the woman — barely more than a girl by the look of her, yet with a hint of steel behind the eyes. 'But he's not always great on the detail and he has so much to do. Why don't you tell me again?'

Most men struggled to multi-task, so why would a policeman be any different? Encouraged, Hazel rattled through the account she'd already given of how Kirsty McKellen had come bursting out of the pod, screaming and almost naked, and how Suzanne had bolted out of the building leaving Hazel to wrap the poor woman up and calm her down, and how, when she'd called the police and finally managed to run out and see what was going on, she'd had to bring her soaked, shivering sister in from the lakeshore, dry her off and keep her warm.

'I looked at Sophie,' she said, anxious to make sure she wasn't seen as neglectful, 'but it was—' She swallowed. 'Pretty clear she was dead.'

'Awful for you,' said the detective, and made a note on her pad.

'Yes. And of course I didn't want Sue getting a chill or something so I had to get her inside and see to her, and not just her physical welfare either. She's a funny old thing, Sue.

35

I love her to bits, but sometimes she takes things very hard.'
In the immediate aftermath Suzanne hadn't seemed to take
Sophie's death very hard, but that would come later, when
it sank in. That was entirely typical of Suzanne, too. 'She's
such an amazing woman. She copes with everything life
throws at her, she really does. Businesslike. Practical. You'd
think she's hard as nails, carrying on like a trooper. Nothing
fazes her.' How easy it was to talk in clichés. The three
sisters, working in the business, living in close proximity at
least until Suzanne had decided to move out, had ploughed
on together in a most amenable way but living on top of
one another meant they never got the chance to talk about
one another. Not that Hazel ever felt the need to bitch
about either of her sisters, but a willing listener was extra-
ordinarily liberating. 'But then it all gets too much for her
and she'll blow up, be completely unreasonable. There'll be
a big row a while down the line and she'll tell us it's all our
fault for letting Sophie walk back on her own, and then we
won't speak for a week and it'll be back to normal.'

'Bottling it up is never a good thing.'

'I know.' Sue had behaved exactly like that after their
mother had died. Even old age had to be someone else's
fault. 'And I bottle things up far too much myself, but not
because I'm like Sue. I think it's healthy to tell someone
things but it's hard.' She had no friends. What a joy it was,
talking freely to someone who wanted to listen, who
wouldn't turn it back on her or tell Suzanne as Tess would,
either out of carelessness or malice. Maybe that was the
shock. But she was enjoying it.

'How did you get on with Sophie?'

Even in the midst of her enthusiasm, Hazel checked
herself. She was essentially a good-natured woman but she
found that as she got older she was less charitable. Experience was deadly for optimism. She was talking to a police

officer and Sophie was dead. 'Sophie was fine.'

'Just fine?'

'Oh, I mean she was nice and everything. A lovely girl, actually. Yes. Lovely.' She paused to contemplate Sophie, bustling up to work every morning with that cheery hello and that smile that always seemed a bit fake. But what was wrong with that? They all wore fake smiles at work, and she knew she never saw the real Sophie when work was over, never had to endure her bad moods the way she did with her sisters — had done, indeed, with her mother. It had made her smile when, at her funeral, a client had said *your darling mother, I never heard her say a cross word*.

'Nobody's perfect, though,' said the policewoman, with a wry smile.

Hazel had brought the remains of her coffee in with her, and picked the cup up to sip at it. After all, it wasn't hard to be honest. 'Sophie was lovely. I mean it. But I think the problem was that Suzanne saw herself very much as her mentor. She was the one who brought her here in the first place. Sue was the one who decided to appoint her. She's the one who insisted we pay for all her training — not that we shouldn't, of course, but she was always sending her on courses we can't afford to send all four of us on.' It was hard not to take it to heart when she'd over-heard Suzanne explaining to a client that Sophie was much better qualified than Hazel herself to carry out this treat-ment or that. 'I think she saw her as a possible replacement for herself when she left.'

'The future of the business, you mean?'

'Yes. And I know Sue must be thinking about retire-ment, because I certainly am, though not for a few years yet, and it's not something we really talked about much. But Tess is so much younger and if anyone's going to take over I think it should be her. Only Sue didn't seem to see that.' She paused. 'Do you have sisters?'

'Like you. Two,' said the constable, and laughed. 'I'm the middle one.'

Hazel liked her. 'Then you'll know. Older sisters don't always give full credit to the younger ones.'

'Oh God, yes. I remember when I made my first arrest and my eldest sister, who was a law student at the time — not even a fully qualified lawyer — said *I really hope you've got the right one or you'll be in trouble*. Like I didn't have a superior officer making damned sure I did.'

Hazel laughed. 'Exactly. Sue's just like that. It's her way or nothing. She's so like Mum, you see.' Their mother hadn't become her own boss until she was in her fifties but once she had the prize she'd clung to it for twenty years. Even after arthritis had forced her out of the treatment rooms and she'd nominally handed the business over she would still spend all her time in the office, going through the books and keeping an eye on her daughters' every move. 'If I suggest something, or if Tess does, she either ignores it or comes down like a ton of bricks. But with Sophie…well. It was different. Sophie could do no wrong.'

'What do you mean?'

It might be because she wasn't family. Sophie hadn't been locked in to the business the way Hazel and Tessa were and so Suzanne couldn't afford to hold her in contempt. 'She was full of ideas. Good ones, most of them, to be fair. Everything from new treatments to colour schemes to marketing and promotional ideas. There was one that she came up with that we did last year that really worked — *Three Sisters at the Three Sisters*, where any three women could book a treatment at the same time and get a glass of Prosecco afterwards, for example. But the thing was that if Tessa or I suggested anything — and we did, often — she'd pretend to listen and then dismiss it.' She shrugged. 'Sometimes Sophie would come up with ideas that one of us had suggested and if we pointed that out Sue would just say that when we'd thought of it the time wasn't right, but she just meant she hadn't listened. I must admit, I'd got to the point that if I really thought something was good for the business I'd ask Sophie to suggest it rather than do it myself, but Tess said that was idiotic. She said it just made us look powerless and reinforced Sue taking all the decisions.'

She sipped her coffee again. Goodness, talking could be therapeutic. 'I'm not badmouthing Sue. It's just that that was what she's like. I love her to bits but working together isn't always easy.'

'Any close working relationship involves compromises,' said the detective.

Hazel stifled a giggle. The woman was using exactly the same techniques to get her to talk as Hazel herself employed on her stressed clients. Maybe she should have been a detective. Or anything, really, that involved working with people she wasn't related to. 'Yes, that's true. And of course we don't always agree on everything. Well. We rarely do.'

'On the business?'

'I know. That's what I could never quite understand about Sue and Sophie. I'm not sure but I think Sue might want to sell.'

'But I thought you said that she saw Sophie—'

'As her successor. Yes, and I think she does. But I also think she might know, deep down, that we wouldn't stand for that so she started making noises about selling the business. And I think Sue's long game was that eventually she would either get Sophie to take over and then she'd still have some measure of control over it even if she wasn't working here.' Just like their mother. 'Or else she'd push us to sell. You know what older sisters are like. They have no faith in you.'

'The absolute truth,' said Aditi Desai, with feeling. 'Yes.'

She paused, a delicate pause that allowed Hazel to begin to think about what she might have said that she'd later regret, how she shouldn't have let her tongue run away with her.

'Of course,' she said, thinking of Suzanne's steely stare and remembering her qualities, 'the business wouldn't have been a success without Sue.'

'Is it a success?'

'Yes. I mean, things are difficult now. There are new trends and we don't have quite so much of the business we used to have. So many new places have opened up and gone upmarket and we don't have the space to expand. It would be easier if we were part of a hotel, and there were other facilities. A pool, for example. We don't have a pool and everywhere has them. The lake isn't the same.'

'No.'

'And Sophie—'

'What do you think will happen to the Three Sisters now Sophie has gone?' asked Aditi Desai, looking carefully around her.

The place must look tatty. When you worked there all the time you never saw it but if you walked in for the first time it must seem so shabby, so in need of love and care and investment. Aditi Desai looked like the kind of woman who indulged in the occasional spa day and surely would never lower her standards and go somewhere like the Three Sisters. Its clientele were ageing or transient. Young people went elsewhere. 'I don't know.'

'Your sister might want to sell, then.'

'I imagine there's a conversation to be had about it.' Hazel put her cup down, regretting how incautious she'd been. 'Still, that's for later. I mean, I'm not that far off retiring, as I said, and I really would like us to sell it, but there's Tess to consider.' And she might play down her own role in the business but if it went there wasn't much else for her to do, and it was depreciating all the time in value. As a going concern it wouldn't fetch that much and she wasn't about to agree to flog it off to someone who was going to convert it into a holiday home. It had to go to the right buyer. 'Is there anything else you want to know?'

'Only about Sophie. Just generally.'

'I didn't really know her that well. We only talked about work. Sometimes I'd overhear her chatting with clients. She'd talk about her holidays and her makeup regime and her boyfriends.'

'Did she have a current boyfriend?'

'Probably. I mean, I don't know, When she was chatting she would always seem to be talking about one and I always got the impression they were different. There, that sounds uncharitable. I don't imagine she had any more boyfriends than anyone else does at her age. Just trying them out to see what fits as my mother used to say. God, as you get older you forget what it's like to be young, don't you?'

She felt a bit guilty as she said it. Maybe that was why she'd resented the young woman — because Suzanne clearly saw more in her than she did in either of her sisters, and because Sophie was young enough not to make the mistakes that Hazel herself had done or, if she did, to break free from them and start again.

'I don't think I'm that age yet,' said the woman, and laughed, rather ruefully. 'Poor Sophie. I expect her parents will be able to give us that sort of detail.'

Hazel rubbed an aching wrist. All in all, she was glad of an excuse to cancel the afternoon's sessions. Her back was troubling her, too. 'Yes. Poor Sophie.' A tear pricked at the back of her eye. In the hustle and the panic she hadn't quite processed it and now it was coming home to her that Sophie was dead. No more of that cheery smile. Just a gap, a real person who suddenly no longer existed. At least with her parents there had been a period of passing, a moment to say goodbye. She'd never before understood how cruel and sudden death could be.

'Oh God,' she said and heard herself whimper. 'I know I shouldn't cry. But it's all so awful, poor Sophie, and now I don't know what will become of the Three Sisters, or of any of us.'

SIX

'I saw her last night.'

Tessa had been crying and she didn't care if the detective saw her. It mattered that Suzanne didn't see it (or rather, hadn't noticed) and she would rather Hazel didn't notice either, and take pity on her and try and treat her like a child rather than an independent woman, but she didn't care if the police knew because they'd find out in the end, even if they had no right to know everything. And in any case the detective sergeant, Ashleigh O'Halloran, immediately struck her as far more empathetic than any other police officer she'd encountered.

There hadn't been many — there had been a few walk-in thefts before they'd tightened up the security and got an entry phone on the door, one attempted break-in some years before, the occasional bout of vandalism or anti-social behaviour in the summer — but Tessa had always felt guilty about dragging officers away from more important crimes and some of them had, she thought, felt the same. This time, though there was no suggestion of a crime, it was nevertheless an enormous comfort to find herself telling her version of a story to a woman who radiated both empathy and interest and who was quite clearly fascinated by everything she had to say.

So unaccustomed was Tessa to this kind of reaction that a little part of her resistance to authority (engendered in her by both her parents, as well as by Suzanne, who always believed she knew better than anyone else) crumbled away to nothing.

'Shall we go and sit in the middle pod?' she suggested. It was her favourite, the smallest and cosiest, the one with the most open views. It was neither soundproofed nor particularly secure, but that didn't matter. All she could hear from the adjacent pod, to which Hazel had been whisked off by the younger of the two women officers, was the quiet mumbling of short questions and long answers. Suzanne, who had come out of her interview looking as stern-faced as she had when she went in, had resisted Tessa's suggestion that she go home and get into some dry clothes and had made herself a cup of tea and said she'd wait to head off any of the clients who hadn't picked up their message and were still asking their way down.

'I do hope nobody turns up,' said Tessa, thinking aloud. That would be interesting, with Suzanne sitting in reception in her robe and slippers.

'Someone's bound to,' said the sergeant, cheerfully. 'You know what it's like. Even if they've got your message they'll have heard there's something going on and they'll turn up for their appointment pretending they don't know there's anything going on, and then they'll go home and tell their friends about it. I think I'd do it myself.'

Any client, Tessa realised, would be turned back by the police. Suzanne's corporate goodwill was no more than a front. She would want to know what was going on. She always did.

'Yes,' she said laughing despite the shocking situation in which she found herself, 'but you're the police.'

'For my sins,' agreed the woman. 'Although I confess, part of the reason I'm a detective is that think people are really interesting and I love listening to them. I think if I hadn't been in this job I might have been a psychiatrist.'

Or a hairdresser, or a beautician. So many jobs required you to be a good listener. 'And yet you chose to deal with dead bodies?' Tessa relaxed into her chair in the middle pod.

'Yes, I know it sounds odd. But I feel I can do some good this way. Not that you can't do good as a psychiatrist, of course, but this is more immediate.'

'I see that.' Carting the bad guys off to prison and hearing the (metaphorical) clang of a cell door was a material difference, in a good way.

'And what about you?' the woman said, relaxing into her chair just as Tessa had done, and glancing along the lake as everybody did. 'I bet your job is all about listening, too.'

'Yes, and I think we do good, too, in a different way.'

'Is that why you chose it?'

Tessa made a face. 'It chose me.' It had been inevitable. 'The Three Sisters is a family affair. Mum and all of us worked in spas and beauty shops in Kendal but when we got the business it made sense that we all worked together.' It was cheap labour, traded for job security and a stake in something that had become more of a liability than an asset.

'What about Sophie?' asked the woman. 'Are there any family connections there?'

'No. I never talked to her about why she chose it as a career. I suppose she just liked doing it. She had nothing but enthusiasm, and when she started she just wanted to watch and learn. But actually she was really good at it. Understanding the customers, what they wanted. Very meticulous with the manicures and pedicures. She was young and strong, too.'

'I expect you all have to be strong.'

'Yes, but it does take its toll.' Their mother used to joke that she could always tell a retired beauty therapist by the slight stoop when they walked and the way they were constantly flexing their wrists or reaching up to massage their permanently aching shoulders. 'But Sophie was great. I sometimes wonder if it bothered her, spending half her working life with three middle-aged women, but she was only here part time, so I don't suppose it mattered.'

'I wouldn't have said you were middle aged.'

Thank you, but we're none of us getting any younger. I'm the youngest and I'm forty-three.' She shrugged.

The detective, who was probably only a decade or so younger, let that pass. 'Tell me about last night. You saw Sophie then, I know.'

'Yes.' At least she hadn't used that deadly, damning phrase *the last to see her alive*. 'She and I were on together at the back end of the day, and she had a client in. The client left and Sophie was just tidying the place up before she went home. I did say that if she wanted me to I'd stay to help her clean up and give her a lift into Pooley Bridge, but she said she was fine about it. Now I wish I had.' And often she would have done, but she'd been expecting to see Leo that evening and had wanted to be home sharp. She hadn't said that in so many words, but nor had she made the offer until she'd had her coat on and was on the way out, and Sophie wasn't stupid. She'd have known the offer was half-hearted and never meant to be accepted.

'What time was that?'

'About half seven, I think.'

46

'Sophie had keys and everything, I believe.'

Suzanne must have told her all this. She supposed they had to cross-check these things. 'Yes. We all trusted her completely. She was wonderful, thoroughly reliable.' And dead.

'And you went home?'

'Yes.' Tessa bit her lip. It suddenly seemed a dangerously selfish thing to do, to drive the short distance to the cottage. But as soon as she'd thought it she was defending herself against any accusation, spoken or otherwise. It had been dark, and the path was rough. It had been raining. She'd been in a hurry because she'd arranged to meet Leo. And in any case it seemed that poor Sophie hadn't even made it off the premises before she came to grief.

'You live quite close, I believe. Pretty much over the shop,' said the sergeant, cheerfully.

'Yes. It just happened like that.' God knows none of the sisters would have chosen it, but yet she thought to admit the truth would have been a betrayal. 'There was so little money left after doing the place up, and the house came as a package with the boathouse, so it was easier just to move into it.' The business had never taken off enough for them to move out. For a moment she allowed herself a heretical thought, that the whole thing had been a vanity project, doomed never to succeed. 'After Dad died and Mum went into a home we just stayed there. It's a nice enough house. And the price of property round here is crazy.'

'God, yes,' said the woman, with feeling. 'I have to share with a friend, too. Can't afford to buy and it's hard even to find somewhere to rent. Did you never want to move out? It must be so restricting, especially with relationships and so on. I know I find it so.'

'Yes. Although none of us are married.' Tessa thought

for a moment, before she handed over a bit of gossip she knew her sisters wouldn't want shared, but it was sufficiently scandalous for her to enjoy telling it, and in any case the police always seemed to want to know everything, no matter how trivial. 'Sue was married once.'

'Oh?'

'Yes, but only very briefly. It was before we came here, when we lived in Kendal. She went off to work in a spa in America and Mum and Dad weren't very pleased about it. Then she phoned up to say she'd got married and, my goodness. You can imagine.' She and Hazel had been a little jealous of Suzanne then, not just at her bid for freedom but its apparent resounding success. 'Dad went over to see what the hell was going on but by the time he got there her husband had decided he'd made a terrible mistake and had disappeared. Dad never even met him. None of us did. Although actually there's a bit of me thinks he doesn't exist. A fantasy. Because Suzanne always wanted to be married and she was just never the attractive one.' That was Hazel. Whatever had transpired, Suzanne had come back from America to the role her parents had expected of her, but bearing a load of bitterness, humiliation and disappointment that she'd never quite been able to shed. And who could blame her? 'I think that's why she moved out of the house.'

'She doesn't live with you?'

'Not any more. She moved out about a year ago, and rents a tiny flat in Pooley Bridge that she found through a client.'

The sergeant raised a questioning eyebrow.

It was a strange sensation, being listened to. Tess thought she could get used to it. 'It's what you were just saying. About relationships. I got a boyfriend, you see.' She felt herself going pink. Forty-three was a ridiculous age to be embarking on a first serious relationship, and the word *boyfriend* made both herself and Leo sound much younger and more frivolous than either of them were, but she couldn't think of a better word for it. *Partner* carried an implication of permanence that Leo would almost certainly resist and *significant other* felt rather too distant. When he introduced her to people Leo always referred to her as *my girl*, whereas she just stuck with his name.

'Okay. And so your sister moved out.'

'I felt a bit bad. I didn't want to drive her away, but I didn't want to have to skulk around like a teenager either. I have every right to bring him home if I want.' The flush on her cheeks deepened as she rehearsed with the sergeant the exact phrase she'd used to Suzanne as they'd argued about it.

'Of course. But at the same time, I can see why she found it so upsetting.'

'That's just it. I can, too. I was very sympathetic and we didn't fall out. But neither of us would give way and Hazel sided with me. I did feel bad for Sue, though.'

'Because of the husband?'

It wasn't an exaggeration to say that this mysterious and short-lived husband had broken Suzanne's heart, but that had been decades before. 'It wasn't just that. I think going away and getting married had been her attempt to break away from home and she really thought she'd done it but I'm afraid they brought her back to heel pretty quickly. I don't think she ever forgave them.'

'Your parents sound quite strong-minded.' Ashleigh O'Halloran picked at a non-existent thread on the sleeve of her jacket — a very expensive jacket, noted Tessa enviously, with a gorgeous crimson silk lining — and avoided eye contact.

'They liked to have us with them, that was all. We were

49

all very close.' But she was lying and she was sure the detective knew it. Her parents had been controlling and Tessa and her sisters had struggled to find the courage or the strength to break free.

She felt a bit sorrier for Suzanne as she thought about it. She didn't exactly flaunt Leo — even if she'd wanted to he wouldn't have stood for that — but she'd been assertive about having him to stay when Suzanne had been difficult about it. It was the only thing she ever had been assertive about. She knew Sue must be desperately jealous of her, but she needn't be. Leo wouldn't have come within a mile of her if her parents had still been alive. He didn't care enough about her to fight for her.

'That's a shame,' said the sergeant, snatching a quick glance at her watch. 'But you still work together with no problem.'

'I'd say so. Bumps on the road. There are always those. But at the end of it blood's thicker than water. Mum wanted us to take on her business and we all wanted to do it.' Up to a point. 'Sometimes I think if she saw us now she might have given us a bit more freedom. And I think if she'd involved us in the decision-making process we might have moved the place on a little more, but we became so set in our ways and it was so easy just to go along with what she wanted.' And now Suzanne was turning into their mother and dragging them along with her.

'Would Sophie being here have changed that?'

'It might have done. And it's funny, because Sue was the one who encouraged her and listened to her and all the rest of it. She'll be devastated, as we all will.'

The sergeant looked at her watch again, as if she were a therapist and being paid by the minute. A sneaking sense of embarrassment crept over Tessa. 'I'm sorry. I've prattled on.'

'Not at all. It was really helpful, Ms Walsh.'

How could the background to three old sisters possibly help in establishing what sort of accident had befallen Sophie? Sensing the interview had reached its natural end, Tessa shifted a bit in her seat. Sue would be in a state. Awful. 'Is that it?'

'For the moment, certainly. I may come back to you with further questions but you've been really helpful, especially under the circumstances. I do hope you all recover from this very quickly. It can't have been a nice thing to find.'

What an understatement. 'Have they taken Sophie — the body — away yet?'

'Not yet, but I don't imagine it'll be very long.'

They got up. 'I think I'll stay here until they've moved it,' said Tessa, inexplicably troubled by the thought of Sophie lying outside in the cold.

'That's probably quite sensible. I'll get someone to let you know when it's done.'

They lingered for a moment in the pod. The rain had come on now, a steady but bleak drizzle that puckered the surface of the water and blurred the glass. 'I'll need to wash these windows.'

'They're very spectacular.'

'Yes, but not very practical, if I'm honest. Sometimes I'm not sure that a beauty studio is the best use for this place. Dad rather forced the use onto the building, rather than working with it.' That had been unusual for him, but she could see why. He would think he could do anything if he turned his mind to it.

'What do you think he should have done with it?'

'Something like this, I think, but just used differently. When Mum stepped back from the business I did suggest

JO ALLEN

something else, but that got shot down in flames.' She made a face.

'What was it?'

'The business struggles a bit. I thought we could make it an artist's retreat. The pods would be perfect for that. There's so much light — which we really don't need in our line of business — and those beautiful views. We could have rented it out, or brought in tutors or something. Had exhibitions, events. It could have been wonderful.'

'But there would have been no work for you.'

That was the problem. 'We could have got jobs elsewhere, of course. I could have run the place. I love art, though I've no talent, but I could have made such a success of helping others, I know. And I did think that with the other two coming up to retirement it's still something they might consider.' But in her heart Tessa knew it wasn't. Their mother had built the business and carried on controlling it long after she'd nominally stepped down. It was most unlikely that Suzanne, who seemed to have nothing left to live for, would be any different.

SEVEN

'Well,' said Ashleigh into her phone, turning up the collar of her coat (too thin and not waterproof, although she'd been in Cumbria long enough to be better prepared than she was) and taking shelter next to the thick holly hedge that shielded the Three Sisters from the public, 'that was something else.'

'Okay.' She thought she could sense Jude's satisfaction, imagined him swinging his chair round and giving her his full attention. He was interested in everything, the essential requirement for a detective. 'You were right, then?'

'I don't know about that, although having looked at the set up I can see why Charlie was bothered. I can't see a clear way to that poor girl accidentally ending up where she did end up. That's the problem.'

'I called Tammy. I don't think she was particularly pleased at being interrupted, but I was at a loose end, as you know I often am, and so I thought I'd make her life difficult.'

'Ha,' said Ashleigh, knowing full well the extent of his workload. 'And what did she tell you?'

'Nothing startling. But like you and like Charlie, she can't see any clue as to how the young woman got there.'

'It's odd, isn't it?' Ashleigh shook water off her dripping fingers and crammed herself even more closely under the shelter of the hedge. 'I mean, there are places along the lake you could fall far enough from to do damage, obviously, and the shock of the cold water could certainly kill you. It was freezing last night. But all those places are so far away from where she was found that I can't bring myself to think she fell at any of those and got conveniently washed up at her workplace.'

'It's definitely odd.'

'I'll be very interested to know what the post mortem says.'

'It'll be very interesting if she drowned, I'll say that,' observed Jude. 'I know that stretch of lake shore pretty well. You've seen it yourself in summer. It shelves pretty gently at that point. And it's not as if she filled her pockets with stones and walked into the deeper water, which would at least be an elegant solution to the conundrum.'

'From the very interesting conversations I've been having with the three Walsh sisters themselves, I'd say that was unlikely,' said Ashleigh. With extreme caution she checked that no-one was listening from the other side of the hedge. The hearse had arrived to transport Sophie's body to the mortuary and Aditi, as the junior officer, had drawn the short straw and gone out into the rain to supervise. In the Three Sisters, Suzanne was standing at the inner of the double glass doors watching the police activity and Hazel and Tessa were just visible behind her, huddled together at one of the tables.

'Is that right?' he said, interested.

'Yes. She had her feet well and truly under their table. They all seemed to like her and the oldest of the sisters seemed to think she was the future of the business.'

'What did the other two sisters think of that?'

'In a funny way, I don't think they minded. That was fascinating, certainly with the two I spoke to. That was Suzanne and Tessa. And I got the impression Aditi felt the same about Hazel. But honestly, there's so much going on there, psychologically. It's such a fascinating set up, and three such different women. They have issues with their parents, and their lives have basically been defined for them by others, not just in their youth but through most of their adult lives. They lived with their parents even when they were working elsewhere and were gathered into the family business when they were adults.'

'Were they happy with that?'

'I don't think so. Suzanne made a break for it, but they hauled her back.' And it was interesting that Tessa had been the one to share that piece of information while her sisters had remained tight-lipped. 'Now they're stuck in the business together and until just recently living in the same house. Stresses and strains galore.'

'If one of them had been found dead in the water I could perhaps have understood it,' he observed, 'but it wasn't. Fascinating.'

'It was. I could have listened to them all day.' How interesting it would be to see the three of them interact. There had been glimpses in that opening scene of a constant manoeuvring for position.

'Hi!' said Charlie Fry, and went marching across the car park with a hand held out in front of him as if he were directing traffic. 'You can't go in there!'

'But I have to,' said a male voice from behind the hedge. 'My girl is in there and she'll need my love and support.'

'Got to go,' said Ashleigh. 'It looks like we have a little local difficulty.'

'I could hear. You'd better go and sort out the forlorn lover. Keep me updated. I'm in a meeting with Faye for most of the afternoon, but if I don't see you there I'll see you tonight.'

'Oh God.' It was the team night out. 'I'd forgotten. You know I'll be busy.' Whatever the initial results of the crime scene investigation there would be paperwork to do back in the office, and in truth Ashleigh had no particular enthusiasm for team nights out and their associated jollities when there was a dead body lying in the mortuary, the death unexplained.

'Me too, but we'd better show face. I don't want to not be corporate. If you're bored we can both sneak off early after I've bought everyone a couple of drinks and you can come back to my place and brief me privately. Or do I mean debrief?'

'Behave yourself,' said Ashleigh in mock severity, closed down the call and turned back to business. 'Is everything okay, Charlie?'

'I'm trying to explain to this gentleman that he can't go down there—'

'But you're there,' said the complainant, cheerfully. He was about the same height as Charlie and probably not a lot younger, but he was lean and tanned and, in his way, good-looking. Rain dripped from his neatly-cropped hair and the hem of his Barbour jacket. 'So why can't I?'

With an internal sigh Ashleigh produced her warrant card and offered it to him. 'I'm afraid there's been an incident and we can't let members of the public into the area until we've finished our investigation.'

'But my girl is in there,' he said. 'I need to make sure she's all right. She'll need someone to look after her.'

'Who's your girlfriend, Mr—?' From her conversation with Tessa Ashleigh had a pretty good idea who this might be but it never did any harm to ask.

'Pascoe. Leo Pascoe. I need to speak to Tessa Walsh. I need to—'

'Ms Walsh is absolutely fine, Mr Pascoe. I'm sure she'll be in touch with you when she's free. But we can't allow you on the property just now.'

He fingered the pocket that must hold his phone, as if to indicate that Tessa already had been in touch. 'She needs someone to look after her.'

'There are trained police officers with her, and her sisters are also there. I'm sure they're all being a great support to one another.'

'Yes, I'm bloody sure they are,' he said fractiously.

There was no love lost there, then. Interesting. 'Honestly, Mr Pascoe, this is routine but it'll take a whole lot longer if we have to interrupt what we're doing to speak to you. I promise you we'll get away from the place as soon as we can.'

He was looking over her shoulder at the hearse. 'It's Sophie, I know. It's not like it isn't public knowledge already.'

'I can't allow you into the spa, I'm afraid.'

'But I—'

'Leo.' Suzanne was still in her towelling robe and slippers but it didn't stop her from forging her way out of the spa and across the car park. 'Go away. Tess doesn't want you here right now.'

He settled into a square-shouldered, confrontational stance. 'I'll believe that when I hear her say it.'

'I heard her say it, and that's enough. Do you think I came out half-dressed in this weather for fun? She doesn't want to see you right now. She didn't ask you to come. I understand why and I hope you do, too. The best thing you can do for her right now is what she wants. Go back home and wait for her to call you.'

He stared at her, mutinously, suddenly oblivious to both Ashleigh and Charlie. 'Christ, you're a bossy one.'

'And you need a firm hand. Since Tess doesn't trust herself to give it to you without you bullying her into agreeing with you, I'm doing it for her. It isn't the right moment. She'll call you later.'

'At least tell her I came.'

'She knows you came. She can see you. Now go. And take that hanger-on with you.'

Her eyes had been dark with fury when she came out but something caught her eye behind him and the fury deepened to black anger. When Ashleigh turned to follow her gaze she saw a second man standing a little way back, showing no signs of engagement but watching the scene with interest.

'He's no hanger-on of mine,' said Leo, with a shrug. 'I expect he's just here to cast an eye over a prospective investment. You know, pick up a failing business on the cheap.'

'He can go, too. I don't want him anywhere near the place. Tell him that.'

'Tell him yourself, since you're so keen on telling everyone else around here what they should do.'

'Just tell him to keep away from us.'

'Tell Tess to call me.'

Suzanne muttered something under her breath then

turned and made her way back across the small car park with as much dignity as her outfit allowed.

Leo Pascoe watched her every step of the way, until the door had closed behind her. 'My God,' he said, cheerfully enough. 'Tess did tell me not to get on the wrong side of her. Now I see why. If I was a copper, sergeant, and I had a suspicious-looking accident on my hands, I know damn well who I'd be looking at as having done it. There's a hell of a lot of anger in that heart, that's for sure.'

He had a wide-eyed innocence about him, the air of a man who intended only good things and only ever reaped bad things from them. Out of the corner of her eye Ashleigh saw Charlie shaking his head, no more fooled by this showing than she was. She had the impression that Leo had known exactly how to wind Suzanne up and had enjoyed doing it.

'Ms Walsh has had a bit of a shock,' she said, to remind him of why they were all there. 'As have the others.'

'I bet. Pretty little thing, wasn't she, young Sophie. Drowned, Tess said. Are you sure it was an accident?'

'We aren't sure of anything just now.'

'I still think I'd look pretty closely at Ms High and Mighty, if I were you.'

'Thank you, Mr Pascoe. We know our job.'

'I'm sorry,' he said, after a moment's pause. 'I was wound up. I'm worried about Tess. A bit in shock about Sophie too, of course. I only knew her as a colleague of Tess's but she was a friendly girl, always brightened the place up and somehow balanced out the old battle-axe in there.' He nodded contemptuously towards the spa. 'And Tess's message got me all worked up. That said, I should probably be kinder to her sister. Although if I'm honest I don't think it was me that was really winding her up.'

He turned and looked back down the path, and Ashleigh and Charlie looked too. The man who had been there — in a suit and smart shoes, on a day like this? — had faded away as if he'd understood his presence wasn't welcome.

'I warned that lad off earlier,' said Charlie, who'd strayed a few yards down the path. 'Some rubber-necker, I think. He knew not to come any closer, anyway. But he can't seem to keep away.'

'He probably doesn't dare get within Suzanne's range,' said Leo, ruefully. 'I bet she can pack a punch if she wants. These masseuses all can. Amazons, the lot of them.' He laughed.

'Do you know who he is?' asked Ashleigh. 'You said something about—'

'About looking out for a possible investment. Yes. I'm afraid I said that to annoy Suzanne. There's no basis for it. It's just that I was at some local tourism committee meeting. He's newly arrived, bought up that rundown hotel out over the back road. The Ullswater Falls.' He jerked a head behind them. 'He made some remark about upgrading and adding a spa and someone suggested he should try and establish a link with the Walsh sisters. Apparently the boathouse used to belong to the hotel, back when it was a private house. Though at a guess I'd say the chances of any kind of working relationship happening are pretty slim. Even when Suzanne's out on a limb, the other two are outnumbered.'

'What's his name?' asked Ashleigh, interested.

'I wasn't really listening. I'm afraid I find these things boring. Tony something, I think.' He shrugged. 'You'll find him at the hotel, I expect.'

'Are you involved in the tourism business, then, Mr Pascoe?'

'I have various interests in various things. Renting out boats on the lake, shooting parties on local estates, a property letting service, almost like Airb&b but on a much more local scale. That sort of thing.' He shrugged in the direction in which Tony whatever-his-name-was had disappeared. 'You can imagine he doesn't always go down terribly well with the members of my network. We understand the area and he doesn't. But he's new and he's bumptious. He'll either learn and succeed or make enemies and fail.' He checked his watch. I'd better go. Unlike you lot, I don't have time to stand around watching. I have things to do.'

'You seem to have found time to come down here,' observed Ashleigh, mildly.

'Yes, because of Tess. I had to make sure she's all right. I'll be off now. And if you need me to give a character reference against Madame Defarge over there at any point, Tess has my number.'

'Well, my God,' said Charlie, sepulchrally as Leo Pascoe sauntered off down the lane. 'That's a trouble-maker if ever I saw one.'

'Isn't he just?' Ashleigh watched him go. 'A confident one, at that. Wow. I know what he said about Suzanne, but I wouldn't want to get on the wrong side of him, either.'

'Yep. Good luck to that bloke who's bought the hotel. Our Mr Pascoe doesn't look as if he's there to make life easier for him.'

'I wonder what the other guy — Tony — was doing. Did you say you saw him earlier?'

'Aye, a couple of times. I spoke to him and he said he was just an interested bystander. And after that he made sure he was on the public path where he'd a right to be. And right in the line of sight for the spa, as well, so as he wouldn't miss anything.'

'They'd hardly miss seeing him, either. I can see why Suzanne might have got a bit wound up by that. I wonder if she knows who he is?' If he was a hotelier looking to develop, a spa might well form part of his plans — and if that was the case the run-down Three Sisters, with its sparring owners, might well not survive the competition.

EIGHT

Arriving at her sister's house full of apologies after that unscheduled morning shift, Becca Reid had been met by a scene of considerable chaos. A weeping mother, a howling toddler and a stressed husband and father who was only too glad to take Rosie off to the pictures and let Becca sort Kirsty out, conspired to make a perfect storm and Becca, as always, rolled up her sleeves and got stuck in.

She was good at that sort of thing. A box of tissues and a shoulder to cry on moved seamlessly on to a snack lunch packed with treats from M&S and the promised Hallmark films. By the time Calum had brought Rosie back, given her her tea and carted her off up to bed Becca had got the wine out and Kirsty was almost fully recovered from her traumatic adventure.

'I just can't...' she said with a shiver as the closing credits rolled on *A Second Chance at Love*. 'I can't process it. It was so awful. At first I thought I was dreaming. Then I realised I wasn't and I'd honestly rather it had been a nightmare. That hand!'

Generally speaking Becca was more prosaic and less given to dramatic outbreaks than her sister. It helped that she was a district nurse who dealt with the sick and the dying on a daily basis. Because she never knew what she was going to find when she opened a door, and because there had been a number of occasions when a patient had passed away (sometimes expected, sometimes not) between one visit and the next, she was equipped to process these departures in a way that Kirsty wasn't.

This was different, though. There was a world of difference between someone slipping away when they were old and ill and the sudden, shocking loss of someone who should still have so much of their life to live. Like Kirsty she'd been a regular visitor to the Three Sisters in her younger, more carefree days, and she vaguely knew a great-aunt of Sophie's, who kept her great-niece's picture on her mantelpiece and spoke with inordinate pride about how well the girl was doing from a limited academic base.

When Becca had been Sophie's age she'd been in a relationship she'd thought would last for ever, with Jude Satterthwaite, and nothing had come of it. Perhaps, after all, you shouldn't dwell too much on potential that wouldn't necessarily be fulfilled.

'It's grim,' she said, tilting the wine bottle towards the glasses and thanking the Lord for the dual blessings that she didn't have to go to work until the following afternoon and that the final part of Calum's contribution to his wife's Christmas treat had been the offer of a lift home at the end of the evening. 'I know that. But it was an accident.' A horrible accident, but an accident nonetheless.

'She's still dead, though.' Kirsty swigged. 'I keep seeing that hand tapping on the glass. I won't sleep tonight.'

'I don't often advise people just to keep drinking,' said

Becca, inspecting the rim of her glass, 'but I think we might make an exception tonight.'

'I made such a fool of myself. And poor Suzanne. She went rushing into the lake to try and get Sophie out and of course it was too late. Oh, God—'

The doorbell interrupted her. 'I'll get it,' Becca said, setting her glass down and getting to her feet. She crossed the room, tweaked the curtain and peeked out, then let the heavy cloth drop and headed for the door. 'I'm on it, Calum,' she called, as her brother-in-law appeared at the top of the stairs.

'Whoever it is, tell them to go away.'

'I don't think so,' said Becca, dryly. 'It's the police.'

At least she was prepared. That quick glimpse out of the window had showed a familiar profile and an even more familiar Mercedes parked in the street. She took a second to compose herself and wrenched the front door open.

'Jude,' she said with a fake smile. 'Good evening.'

He did a quick double-take, as if he thought he might have come to the wrong house. Good. That gave her the advantage over him. 'Becca. Hi.'

'My God,' called down Calum, who hated him, 'what the hell are you doing here?'

'It's a welfare call,' he said, in the neutral voice he always used when he was busy. 'If it's not convenient I can—'

'Come on in.' Emboldened by the wine, Becca felt quite comfortable at overruling Calum in his own house. She had almost as many reasons to be irritated with Jude about the end of their relationship as she had to be annoyed with herself, but whatever had passed between them remained just that — a matter for the two of them.

She resented anyone else taking on grievances on her behalf.

A whimper from Rosie's bedroom sent Calum back out of sight, and Becca led Jude into the living room where Kirsty looked across at them, wide-eyed and anxious. 'You'd better sit down.'

'I won't stay,' he said, surveying them. 'I can see I've interrupted a party.'

'It's supposed to be my Christmas treat,' said Kirsty sipping her wine too quickly. There was a pitch to her voice that suggested she was trying too hard and that tears weren't too far away. A sideways look at Jude told Becca that he sensed it, too. She sat down next to Kirsty on the sofa and placed a reassuring hand on her arm. 'And since the beginning of it went so bloody pear-shaped we thought we'd try and make the rest it better.'

'Lots of wine and an Indian takeaway,' said Becca, for Jude's benefit. 'It's been a bit of a disaster, really.'

'The wine and the takeaway will help.'

Once upon a time they'd understood one another so well they barely needed words to communicate, but these days Becca could no longer tell whether he was amused and, if so, whether he was laughing at her or with her. The consequent feeling of helplessness always made her sharper with him than she intended. 'I can see it's put you out, as well as us. You're working late again.'

'Not today. I'm on my way to a team night out. Our Christmas do, as it happens, since we spent all our time before Christmas making sure everyone else's Christmas parties were fine. I'm not putting myself out and I'm not on official business.' He smiled at Kirsty. 'So I thought I'd pop round and make sure you were okay. For old times's sake.'

Kirsty, who got sentimental after a drink like an old

lady after a couple of sherries at Christmas, sniffed. Before the big bust-up, she and Calum had regularly socialised with Becca and Jude. 'Thank you, but you didn't have to.'

'As I say. I just wanted to reassure you.'

'It wasn't an accident, was it?' asked Kirsty. She set the glass down with exaggerated care and helped herself to a peanut, but she didn't take her eyes off him.

'It's unexplained,' he said, as he always did.

'I'm not an idiot. That's what's bothering me. It was bloody awful but if it had been an accident I could have handled it. But I've been thinking about it all the time we've been watching these films and it can't have been. You don't just fall in the water and even if she did there's nowhere near there to fall from. And you don't just drown. It isn't that deep.'

'It's something we—'

'But why the hell would she have been near the water? I don't see how it can have been an accident. Do you?' She turned in appeal to Becca.

'If someone is taken ill,' said Becca, quick to add her reassurance to Jude's, 'and perhaps passes out near the water—'

'There was no need for her to be anywhere near the water!'

'That's what we're looking at.' Jude took an over-obvious look at his watch. 'I was literally passing your door, and I just came to say we're doing everything we can and if you have any concerns about it don't hesitate to call me.'

'Thank you.' Kirsty was mollified. 'Actually,' she said, as if to her own surprise, 'I appreciate you coming.'

He grinned, the first sign of any relaxation. 'Then it was worth it. I'll leave the two of you to get quietly plas-tered, and go out and get quietly plastered myself.' He turned to the door.

Becca got up and went after him, unable to leave him be. 'Quietly plastered? I know you. You'll be at home with your feet up and the telly on by ten o'clock.' Or, more likely, at home getting cosy with Ashleigh O'Halloran, who had so neatly replaced Becca herself in his affections. She had no-one but herself to blame for that.

'Probably,' he said, pausing in the hallway. 'I'm a busy man.'

'You should get a massage yourself,' she said, thinking aloud just as Kirsty had done, allowing the two glasses of Chianti to speak through her. 'I bet there's a hell of a lot of tension in your shoulders to be got rid of.'

'As usual, yes. But somehow I don't see myself down at the Three Sisters allowing one of them to wrestle me to a couch.'

'They do do men, I'm sure. Lots of places do. It's quite the thing. Very metrosexual.'

'I'm sure, but it's not really my scene.'

They stood there for a moment while Becca wondered what she could say to him that would do as an apology without sounding abased and decided to say nothing because the drink would lead her down a direction she'd surely regret. 'No.'

'Was it you who chose the Three Sisters?' he asked.

She nodded. 'I wish I hadn't. I'd normally have picked somewhere else, somewhere with a whole-day experience, but I wanted to put a bit of business their way.' No good deed, after all, went unpunished.

'Oh?'

'I'd tell you about it, but it's not really the moment.'

He shot a look through to the living room, where Kirsty was just setting up the next movie and the next glass of wine. 'I get that. I probably shouldn't have called but I didn't know you'd be here.'

She felt faintly crushed. 'I can call you some time about it, if you like.'

'Maybe when you get home.'

That meant he was serious, but about what? About what she had to say to him, or merely about hearing her say it? 'But you'll be out.'

'As you said.' He laughed, ruefully. 'I'm not exactly a night owl these days. I won't be late back and even if I am, I can still talk to you.'

'I'll do that then.'

'Goodbye. 'Bye Kirsty. All the best, Calum!' he called up the stairs, then stepped out over the threshold and into the darkness.

'Do you think we made him feel uncomfortable?' Kirsty asked, hitting the pause button on the telly.

'Yes.' Becca dropped into her seat and reached for the wine. It was probably not a good idea to have too much more now she'd undertaken to call Jude later on, but really. Sometimes you needed a drink or several.

'Uncomfortable? I should hope you did,' said Calum, coming into the room and handing out menus for the local Indian takeaway. 'Right, ladies. Time for some food to soak up all that alcohol.'

Becca took the menu and let her eye slide over lists of different choices. Jude might feel uncomfortable about it but she felt even more so, knowing that the tension between them was her fault more than his and that her family's unstinting support for her, touching though it was, was more than a little fraudulent. If she called him later she might find a way to say that.

Or she might not.

NINE

The team evening out was reaching its tipping point, at which its attendees would decide whether to call it a night or carry on into the small hours. In the corner of the pub, Jude was sitting as far away from the action as he could manage, an empty pint glass in front of him. He was waiting for the optimal moment to cut and run, and until that moment came he was thinking about work.

'Listen, son,' said Doddsy in his ear, 'if you can't join in the party and get yourself legless like the rest of us, maybe it's time to take yourself away for a cup of cocoa and an early night, eh?'

Jude grinned. This was comedy at any number of levels. For a start, Doddsy was resolutely teetotal and had been all the time Jude had known him. To go on with, nobody else was getting legless, yet, though Chris Marshall and Aditi were giggling together loudly over some anecdote Jude had heard and which bluntly hadn't justified that level of merriment. 'Okay. Is this my regular ticking off for working too hard?'

Doddsy was Jude's junior officer in work and his best mate out of it, though these days the social part of their relationship played out on a more occasional level since Doddsy had found himself a much younger partner and Jude had managed to find himself settled into an on-off relationship with Ashleigh. He had regrets. He missed Doddsy's company and his sound, good common sense. 'I've got things on my mind.'

'At least try to hide it when you're supposed to be having fun, eh?'

'You sound like my mother.'

Doddsy, who was eternally good-natured, laughed at that where someone else might have taken offence. 'I never get the time to take you aside for a quiet word these days, so I'll take my chance now. What's on your mind?'

Jude considered. There were two truthful answers — that he was thinking about work on a social night out, and that he had been thrown off his stride when his conscience-saving visit to Kirsty McKellen had been sabotaged by Becca's unexpected presence — and admitting to either of them would expose him to some kind of common-sense commentary he wasn't in the mood for. He opted for a half-truth he thought he might get away with, a perennial thorn in his flesh. 'My bad. I was letting my thoughts run away with me. Mikey.'

'The lad causing you trouble again, is he?'

In fact Mikey, Jude's much younger brother, had emerged remarkably unscathed from a highly problematic adolescence and early adulthood and Jude was considerably less worried about him than usual. 'You know how it is. I worry about him unnecessarily because someone has to and Dad doesn't care.'

Doddsy fished a piece of orange out of his St

Clement's and chewed it thoughtfully. 'I thought he was doing fine.'

'He is. Good job, nice girlfriend.' Izzy Ecclestone was eccentric and probably a little more edgy than Jude was comfortable with, but she was good for Mikey and he was good for her. 'He's calmed down. I don't know why he's bothering me tonight. Unless it's that I have a subliminal fear I'm going to run into him down here and have to buy him a pint.' This particular pub — not his choice — was one of Mikey's favourite haunts.

Doddsy laughed, but nevertheless took a cautious look around the pub. It wouldn't be Mikey he was looking for but another of the many weights on Jude's conscience. Adam Fleetwood, his former close friend and now a reformed ex-convict, was also in the habit of frequenting this particular drinking hole. Knowing that, Jude made a point of avoiding it.

Adam wasn't in tonight but the thought of him amplified Jude's bad mood. Adam had been part of that crowd, with Kirsty and Calum and Becca and Jude himself, until he'd gone to prison and everybody — even Becca — had decided he was hard-done by and that Jude was somehow to blame. Which was unfair because nobody had made Adam deal drugs and Jude hadn't been involved in apprehending him — only in keeping Mikey out of the whole mess.

In a small town like Penrith it was all but impossible to keep the warp and weft of personal and professional from becoming tangled. He wouldn't have been thinking about Adam and Mikey if he hadn't made that unfortunate decision to call on Kirsty and see if she was all right, and if he'd known Becca would be there he wouldn't have gone within a mile of the place.

'I'm out of sorts, that's all.' He pushed away his empty

glass. 'You're right. If I can't get in the spirit of it I might as well go home like the grump I am, eh?'

Doddsy gave him a pained look. 'That wasn't what I said.'

'No, but it's what you meant.' He could hear himself sounding like a petulant teenager. In his imagination the three women at the Three Sisters bickered in the same way over subtle misinterpretations of the words and the tone of what any one of them said to any other, unable to let a perceived slight pass unavenged. 'Sorry, Doddsy. I'm getting too old for this game.'

'You've got ten years on me and I'm still up for it.'

'Great staying power, then.' Jude looked across the bar for Ashleigh who, he'd sensed from their brief conversation earlier in the evening, was in just as unsettled a mood as he was. 'Well done. But you're right. I'm not in the mood. I think I'll head.'

Doddsy said nothing, too wise to patronise, and turned away to engage in conversation with someone else. Sliding out of his seat, Jude threaded his way across the bar to Ashleigh.

'I'm done here,' he said to her. 'Want to come with me? Or would you rather stay and enjoy the fun?'

She was more sociable than he was and he'd expected some kind of hesitation, some weighing up of her options, but she shook her head immediately. 'I'm not in the mood either.'

'I thought as much. Bee in your bonnet?'

'More like a stone in my shoe. Just one of those things that won't let me go.'

'Sophie?'

'I knew you'd get it. I keep thinking about her, and it seems somehow wrong to be having a good time. Is that your problem as well?'

'Part of it,' he confessed, 'though I lied to Doddsy and told him it was Mikey.' He wasn't going to tell her the rest of what had unsettled him. There was no need. She had an uncommon knack of understanding other people's motives and ferreting out their problems, so there was every chance she'd work it out for herself.

'May you be forgiven,' she said lightly, and lifted her coat from the back of her chair. 'Let's sneak out before anyone tries to buy us another drink.'

They extricated themselves from the pub almost unnoticed and strolled down the hill towards the town square. These days their relationship was more casual than it had been, friendship with benefits rather than the grand love affair to which both had aspired with other partners and which both had somehow let go. For a while, when he'd first met Ashleigh, Jude had thought he was over Becca but time had shown him how wrong he was.

It was the other side of the equation that troubled him. What did she feel for him? She hadn't needed to offer to phone him; there could be nothing she had to say that couldn't have been said on her sister's doorstep. And she materialised in his life with an uncomfortable regularity, often appearing from her cottage for no particular reason whenever Jude called in to visit his mother, who lived opposite her. Mikey swore it was deliberate, but Mikey had always been a bit of a wind-up merchant where Becca and his brother were concerned.

The signs, then, were that she hadn't got over him, but none of that tied in with the fact that when he'd had the courage to approach her, at a point when Ashleigh had chosen to step back from their relationship, she had turned him down flat.

That was the worst of it. He'd been so sure she still cared, so confident of a positive response, and had ended by making a fool of himself. He didn't dare risk making that mistake again.

'Sorry,' he said as they paused at the square. 'I'm a crabbit old beggar these days, as my dad would say.'

'It's old age,' said Ashleigh and laughed.

He was much younger than he felt, not yet forty. 'Shall we go back to my place?'

'If it would cheer you up. And assuming you've no other appointments.

It was almost as if she knew. 'Becca's phoning at some point.' At least this wouldn't be a bone of contention. Neither he nor Ashleigh kidded themselves that their relationship was anything approaching a romance.

'Is she, indeed?'

'I called in on Kirsty McKellen on the way here and she was there. She wanted to talk about the Three Sisters.'

'Oh God, yes, of course.' Ashleigh slipped her hand into his as they crossed the road. While they were in the pub the temperature had dipped below freezing and though the afternoon's drizzle had petered out it had never dried and now it was hardening under their feet. 'I don't know how I'd forgotten Kirsty was her sister because obviously that was what made me call you this morning, but somehow it slipped my mind. I can't stop thinking about Sophie.'

'Same.'

'Accident is impossible, isn't it?' Her fingers tightened around his.

'You'll know more than I will, but there's certainly something really odd about it. I wouldn't be at all surprised to find it's much more serious than that. Especially in the light of what you say about the whole set-up of the place.' Those mighty tensions among three adults forced into close contact, for years. He'd bet his house that the three of

75

them bitterly resented not only each other but their own failure to forge another path.

'I know,' said Ashleigh as they passed up through the narrow lane and into the churchyard, where the damp was curdling to white on the grass of the curtilage. 'There's so much going on there, as I say. A huge amount of tension. I felt quite glad to be out of it. And then when I was outside we got another helping of it with our two bickering onlookers. Or not quite. One of them disappeared pretty quickly.'

As they walked, she filled him in on the encounter with Leo Pascoe and the mysterious hotelier, Tony, and Jude both listened and kept a wary eye out. There was a group of men standing at the taxi rank, smoking and eating chips, and he took a quick look at them as he always did because this, too, was one of Adam Fleetwood's favoured haunts. He held her hand more tightly as they negotiated the thickening black ice and they forged through a cloud of nicotine and vinegar unscathed.

'I think I've heard of Pascoe,' he said, once they were out of earshot. 'I've seen his name in the paper. He's one of those guys who's on the board of just about everything worthy around here and has a finger in every pie. He seems to be very rich, though I don't know where the money comes from, which always interests me even though it's none of my business. He's always in *Cumbria Life*.'

'You don't mix in those social circles, then,' she teased.

'No, but he'll be best pals with the Chief Constable. Not literally, I don't think, but certainly that type, and they're bound to be members of the same golf club.'

'From what you say he doesn't sound like the sort of person you'd expect to be dating Tessa Walsh.'

'Love's a funny thing. But no. You wouldn't match them, I don't think. Which makes it even more interesting.'

'You're right, but despite what I said I don't think I'm that surprised. I know nothing about him but from the way he tried to turn the charm on me I'll be very surprised if Tessa's the only woman he's going out with. He fits that type, too, the sort who's always looking out for a new woman but hedges his bets and never risks losing one. I wouldn't insult Tessa by saying she's desperate, but I bet she lets him get away with a lot and he knows she won't ditch him.'

'It gets murkier, doesn't it? I'm interested in the mysterious Tony, too.' The motives for homicide were almost always pretty straightforward. If it wasn't an accident, the chances were that if Sophie hadn't died for love, she'd died for money.

'We shouldn't get ahead of ourselves,' said Ashleigh, after a moment, 'but I think I'm going to bet that Sophie was murdered.'

'I'm not going to risk my money by betting against you.'

As they headed up Wordsworth Street he kept a wary eye out for the flat opposite his own. Adam seemed to have rented it purely for the sake of being a constant presence in his adversary's life, but the curtains were drawn. For once the cold and the sleet had got the better of Adam's malicious intent. That was something, at least.

'Drink?' he asked, when they were safely inside and had divested themselves of their coats, 'or coffee?'

'I'll go for the coffee. And better make it decaf. I've a funny feeling tomorrow's going to be a long day and a difficult one.'

'We're expecting the PM results first thing in the morning. If you're right we're all going to need a lot of strong coffee.' He went into the kitchen and fiddled about with the machine, taking two cups through when he was done.

'Did you say you'd ring Becca?' asked Ashleigh with studied disinterest as she accepted her cup, 'or was she going to phone you?'

He glanced at the clock. Ten o'clock. 'She said she'd phone. But she might not.'

'Why don't you phone her and get it over with?'

Ashleigh had an unsurprisingly ambivalent attitude towards Becca. Jude himself reacted in exactly the same way every time she mentioned her ex-husband with any form of wistfulness, though the situations weren't comparable. Ashleigh's ex had been controlling, selfish and damaging, incapable of holding down any kind of a relationship, whereas good-natured, community-spirited Becca was entirely the opposite. 'I could do, I suppose. I don't know if she'll be back from Kirsty's yet.'

He was spared the decision by his phone. 'Speak of the devil,' he said, and answered it. 'Hi, Becca.'

'It's not a bad time, is it?' she asked, sounding anxious. 'I know you said you were going out.'

'Not at all. A good time, in fact. Ashleigh's here,' he added, for clarification, 'and I've got you on speaker.'

'Right. I'm sorry I was a bit terse with you earlier. It was just a difficult day all round.'

'I understand.' Out of the corner of his eye he saw Ashleigh staring intently at the phone. He patted her knee for reassurance and regretted it immediately. There was nothing to reassure her about; she knew it all.

'I wanted to tell you why I picked the Three Sisters for Kirsty's present. That's all. It's a bit run down, you know?'

'So I'm told,' he said, and slid an arm round Ashleigh's shoulder.

'It's really stupid but I felt sorry for them. When people talk about it it's all about how shabby it is and how limited the facilities are and how the Walsh sisters never look like they're enjoying themselves and it's a pity they aren't all as young as poor Sophie was. My mum used to go there when their mum was in charge, you know, but that was twenty years ago when it was cool and edgy. And actually it was Mum who suggested it. I asked her and she said she thought they could use the business and even if that part of the Christmas treat wasn't as good as it could have been, the real fun would come with the two of us having a girly time together.'

'Your mum's as soft as you are,' he said, amused.

'Oh God, I do hope not. Anyway, that was it, really. But from what Kirsty said I'd no idea the place had become so shabby and that just makes me wonder if they're in some kind of financial difficulty. That's all.'

'Thanks. That's very helpful.' It was his stock response to every offer of information from every member of the public.

'Okay. I'll see you around, then.'

'Bye,' he said and ended the call. 'Well, Ash, what do you make of that.'

'Are you for real?' She slapped him affectionately on the arm. 'That was nothing to do with poor Sophie. She just wanted to talk to you.'

'I don't think it was that. She's known me long enough. She knows I like to know everything about anything just in case it's relevant.'

'She didn't have a lot to say that was relevant to the case. Just that the place is tired and run down, and I already told you that.'

'If it turns out that Sophie was murdered then it may well be that the state of the place is relevant.' Surely the sisters would have life insurance, and it was conceivable that Sophie, leaving late at night, could have been mistaken for one of her employers. Tessa, perhaps, who had been

79

the one to leave immediately beforehand? 'Do you fancy going down for a treatment and sniffing the place out as a customer?'

'That would look great on my expenses, wouldn't it? I don't have time for that sort of thing these days.'

'Maybe we should go up to the Ullswater Falls, then, and check out the sisters' potential competition. We could go up and have a drink at the weekend. See if there's anything going on up there.'

She laughed. 'Next you're going to unmask the mysterious Tony as a contract killer.'

'Not a chance. If he was he wouldn't be anywhere near the scene of the crime. I think it's a lot simpler than that. I think he's nosey. And so am I,' he said, and picked up his coffee.

TEN

'**O**kay,' Jude said with a sigh, 'so now we've got the post-mortem results and it's as we thought it might be. Sophie Hayes was murdered. Just what we all need on the morning after the night before.'

The email with the detailed results had dropped into his inbox ten minutes earlier, but he'd been forewarned by a quick call from Matt Cork, the pathologist and an old friend. Now he'd had time to give some thought to the ramifications he and Doddsy, Ashleigh, Aditi and DS Chris Marshall had convened a meeting in the incident room. He already had detectives scanning through all the available databases for everything they could find on Sophie Hayes and on the Walsh sisters, but nothing beat half an hour's brainstorming.

An untidy accumulation of information spilled out on the table at which they sat — photos of Sophie's body, fully-clothed and bloated on the lake shore and naked in the mortuary. There were pictures of the Three Sisters spa and the women who ran it, photos taken by Tammy and the CSI team of the scene where Sophie's body had been found, and a large-scale Ordnance Survey map of the immediate area on which Jude had already sat down and sketched in possible lines of escape for an attacker. On the board behind them, where the information would soon be displayed, Jude had already written Sophie's name and those of the three Walsh sisters.

To a degree that was futile. In the dark, and on that remote path, it would have been easy for the killer to make his — or her — escape without any real risk of coming across a witness and, if they heard someone coming or were alerted by the light of a torch, it would have been easy enough to melt away into the shadows until the danger was past. When this meeting was over he'd send someone down to Pooley Bridge with a team of uniformed officers to see if anyone had seen or heard anything on the path that linked the near-empty campsite and the village, and passed by the Three Sisters, but he doubted it would bring them any joy. It might not be the perfect murder but it seemed whoever had done it had made a clean enough escape.

So they would catch them another way. 'I don't know if you've had a chance to read the PM report.' He looked at them; Chris bleary-eyed, Aditi yawning, Doddsy with the smugness of the lifelong teetotaller. His and Ashleigh's decision to leave early seemed to be the right one. 'Sophie died almost instantly from pressure on the carotid arteries. There's bruising on her neck.' It hadn't been visible under the scarf she'd worn when she was pulled from the lake, but it was clear enough from the subsequent photographs of her body. 'She'd been in the water for several hours and she was dead when she went in.' He took a quick look down at the email Matt Cork had sent. 'Matt's always cautious about the time of death.' Rightly so. He allowed himself a wry smile at the pathologist's abundance of caution. *For certain, some time after she was last seen alive and before the body was found.* 'The last report of her alive is from Tessa Walsh who saw her at half past seven.'

'She says,' interjected Chris, more alert than he'd seemed.

'Yes. But her client left at twenty past and Sophie was very much alive then.' Though a lot could happen in ten minutes. 'Kirsty McKellen saw the body in the water at almost half past ten yesterday morning, by which time it was already distended. So I'm going to stick my neck out in a way Matt wouldn't and say that her death occurred approximately an hour after Tessa left the Three Sisters.'

'An hour?' asked Ashleigh. 'Tessa said Sophie only had to tidy up and that wouldn't have taken long. And it seems sensible to me that she might have been attacked very close to the spa, probably as she left. So what do you know that we don't?'

Jude tapped at his iPad. 'I'll forward you all the detailed PM report. There are indications — this is Matt being hyper-cautious again — that she'd had sexual inter-course relatively soon before her death, and by relatively soon he doesn't mean the night before. There are no other signs of force on the body at all. Her clothing hadn't been in any way disarranged. So I think we can assume it was consensual and had taken place at some point after Tessa left and before Sophie got ready to go home.'

When he'd read over the notes of the witness inter-views Ashleigh and Aditi had compiled it had immediately struck him as odd that Sophie had so regularly declined repeated offers of a lift back along the road from the spa in the dark. Now that, at least, made sense.

'Hazel said something about Sophie,' ventured Aditi. 'I thought she was pretty derogatory, and I think she thought so too because she tried to backtrack on it. She made some remark about how many boyfriends Sophie had and that it was never the same one. She didn't quite accuse her of being sexually promiscuous but it was pretty obvious she didn't approve.'

'I wonder if she knew what was going on?' mused Ashleigh. 'I'm assuming we're all thinking the same thing here — that it suited Sophie to be the one who always stayed to clear up because she could invite her boyfriend back to the spa after hours for a little bit of privacy, assuming for whatever reason she didn't want to take him home. Right?'

'Exactly that,' Jude said. 'Though quite why anyone would want to kill her for that is open to question. Apart from the obvious, of course — that it was the lover — and assuming it was her they wanted to kill and not one of the others.' It had been a cold night and Sophie had been well wrapped up in a big puffy jacket with a hood and a scarf. There wasn't a great height difference between her and any of the Walsh sisters, or certainly not in the dark. Mistaken identity was a definite possibility.

'If it's that it must mean it was Tessa they were after.' Doddsy sat back and shook his head. 'She was the only other one there.'

'We don't know that. We don't know what the killer knew.' They may have been mistaken about the rota or they may have guessed, or they may just have hung around until they saw the person they thought was their intended target. Or they may not have planned it at all, if Sophie saw something she shouldn't, but he was inclined to dismiss that. Tammy and the CSI team hadn't uncovered so much as a discarded cigarette end to indicate that anyone else had been on the scene, still less that they'd been engaged in anything nefarious.

'Okay,' said Chris, already writing himself a list of notes, of things to look up. 'Who are the possible suspects? The lover is the first and the most obvious one, isn't he?'

'I think so,' said Jude, with faint distaste. It was something they came across too often — a partner, almost always a man, who couldn't bear refusal or rejection.

'But we don't know who he is? No DNA match?'

'Nothing's been run through the database yet. We might be lucky and the guy's in there. We might not.' There was every chance they wouldn't be, if Sophie's lover hadn't put a foot wrong with the law in the past. 'Even if we identify him, it doesn't mean he killed her.' But he would be another witness, someone who could further narrow the time of death, who might have heard or seen something as he left the Three Sisters.

'I'll go down and talk to her parents, if you want,' Ashleigh said. 'They may know. There might be all sorts of reasons why she didn't take him home. It needn't have been furtive. It could be no more than convenience, if he works locally and they could meet up on the way home.'

He nodded. Ashleigh seemed to have a hypnotic effect on some witnesses. They wanted to tell her things, and even the most hostile and resistant of them sometimes got lulled into a false sense of security. In this sort of situation, where parents might withhold information to protect their daughter's reputation even if it lessened the chances of her killer being caught, her skills were particularly valuable.

'Good shout. It's bad enough for them that she died. They'll take the fact that someone killed her very hard, no doubt.'

'They're only over in Penrith. I can go down there after I've set up the door-to-door inquiries.'

Jude flicked a quick look at the whiteboard behind them. Seeing it, Chris obligingly jumped up, picked up the marker and wrote *mystery man?* in capitals next to Sophie's picture, then stood with the pen poised. 'Any other suspects to put up while I'm here? The three sisters themselves, of course.' He flourished the pen in the direction of their names.

'Yes. There's the man from the hotel. His name's Tony Charles.' Ashleigh sat back and laid her iPad on the table, with the website for the Ullswater Falls Hotel open on the screen. 'Let's think about him. I don't know why we're talking about a mystery man as if there's only one. There's another, and he's it. Hanging around but not getting too close, and no-one seeming to know much about who it was? I think we need to have a little chat with him and see where he was when Sophie died.'

'I'll do that,' said Aditi, promptly. 'How do you get to the place? I don't recall seeing any signs.'

'On the hill.' Doddsy reached for a pad and drew a quick sketch — the Three Sisters, the path along the shore, the roughly-metalled track that intersected with it and cut back through the countryside to join the Pooley Bridge-Howtown road. In a rough triangle between the village, the road and the spa he drew a square. 'The main access is behind the car park in the village.'

The Three Sisters, Jude remembered, had once belonged to the hotel; so had the house where he suspected Hazel and Tessa spent their time bickering the long evenings away. 'It would be quite neat for the business if they could swallow up the spa and extend and improve it.' He scratched his head. 'But that would be a reason for one of the sisters to kill him if they didn't like the idea, not for him to do away with the most junior member of staff.'

'It doesn't rule him out as a bit on the side, though. If he lives locally that rules him in, I'd say.'

'What,' said Chris, 'with a whole hotel of his own to play with?'

'He may also have a wife,' pointed out Ashleigh, 'in which case I would say Tony-of-the-Ullswater-Falls immediately becomes very interesting. As indeed, does a wife who might know and be as well placed as he would be to do the deed quickly and make a clean getaway.'

Jude looked at the sketch again. 'I wouldn't swear to it but I think there's a gate onto that path from the hotel grounds.'

Chris sat down and drew a sweeping black arrow onto the map from the Three Sisters to the hotel, then stood up again and wrote *Tony Charles* on the board. 'Right. What about the others? The three sisters themselves.' Their names were already up, so he sat down again.

Jude looked to Ashleigh and Aditi. 'You two spoke to them. I've had a quick look through your notes of the interviews, but what did you make of them? There seems to be a whole load of stuff going on there, Ash said. Let's start with Suzanne.'

'I thought Suzanne was very interesting,' said Ashleigh. 'All of them are, but I think she might be the most complicated. She was very tight-lipped with me, for most of the time, but I could sense something boiling up inside her. A kind of slow frustration that might have been there for years, almost.'

'Hazel said that that's what she's like,' added Aditi. 'Absorbs every knock, then blows her top, then it's all over.'

'Yes, and Tessa's boyfriend said something similar, didn't he? Suzanne was shouting at him in the car park and he just about said if we were looking for a killer we should be looking at her.'

That kind of thing might be inspired, or it might be malicious. It might, of course, be intended to deflect from another person entirely. 'Did I see in the notes that Suzanne moved out when Tessa found a partner?'

'You did, but I'm not necessarily sure that means she was intolerant of what other people might think of as loose sexual behaviour.' Ashleigh fiddled with her pen. 'It may just be that she disliked him — which was the impression I got — and couldn't bear having him around, or it may be that he was the excuse she needed to move out. Because he clearly dislikes her, he was obviously trying to wind her up and he knew exactly what to say and what impact it would have. In that context, I can quite understand why she wouldn't want to stick around to have him constantly winding her up. And she'd hate it if she felt he'd forced her out.'

'She's nearly sixty, though, and was living with her sisters, not sixteen and living with her parents,' sad Chris and laughed.

'Agreed. But sometimes people get set in their ways as they get older and it's quite easy to get stuck in a rut. For what its worth I didn't get the impression that Suzanne was in any way jealous of Tessa, but rather that she was protective of her,' said Ashleigh.

'Might she have been jealous of Sophie?'

'If she knew, possibly, and it would depend on who the man in question was. And of course although she wasn't there that evening — she'd already left — that doesn't mean she couldn't have come back.'

'She had a short-lived marriage, right?'

'Yes, but she never mentioned it, nor any other sexual relationships, though obviously I didn't ask as we were talking about Sophie's death as an accident at that stage. But my own opinion is that Suzanne has been to the school of hard knocks and whatever went wrong in her marriage

— or at a guess whatever was never right in her marriage — has embittered her for a lifetime.'

She shrugged, and avoided everyone's eye. If you loved someone and lost them it could scar you for life. Jude knew that from his own experience and so did she. It was entirely reasonable that Suzanne felt the same.

'What about the other two?' asked Doddsy. He'd been skimming through the interview notes as he listened, a slight frown indicating that his views on the three Walsh sisters were in line with Ashleigh's and Jude's own — that such a high level of dysfunctionality created a climate for violence. 'Hazel. The middle one. Classic middle child syndrome?'

'Possibly. Though speaking as a middle child I don't care too much for that kind of pop psychology.' Aditi winked at him. 'I'd say Hazel is very much in the shadow of her older sister, and I'd guess she was probably very much in the shadow of her parents, too — certainly her mother, who seems to have been a very single-minded woman in both her business and personal affairs. I'd also venture to suggest that she might have been the adored youngest child — which is a very comfortable place to be — until she was eleven or twelve and then, lo and behold, up pops a younger sister. That would put a child's nose out of joint for a long time, possibly permanently.'

'You didn't detect any particular negativity towards either of her sisters?' Jude asked of Aditi.

She shook her head. 'The opposite, if anything. She looked a little downtrodden, I thought. The only lack of charity she showed was towards Sophie.'

'Of whom, of course, Suzanne spoke very highly,' Ashleigh reminded her. 'It does make me wonder. If Hazel had plans to take over the business when Suzanne retired then it's possible she saw Sophie, who Suzanne clearly considered a natural successor and who had a considerable influence, as competition, but I can see two problems with that. One is that Hazel is only a couple of years younger than Suzanne and so she almost certainly wouldn't have had much time either to run the business or to be bossed around by a much younger woman if Sophie did take over from Suzanne. The second is that I didn't get the sense that Suzanne really planned to retire at all — only that she was keen to ease off on some of the more physical work. So while Hazel's jealousy, if she was jealous, might make perfect sense, there was absolutely nothing to be gained from killing Sophie, unless there was some reason we don't know about.'

'That said, even such a slender motive is a motive. Remember what Hazel said about Suzanne allowing her resentment to build. Hazel wasn't on duty at the spa that evening either, but she could easily have loitered near the building, or even gone home and come back later.' It was Jude's turn to frown. 'And then we have Tessa, don't we?'

'I'm going to guess Suzanne was jealous of Tessa's boyfriend, if nothing else,' said Ashleigh with a sigh. 'He knew it. That's why he was taunting her. *My girl. I need to look after her*. All that sort of thing.'

'It's a point against Suzanne, rather than Tessa, I would say.'

'Yes. But what stands against Tessa is that if Suzanne and Hazel retired then she was the one who stood to lose out if Sophie took over. So if Sophie was a threat to any of them, she was a threat to Tessa.' And Tessa had been the last to see her alive. They only had her word for what had passed between the two of them.

'Any of the three of them could have come back to the spa for whatever reason,' said Doddsy after a moment's thought. 'If we're right about Sophie taking her boyfriend back there they might have caught them *in flagrante*. Maybe sexual jealousy, maybe just out-and-out fury at an abuse of responsibility. I'm thinking of what we've established about Suzanne, in particular, though the other two sound as if they might be pretty buttoned-up, too.'

'Hazel was the family beauty.' Ashleigh said it with a degree of sympathy. 'And yet she never found a partner, at least as far as we know. Jealousy is a pretty complicated emotion and a strong motivator.'

'Possibly. But if that's the case I'd have expected the distraught boyfriend to come forward with his account of what happened. He'd hardly not have heard a row. Unless he left beforehand and missed it, of course.'

'And unless he has a very good reason for not wanting anyone to know who he is.'

'True. We'll follow that up, then.' Jude made a note. 'All of them, in fact. I want someone to check on the sisters' movements after they left the spa on Wednesday evening. I've a suspicion we won't be able to rule any of them in or any of them out, unless Tessa and Hazel can corroborate one another's statements and even then we can't be certain they aren't in it together.'

'I'll sort that out.' Doddsy gave him a businesslike nod.

'And I'd like to look into the business. Chris, this is your kind of thing. I want to know how the Three Sisters is set up, who owns it, what kind of conditions are attached to the ownership. I'm interested in how they're insured and whether that insurance pays out in any way if one of the co-owners dies. I want to know what happens to that individual's share of the business. And I'd also like know what kind of financial shape it's in. Because if Sophie was killed in mistake for one of the other three, then my guess is that it's either going to have something to do with their personal or professional relationships or with the two combined.'

The warp and the weft. He thought again of Becca and Adam and Mikey. No matter how hard you tried you couldn't compartmentalise your life and bitterness endured for years — and sometimes, for ever.

ELEVEN

'Y ou haven't ever been to the Three Sisters Spa, have you?' Jude put his head round his boss's door after a perfunctory knock.

Exactly as he'd known she would, Detective Superintendent Faye Scanlon, who relied on formality to shore up what Jude suspected was a fragile ego tinged with an emotional paranoia, scowled at his casual approach.

'I'd say come in, but it appears you're already in.' She pushed her chair back and regarded him with uncharacteristic wariness. 'I've heard of the place but I wouldn't be seen dead there.'

'That's an unfortunate turn of phrase.'

'It was unintentional.' Faye was always too sensitive to her dignity to be able to laugh at herself. 'To answer your question, I like the odd spa day but I prefer to go somewhere a little more sophisticated, and preferably with a high-quality afternoon tea to follow. Which, incidentally, is what I had planned for the weekend, so I rather hope you're not going to tell me something that's going to make me have to cancel.'

'I don't think so.' He came further into the room, unbidden, and closed the door behind him. 'I'm pretty sure I have everything under control. I'm just in to give you a heads-up about the body that turned up down at the Three Sisters yesterday morning.'

'Homicide, then?' Her expression sharpened.

'Yes, though not a messy one.' He was always grateful for this small mercy. 'Pressure on the carotid arteries. Matt Cork says death would have been almost instantaneous.'

'Lovely,' said Faye, with distaste. 'And do you have any idea who did it? Any suspects?'

'Take your pick.' They hadn't discussed it at the meeting but it was clear to him, and it surely would be to the others, that any one of the three sisters, all skilled in massage techniques, would have known exactly where — and where not — to apply pressure and how much damage they could cause if they got it wrong. Taken by surprise, especially by someone she knew and trusted, Sophie would have been easy prey. 'It could have been one of the girl's employers. It could have been a passer-by.'

'Have you identified a motive?'

'Nothing so obvious, but I'm wondering about mistaken identity.' Though when he thought about it it was unlikely that one of the sisters would mistake Sophie for either of the others after so many years living and working together and fighting like rats in a sack. They'd know every characteristic, every movement, every shake of the head. A mistake was possible, but only if the murderer had no more than a split-second to do the deed.

'I see. And is there anything you specifically need me to do?' She framed the question carefully, leading him to the answer. *No, nothing.*

'I've said you'd do a press conference at half seven tomorrow morning,' he said, unable to resist, and then had to hold up a hand to deflect the fierceness of her scowl. 'Only joking. I have everything under control, as far as possible at the moment, but I'll make sure I keep you updated.'

'Preferably not tomorrow. I have a lot on.'

Her phone rang, and he took that as dismissal, retreating to the corridor and closing the door behind him before heading back to the incident room. There were half a dozen people in there, working away at their laptops. Ashleigh and Aditi had gone back down to Ullswater where the incident scene had become a crime scene and the spa building was sealed off and being searched by the CSI team. Along the lakeside path and in the village a squad of uniformed officers armed with clipboards was embarking on the almost certainly fruitless task of finding someone who might have seen something in that dark, cold night. To Aditi, he had delegated the task of cross-examining the Walsh sisters on their whereabouts.

If he was a bit younger he'd love to have done that himself; interviewing witnesses was something he enjoyed, if only as an observer of human nature. Occasionally the temptation proved too much, and there were times when he headed out of the office with his notebook, something which irritated Faye, for whom precedence was sacred. The Walsh sisters were a particularly tantalising case. It would have been fascinating to see how they talked about one another, what their indiscretions might be, how they were affected by the news that Sophie's death had been no accident. For a moment he thought seriously about it, but the idea was brief. There were other things on his desk that demanded his attention and in any case he had no wish to let Aditi think he thought she wasn't up to the job.

'I'm just checking in,' he said to Chris, who was nearest

and who had looked up from his computer when Jude walked in. 'Any joy?'

'Yep,' said Chris with a broad grin. 'Nothing to ease the hangover like a successful computer search.' He was looking surprisingly perky, but the dark stain on the inside of his empty coffee mug gave him away. He was running on double-strength caffeine.

'I gave you the easy job out of consideration.' Jude, who had given Chris the job because he was good at it, pulled out a chair and sat down. 'Let's hear it.'

'The main thing is that the Three Sisters is in financial difficulty.'

'Is that right?' It was no surprise.

'It's been running at a loss for years. There's been zero investment. I did a quick sweep of their website to see how busy they are and either their booking system isn't functioning or else there isn't any business for them. I could have got myself booked in for any time next week if I'd wanted. Manicure, pedicure, facial, anything.' He laughed. 'I was tempted by a seaweed wrap, but Caitlyn would have a fit.'

Jude, too, had managed a quick look at the website and found it competent but uninspiring, a feature of a limited marketing budget. 'The property has a value, depending on use.'

'It does, but with limits. From what Ash and Aditi said It looks as if it needs a lot of work and I'm no architect but I bet converting it would cost a fortune. The business has very little in the way of assets. I checked to see if they inherited anything from their parents, but there was nothing but the business and the house they live in.'

Jude rubbed his chin. That might explain why Hazel and Tess, at least, still stuck it out in the family home. He wondered what kind of place Suzanne had found, and how she'd managed to afford it. 'Sophie worked there two days a week.'

'I'd bet a quid there wasn't two days' work a week. If she was doing it the others must have been sitting around painting each other's nails for fun, not profit.'

'Was it insured?'

'I haven't got that far yet. I'm still on the property details. But the three of them own it jointly and given what we know I'd say that'll cause a few problems.'

In theory it should be the opposite. Two against one would make a working majority and avoid the business being stalemated into atrophy by one against one or two against two, but it was easy to see how differences of opinion might ebb and flow, how one partner might threaten to leave and sell to a third party or make the others scrape around to buy them out. No doubt all those things had gone on in the tight, bickering relationship between the three siblings...but how had it ended?

TWELVE

'I just can't—' Anna Hayes, Sophie's bereaved mother, had insisted on making Ashleigh a coffee and handed it to her before she sank into the armchair. Her face was as white as her daughter's had been after a night in the water, her eyes dim as if the spark had gone from them the moment her daughter died. 'I just can't believe it. I know it happened but I can't believe she's gone.'

Despite their shock and grief Sophie's parents were functioning, sitting in the kitchen of their neat semi in one of the sprawling new estates on the outskirts of Penrith, doing exactly what they would normally have done. They checked messages of condolence (at least half a dozen in the few minutes since Ashleigh had arrived) and then apologised for their rudeness and swiped them aside to return to later. They made coffee; they ate biscuits; they talked and breathed and moved just as they had done before Sophie's death. But they were human. Anna couldn't suppress the occasional hiccoughing sob while Dean, Sophie's father, wore a permanent expression of woe.

Who could blame him for that, thought Ashleigh as she gave them a moment to recover from the news that Sophie's death hadn't been accidental. 'I can promise you we're doing everything we can to find out who did it.' She was too well-rehearsed at this kind of glibness, a part of the job she hated but one that had to be done. 'I know it will be painful for you but I need to ask you about Sophie, and I need you to try and think of anything about her that might have caused someone to want to harm her.'

'She was our angel,' said her father, unsurprisingly. No-one liked to speak ill of the dead — or at least, not their nearest and dearest. Friends and acquaintances might be more trenchant, and different people presented themselves differently to different people.

'Oh, darling!' said Anna, and touched him affectionately on the arm. 'The sergeant has to ask.' She got up and tweaked the blind, though it was open and there was no-one to look in through the kitchen window. Outside a cat prowled along a wall, hunting. 'Don't get me wrong. I loved her so much. Everyone loved her. But I don't imagine she was perfect.'

The look she shot at her husband was apologetic, the one he returned more sorrow than anger, but after a second he dipped his head in agreement. 'She was perfect to me.'

'She was impatient,' her mother went on, resuming her seat. 'Keen to make progress. She was only twenty-three but she wanted everything immediately. I think kids do, these days. Everyone tells them they can have whatever they want and be whatever they want and nobody tells them it takes time and hard work and sacrifice. But that's not Sophie's fault.'

'You say she was ambitious. In what way?'

'I don't...I mean, she loved her job and she did work

hard at that. Don't get me wrong. She had dreams — I had dreams myself at her age, wanted to be a fashion buyer for one of the big shops. She wanted to run her own spa business, or even a chain of them. And she had that part-time job.' Her voice faltered.

'Her employers thought very highly of her.'

'Yes, she loved what she did. But I was never quite sure that she loved the place as much as she said she did. I think she saw the Three Sisters as...well, as an opportunity. A means to an end.'

Who wouldn't, in Sophie's position? 'I understand she was increasingly involved in the business?'

'I suppose...I mean, she wasn't always that kind about the women she worked for. Two of them didn't like her, or so she said, but she'd say it only mattered that she kept in with the one who made the decisions, the one who had the power. Then she'd be in a good position if she wanted to stay and have experience and a good reference if a better position came up. Isn't that right?' She looked at her husband, and he rewarded her with a sad nod.

'Which sister was that?' asked Ashleigh, though she knew the answer.

'The oldest one. Suzanne.'

'Did you ever meet the sisters?'

'Oh yes. I go there to get my waxing done, to support the place more than anything else. It's in a poor state, if I'm honest. It won't be long before Suzanne retires and when that happens the business will struggle. I always said to Sophie that there's better opportunities, and with her skills she could go to one of the big hotels and get more money and a few decent perks, full-time work, and a lot of experience. She didn't rule it out but she said she'd stick with the Three Sisters just now. She was sure someone would take it over and make some investment in it and she wanted to be there when that happened. She thought she'd be the one who knew how everything worked, make herself indispensable.'

'That Suzanne thought the world of her, though,' said Dean, loyally.

'Oh aye. Rightly so, though I'm not saying our Sophie didn't make a particular effort to be nice to her when perhaps she was a bit sharper with the others.'

Ashleigh looked at the photo of Sophie on the mantelpiece — a twenty-first birthday portrait, perhaps. He smile was much more natural than the forced one in the studio portrait on the board at the Three Sisters.

'What about the others?' she asked. 'How did she get on with them?'

'Fine as far as I know. I mean, you don't get on the wrong side of people who pay your wages and they were as much partners in the business as Suzanne, as I understand it. But I reckon Sophie maybe didn't make quite the effort with them. Not that I'd say that was enough for someone to kill her.' She looked anxious, as if Ashleigh might think Sophie had somehow brought her doom upon herself.

'You wouldn't think so.' But you never knew. Sophie herself might have been so self-centred she had no idea of what kind of tensions simmered between the three. It struck her as unlikely that either Hazel or Tessa would have been so indiscreet with their employee as they had been with the police, their tongues loosened by shock and an apparent desire to help. 'Is there anyone else you know that she didn't get on with?'

They both thought about it, and Dean shook his head more quickly than his wife, although she, too, ended up sighing.

'I honestly don't think so,' she said. 'She had plenty of friends, of course, and they'd fall out like kids do. They are still kids at that age, whatever they think. Sometimes she'd go on about this one being needy or that one only thinking about herself. But her friends were all local. They'd been mates since school and they were always there for one another. I can't imagine anyone of them having a grudge against her.'

'What about her other job? She did pub work, I think?'

'Yes, shifts at different places wherever she could get them. She made a few friends there, I think. I mean, she was a people person, good with everyone, whatever she really thought of them. But again, I can't think she'd have upset anyone.'

'And boyfriends? She was a very attractive young woman, wasn't she, and I think she told some of the clients at the spa that she had a boyfriend.'

'Not right at the moment,' said Anna, cautiously.

'Was she pretty open with you about things like that?'

'Oh yes. I mean, when she was a bit younger it was a bit awkward, her bringing boys home, but young people do what they do, like the birds and the bees. And I'm not saying that we didn't do it too, only even in our day folk were a bit less open about it.'

'She wanted her own private life, our Sophie,' chimed in Dean. 'She was always looking for a place to rent of her own but you know how it is. Hardly anything on the market and what there is gets snapped up in hours and the price of it was way above anything she could afford on two part-time jobs. We'd have helped her if we could have afforded it. If she wanted to bring a young man back, we were happy enough with that. Nice lads, most of them.'

'But you say she wasn't courting right now?'

'No. There was a young man she was walking out with, as my mam used to say, but he moved away to Preston with work and the two of them never managed to get their shifts aligned and it all petered out. I don't think she'd been seeing anyone since him, and that was a few months ago.'

Ashleigh noted down the young man's name and the names of some of Sophie's friends and brought the interview to a close. 'One last thing. I think she was in the habit of parking in Pooley Bridge and walking back from the Three Sisters on her own after her shift.'

'Aye, that's right. Did it all the time. She never minded it.' Dean shrugged. 'It's not far. I did say as how they ought to let her park at the spa because she was young but she said it would put customers off if they had to walk back to Pooley Bridge in their flip flops after they had their nails done, though if you ask me they shouldn't be driving in flip flops either, but what do I know?'

'She was the last to finish that night,' said Anna, biting her lip in anguish. 'She often was. She used to volunteer to lock up and do the cleaning up. She said she liked doing it, and the others didn't.'

Something else to make her seem useful to her bosses. Sophie had seemed remarkably determined to make her mark on the Three Sisters. 'Did she ever express any concerns about her safety?'

'No. If she had I'd have been down there reminding those women of their responsibilities.' Dean's chest puffed out in a father's righteous fury.

'No,' said Ann, more reasonably, 'she didn't. Sometimes I'd ask her if she was all right about it, but she said she liked the walk, and it wasn't far. But I can't say I liked the idea of her walking the path on her own, especially after dark. It's busy enough in the summer but even then it's full of strangers.' Her voice quivered. 'I don't like to think of someone knowing she was there and lying in wait for her.'

'We don't know it's that,' said Ashleigh, getting to her

feet. It would be little enough reassurance for them, but it was all she could offer. 'There's every chance that it was a random attack. Sophie may just have been in the wrong place at the wrong time.'

'I hope you get the bastard that did it,' said Dean, showing her to the door, 'and for his sake, I hope you get to him before I do, because if I meet him alone in the dark he won't make it to prison.'

She should have warned him, very gently, about this kind of threat and that kind of language, but she didn't. 'Goodbye, Mr Hayes. Mrs Hayes.'

As she stepped out into the chill afternoon, she looked back and saw him turn to his wife. 'I never knew any of that about our Sophie,' he said, plaintively.

'Of course you did,' said Anna, robustly, 'or you would have done if you'd ever listened to anything she said,' and then she closed the front door and Ashleigh got into her car and headed off back down towards Ullswater.

THIRTEEN

'Tony Charles,' said Tony-from-the-Ullswater-Falls, clasping Aditi's small hand firmly in his large one. 'I thought you'd be round. I'm surprised not to have seen you before. Door-to-door interviews, isn't it, like in all the police procedurals. *Did you see anything unusual on the night of the whatever-it-was of January?* And if anyone says no they didn't, they were at home with a can of Stella and Match of the Day you'll know they did it because the whatever-it-was of January was a Wednesday and MOTD is only on at weekends.' He smiled, broadly, and then the smile disappeared like a perfectly-timed fade in an Oscar-winning film. 'I shouldn't joke. I know how serious this is, at every level. That poor kid, minding her own business and just trying to make an honest living. And to be honest I've my own honest living to think about as well. If I've got hotel guests walking to and from the village at night I'd be happier if I didn't think there's a lunatic out there pushing them in the lake and drowning them.'

So that was the chat in the village. It was as good a theory as any other on the basis of what the public knew.

Intrigued by Tony's perfect front-of-house persona, Aditi followed him down the corridor and into an office. The sign on the door said *Manager*, in stick-on gold letters so old they might have come from Woolworths. The *M* was slightly askew.

'Yes,' he said, seeing her take a second look, 'it's pretty shabby. I've only been in the place a matter of weeks and there's a huge overhaul planned but we can't do it all at once so we have to prioritise. The public areas are obviously way more important and this is at the back of the queue. In many ways this place wasn't the best buy, because it was a little way beyond my budget but that's me. I can't resist the lure of an opportunity. I'm pretty handy and I do a lot of the maintenance myself. Though, on reflection, I think I might manage to find a few pennies down the back of the sofa to pay for a new sign.'

He waved her to a seat that had also seen better days and sat down at his desk, leaning forward with hands clasped, a man more used to being the interviewer than the interviewee. The desk gave a wide, sweeping view down the slope and across Ullswater, and the grey slate roof of the Three Sisters was visible above a belt of glossy rhododendrons. 'You wanted to talk to me?'

'Yes. First of all, if I may, I'd like to run through a few routine questions.'

'First of all? That implies you have me lined up for some special attention.' He smiled again and the smile, thought Aditi, was like a tiger from an animated film, all gleaming teeth hiding a dangerous and unpredictable nature.

'I do have some specific questions for you, as well as the routine ones, yes.'

'I think I can guess what those are about, too,' he said with a nod. 'But let's do the easy stuff first.'

'The first is to ask you if you saw anything at all unusual on Wednesday evening.'

'I can't say I did. I was inside most of the afternoon and evening, keeping an eye on the bar and dining room. It was dark, and I did go out into the grounds of the hotel, on my evening walk-round. I go out every day, morning and evening, to check the place over from the outside as well as the inside. You see things differently at night.'

'Did you go down to the lake?'

'No. The grounds are quite extensive and, as you may know, there's a path down through the shrubbery to the lake and that comes out near the Three Sisters.' He gestured to the window. 'But I didn't go there.'

'What time was that?'

'About seven, I think. I came back up and went to the flat to change my shoes. It was hellish muddy out there, even just on the path. I went into the bar after that, to chat to some of the guests, and then I went through to the dining room and did a bit of waiting. I like to show my staff I'm hands-on, and I won't ask them to do anything I'm too high and mighty to do myself. Though for health and safety reasons it's probably better if I don't go play chef.' That larger-than-life smile again.

'Did you see anyone in the grounds? Perhaps coming from the direction of the Three Sisters?'

'You think someone might have made their escape that way?' He scratched his head. 'I hadn't thought of that.'

'We have to look at all possibilities.'

'I suppose you'll want to speak to my guests, then, although I think I can account for all of them. We only have six or seven at the moment — midweek, January, trying to recover from a bad reputation. All that. Most of them will have been in the dining room or the bar at the time, especially given the weather was so bad. I didn't stay out that long and I only went down to the edge of the terrace to check that the external lighting was working. I didn't see anyone. If I had done I'd have gone over and engaged them in conversation. But because I didn't see them doesn't mean they weren't there.' He looked thoughtful.

'It very much doesn't.'

'I don't like that thought,' he said with a sigh, 'but I'm going to hope I'm right and there wasn't anyone to see.' He met her gaze. He was a confident man and the smile was too slick to be believable.

'Did you know Sophie?' she asked.

'No. As I said, I've only been here a few weeks. I knew about the spa, of course. I'd heard about it in the village and at the tourism forum, and I'd planned to go down and have a chat with the owners to see if we could come to some mutually beneficial agreement. They need the business, if the local gossip is correct, and I'd benefit from the added value a facility would give me. That's all. I knew the Three Sisters was owned by three sisters, though I've never met any of them. I didn't know there were any other staff.'

'You say you planned to talk to them. Had you approached them in any way?'

'No.' But he looked distinctly shifty at that.

'I think you know what I'm going to ask you next, Mr Charles.' Aditi did her best to look severe.

'I suppose you want to know what I was doing down there after they found the body,' he said with an uncomfortable sigh.

'You certainly made yourself very obvious.'

'It probably didn't look great. I was being nosey. I run a business. I wanted to know what was going on down there in case any of the guests asked me, and I wanted to be able to reassure them there was no threat to themselves.'

'We had uniformed officers down there,' she reminded him. 'I was there myself. Any one of us would have been happy to reassure you.'

'Yes, you're right. But your uniformed officer was being pretty shirty with the other fellow who was there. Pascoe, is that his name?' A look of studied disinterest appeared on Tony Charles's face, at odds with his professional bonhomie. 'I know him from the tourism forum, though only vaguely. If you want to know the workings of the spa you'd be better off asking him, by the sound of it.'

'PC Fry has a responsibility to keep people away from the scene of an incident,' said Aditi, serenely, 'but you rather gave the impression that you were making yourself deliberately obvious. And not to him.'

He took a moment to think about that, and for a second or two the smile settled into a more neutral look before he seemed to remember who he was talking to, and that it was in his interests to be positive. 'It probably wasn't very well-judged of me. At the time I thought it might not be a good idea for them to think there was a strong man hanging around in that lonely place after what had happened, so I wanted them to know who I was.'

'At the time Sophie Hayes's death was thought to be accidental,' Aditi reminded him, 'and we weren't looking for anyone. We were trying to establish the circumstances of her death.'

'Right. But it's a general thing, isn't it? It's good practice, not to alarm women. Most of their clients will be female too, if not all of them, and the lighting down there is pretty poor. I'm not in the business of causing unnecessary distress to anyone.'

Noting both the use of the word *unnecessary* and the slight hardening of his expression, Aditi concluded that Tony Charles wasn't to be trusted. 'You went down there for a reason, though, and you didn't go away when PC Fry asked you at first.'

He shrugged. 'I heard what Pascoe said about me looking out for my investment. It would have been a guess on his part, but he was right. I mentioned it earlier. The Three Sisters could be something very special if it was properly run, had a lot of money thrown at it, and could be tied into a successful business. So yes, although I hadn't approached them I'm certainly considering it as a possible option.'

Suzanne hadn't liked the look of him, that was for sure, but it was interesting that Hazel thought she might consider selling. 'But you didn't know Suzanne Walsh, you say?'

'No.'

'She seemed to know you.'

'Maybe she just doesn't like the look of me.' He grinned and sat back. He wasn't tall but he was muscular and the expensive suit was taut across broad shoulders. Sophie, who had needed a certain strength of her own for her job, would nevertheless be easily overwhelmed by him. 'What's your background, Mr Charles?'

He waved a hand around him, airily. 'Hotels. All my life, all over the word. I worked for a major hotel chain, made a success of it, saved and invested my money wisely — and with a degree of luck, I should say. When I turned forty-five I decided it was time to be my own boss if I didn't want to spend the rest of my life as an employee. That was five years ago. I bought a crumbling old hotel in London, did it up, made it welcoming — it was one of those places where the staff hated the guests and didn't bother to hide it — and turned it into a money spinner. And then I decided it was time to move to the country. When I saw the Ullswater Falls was up for sale I thought I'd try and turn the same trick. And it's going well, so far.'

The door opened and a woman — tall and immaculately dressed in a neat grey suit and navy blue heels — appeared.

'Tony, do you have a minute?' She stopped, looked at Aditi. 'Sorry. I didn't realise you were busy.'

'This is my wife,' he said, getting to his feet and beaming. 'Esmerelda.'

'It's Philippa,' she said to Aditi, slapped Tony lightly on the forearm and they shared a fond laugh. 'Take no notice of him. He's a bit of a joker.'

Aditi, also getting to her feet, introduced herself. 'Detective Constable Desai. I'm making routine inquiries about the incident down at the Three Sisters the other day.'

Philippa Charles's expression softened to one of genuine regret. 'I heard about it. What a terrible thing to happen. And she seemed such a nice girl, too.'

'You knew her?' said Tony, before Aditi could speak.

'I wouldn't say that.' Philippa looked at him, quizzically. 'She came up here just after we moved in and said she'd heard that we were thinking about adding a spa to the hotel and would there be any jobs. I told her it was in the plans but we hadn't made much progress as yet. She sent us her CV.'

Aditi looked at Tony and raised an eyebrow, but he turned away from her and addressed his wife. 'Did I know that?'

'Possibly not. I thought I'd mentioned it, but I have so much going on in my head I might have forgotten.'

'She sent her CV just to you, or to you and Mr Charles?' asked Aditi.

She looked uneasy again. 'I'm not sure. I gave her the

main hotel admin address. Sometimes Tony checks it, but it's usually myself or the receptionist.'

'I don't remember seeing it,' Tony said, 'but it might have gone to spam. Or someone else might have seen it and filed it. But to be honest, I don't really look at that kind of thing.'

There was an awkward silence in which he looked at Philippa and she looked back as if to reassure him. 'I'm sorry I interrupted,' she said, including Aditi in her apology, 'but it is rather urgent. The architect is here to have a look at those buildings at the back.'

Aditi almost felt his sigh of relief. 'Is that the time? I'd better talk to her, then.' He turned back to her. 'Sorry I couldn't be more help to you, Constable, but as I say, we're new around here. Though obviously your people are more than welcome to have a look around the grounds, although it would be good if they could be as discreet as possible. And there's work going on, so I'd appreciate it if you could let us know beforehand.'

'Tony.' Philippa tapped her watch. 'The architect.'

'Yes, of course.'

He led the way out of the room and back down the corridor to where a young woman with a clipboard was sitting doodling what looked like sketches of buildings. 'Goodbye, Constable,' he said, turning to Aditi. 'As I said, I'm sorry I couldn't be more help.'

But, thought Aditi as she left the building, making way for a couple of builders carting construction materials from a delivery lorry round to the rear of the hotel, he had been very useful and very interesting indeed. And possibly rather more than he'd intended.

FOURTEEN

'**M**ikey.' Jude had left it far too long before he called his brother. He knew the response he'd get, and now he'd reached the point where he was only making matters worse by the delay and Mikey would have every reason to be annoyed with him because he wouldn't now have time to make alternative arrangements. Still he held on, just in case something came up, and nothing did. And there he was, five minutes before they were due to meet in Penrith, still in his office. 'Look. I'm sorry.'

'What?' They played this scenario out so often that Mikey, knowing what was coming, was already aggrieved. 'I'm already in the pub and I don't have the car. How am I going to get to the football if you're not going to give me a lift?'

'Can you get a train?' It was an easy walk from the station to the Carlisle United ground. 'I can come and pick you up afterwards, if you want.'

'Don't put yourself out.'

Jude waited for Mikey to hang up, but he didn't. That

meant there was more to be said, more punishment to be meted out, and with reason. He had two forms of relaxation, walking and football, and the latter, being fixed, was the one that too often fell victim to the requirements of his job. It was unfortunate that it was usually the one whose cancellation affected others.

'Like,' said Mikey, sarcastically, 'it's not that often you want to come to the game with me anyway. You'd usually rather go with Dad.'

Jude bit his lip. He didn't have to be a psychologist to know what Mikey was at — using him as a proxy for all their father's failings. David Satterthwaite was an absent parent and his abandonment of his family when Mikey was barely a teenager had been damaging for everyone. The worst of it was that he wasn't remotely repentant. 'I did try.'

'Would you have cancelled on him?'

'I expect so,' said Jude, evenly, 'under the circumstances.' Saturday afternoons were the only time he ever saw his father, the only safe space where the two of them could maintain some kind of civilised relationship, and he was the only one who still kept any kind of contact. Because of that he never cancelled their arrangement lightly. Today it was David who'd found something better to do than use his season ticket and so Jude had arranged to meet up with Mikey for the game and a couple of beers afterwards in Penrith.

'What circumstances are they this time? Just couldn't be bothered? Is that a circumstance?'

If it had been David, would he have cancelled? If he was honest, Jude thought he might not have done. He would have done what he had to do later on in the evening, at home, but he'd reasoned that he saw Mikey often enough at other times and he hadn't bargained on just how annoyed his brother would be. Or maybe Mikey was just in a mood. Either way it was someone else warning him about what a grumpy workaholic he was becoming. 'It's this thing at Ullswater.'

'At the Three Sisters? Or the Three Spinsters, as they call it in the tourism industry around here.'

Cruel, but apt. 'I didn't know you were plugged into that network.'

'Maybe a bit. We've got a new account dealing with the hotels around here, trying to get some kind of consortium going to manage the summer peak for sustainability or something.' Mikey worked for a marketing and communications company. 'The name came up. Most folk in the industry seem to think they're a bit of a problem, tbh.'

'In what way?' Jude, who had been scrolling through a page of documents relating to the investigation, sat back and gave Mikey his full attention. His brother had the same inquiring mind as Jude himself and augmented it with a quite extraordinary knack of both inducing indiscretion in a way Jude, as a detective, could never do without arousing suspicion, and acquiring and retaining an extraordinary amount of information.

'Oh, just that the older of them is set in her ways and can be quite bolshie. They reckon she only comes along to the forum to find out what everyone else is doing and she never agrees to participate in anything. Certainly never comes up with the money. My boss thinks that's because there's no money to come up with. So rather than admit that she just sits there and shoots everyone else's ideas down in flames so she doesn't have to admit she's got nothing to contribute.'

That certainly chimed in both with Ashleigh's impression of her and the information Chris Marshall had come up with. 'I don't suppose he said anything else?'

'No, except he thinks it would be common sense for them to be working with the Ullswater Falls, but apparently when that was suggested she wasn't having it. People get precious about their businesses.'

'When was that?'

'Oh, some time back. I wonder if she might change her mind now there's a new owner. I mean, if the gossip is true they need to do something, or they'll go under. I thought of buying Izzy a couple of sessions there for her birthday, but I'm not sure now. I don't hear good things about the place. I know Becca was going there with Kirsty but that was just Becca being nice and trying to support them. I'll have to dig a bit deeper in my wallet and see if I can afford somewhere a bit more upmarket.'

'Is Izzy into spas?' Jude asked. Mikey's girlfriend was eccentric, much more into ghosts and auras and portals to the underworld than facials and eyelash tints.

'Probably not but she's getting a bit more down-to-earth these days. She might like an aromatherapy session or a couple of those hot stone things. She was thinking of applying for work at the Ullswater Falls. Did you know they're hiring? Live-in, too, so she'd be closer to me.'

'I didn't, but I'm not surprised. They're under new management.'

'Yeah, I know. But they might struggle. She hasn't actually done anything about it. I don't know if she'd be that happy working there at the moment, because of this Sophie Hayes thing. And I don't think I would be either, not that I want to come over all protective alpha male even if it was any of my business, which it isn't. But I don't like the idea of some lunatic going around bumping off young women.'

'Neither do I.' That theory hadn't been ruled out, but against the complicated personal lives of the three sisters

Jude's instinct was that there was no risk to Izzy, or to anyone else who wasn't already directly connected to the spa. Hopefully there wouldn't be anyone else at risk at all, but you couldn't be sure — especially not if Sophie had been killed in the dark by mistake and the real target was one of the sisters. But which one, and why? 'Which is why I'm sitting in the office on a Saturday afternoon trying to solve that problem.'

'Yeah.' Mikey, it seemed, had talked himself into justifying his brother standing him up. 'I do understand.'

'I'm serious about coming to fetch you. If you get yourself there I'll bring you back.'

'So you're not that busy after all, not a whole day job. Right. But it's okay. I've got a couple of mates who are going and I can just tag along with them. You can get me the pints some other time.'

'Right. Let's make it soon, and you can fill me in on all the ins and outs of the local tourism scene.'

'Like you're really interested.' Mikey laughed.

'But I am.' It was unusual for Mikey to get over a slight so quickly. He might as well make the most of it. 'I don't suppose you've come across a Leo Pascoe, have you?'

'Tall guy? Blond — dyed, I bet. A bit posh? Country sports and country gels?'

'That's the one.'

'Yeah. I think I met him at some drinks do or other. Fake as a nine-bob note.'

'Your work sounds a whole lot more fun than mine,' said Jude wryly. Mikey always seemed to be meeting and greeting at marketing events, or representing his employers at awards dinners or book launches or glad-handing the wealthy for sponsorship deals. Unsurprisingly; he was a gregarious, interested young man and a good listener.

'Most of these things are dull as ditchwater. I do

117

remember this guy, though, largely because he wasn't interested in talking to me but was too busy staring down one
of my colleague's cleavage.'

'Grim.' Ashleigh had made that observation, too.
Pascoe must have a roving eye, if not worse.

'I thought so, but bizarrely enough she didn't seem to
mind. Said he was very charming, and I suppose he was,
but not interested in turning his charm on for me. I'm not
well-connected enough, which is the category of people he
seemed to want to talk to.' Jude could imagine the grin that
went with that statement. 'Anyway, if you're going to leave
me on my own I'd better get up to the station. I'll see you
next time you can think of an excuse to hang around on
Becca's doorstep.'

'Enjoy the game,' said Jude, and chose to ignore that
last comment.

FIFTEEN

'Time for a break, I think.' Bored with his own company and frustrated by his own thoughts, Jude had lasted until four o'clock before he headed down to the incident room. Ashleigh, too, had sacrificed a chunk of her Saturday in pursuit of Sophie's killer and was yawning at her desk as she shuffled through a pile of papers.

'A break? What's that? Though I think I do need one.' She sat back and stretched. 'I've been going over the witness statements and cross-checking everyone's movements to see if we've missed anything, but nothing's jumping out at me.'

'It's time we went out for some fresh air, then.' Jude's phone pinged with a message. Mikey. *Cracking game. Your loss M8.* He sighed.

'If you think I'm going hiking at four o'clock in January, you can forget it.' She shook her head. She was strictly a fair-weather walker.

'You'll be surprised how different things are in the dark.'

'That's pretty much what Tony Charles said to Aditi.'

'He's not wrong. I thought we could go down to Pooley Bridge. Take a wander along past the Three Sisters and see what it looks like in the dark. Call it fieldwork. Then maybe go for a quick drink at the the Ullswater Falls. All in the name of duty, of course.'

She nodded. 'Ah, I see. Aditi certainly flagged a few interesting things about Tony Charles, didn't she?' She switched off her laptop, got up and put her coat on.

'It's possible he genuinely is overwhelmed by emails and doesn't remember everything his wife says to him, I suppose,' said Jude, doubting it.

'And that he did genuinely just happen to be loitering around the Three Sisters purely so they would know who he is and not be alarmed if they bumped into him in the dark.'

'Taking both together,' he said, holding the door open for her, 'it seems a little unlikely to me.'

'Well, indeed. And I'll tell you something else. I've been thinking a lot about Tony and Mrs Tony. If Aditi is right, his wife was covering for him when he said he didn't know who Sophie was and I'd love to know why she was doing that. Because it might not be out of the goodness of her heart.'

Jude thought about it as they walked down the corridor. It was possible that Tony Charles would have hell to pay to his wife if she suspected he was denying any knowledge of the girl because that might look suspicious, but Aditi had noted what she'd thought was a genuine fondness between them. 'It's more likely she's trying to keep him out of trouble, I'd say.'

'Do you think she knows anything?'

'I expect she knows everything he knows, now. I just wish we did.'

'He struck me as trouble when I had that glimpse of him down at the spa,' said Ashleigh as they headed out of the building towards his car. 'I asked Suzanne about him afterwards and she said she didn't know who he was but she didn't like the look of him. The other two never even saw him, or so they claimed.'

It was less than fifteen minutes to Pooley Bridge from the police headquarters. Jude flicked the radio on as he drove, catching the football results just as the car dipped down the hill. Four-three, with a late winner for Carlisle United. Mikey always got the good games.

'Is that the way to the Ullswater Falls?' asked Ashleigh, peering into the gloom as Jude turned the Mercedes into the car park and pulled up at the far end, where a gate led on to the Ullswater Way.

He got out and checked his phone. Mikey again. *Just as well u didnt come. ud have jinxed it.* 'Yep.' He laughed and turned to see where she was looking. On the hill behind the car park the driveway to the Ullswater Falls was dimly marked by the glow of solar lanterns shivering through the bleak skeletons of the leafless trees. The hotel stood on the brow of a low hill, its ground floor bright like a beacon and half a dozen lights on the upper floors.

'No concerns about the electricity bill there,' he said.

'It doesn't look that busy. There are a lot of rooms empty.'

'They'll be doing some of them up, I expect. Aditi said there was building work going on. It's been closed for decades. In my view it's way more welcoming than it used to be, so maybe the guests are all in the bar.'

'I had a quick look at Tony's background earlier,' said Ashleigh, digging her gloves out of her pocket and pulling them on as they strolled over towards the ticket machine. 'His professional history is pretty much as he said it was.

121

He seems to have exactly the right skillset for a hotelier, and when he left his previous employer they sent him on his way with a glowing endorsement and plenty of words of good advice. He's a London lad, originally, but he really has been all over the world. Most recently he was in Hong Kong but he's worked in Australia, South Africa, America, Dubai. You name it, he's been there, and he's been involved in managing some world-famous hotels.'

'No disrespect to the Ullswater Falls,' said Jude, looking up at it, 'but it doesn't exactly fall into that category does it? I wonder why the sudden change?'

'Maybe he just fancied a challenge. Or maybe he thought a hotel in the country would be a change of pace and he'd get to slow down a little as he gets older.'

'I bet he knows that isn't the case.'

'Some people like a change, I suppose. It's a world away from a five-star hotel in New York.'

As Jude waited for the parking app to connect, he cast a glance along to the path that led from the car park down past the Three Sisters. Its starting point was marked by a sad collection of cellophane-wrapped flowers, their petals already nipped by the frost, and the tunnel of trees and thick hedges that framed the first fifty yards seemed to suck in all the ambient life from the village and the car headlights on the road. Even the additional boost from the half moon that drifted out from behind thinning clouds was lost in it, but there was enough light for him to see a figure, wrapped in a big coat, walking briskly along the path.

The app connected and pinged at him. With the parking paid for, he turned to Ashleigh, who was still staring up at the Ullswater Falls, touched her gently on the arm and pointed. Together they stood and watched as the muffled figure emerged into the car park, saw them and stopped.

'Oh,' said Tessa Walsh to Ashleigh, 'it's you. I thought you people had finished. Someone phoned Sue and told her we could all go back. Not that I particularly wanted to.'

'We never finish,' said Ashleigh cheerfully. 'I'm technically not on duty at the moment, though obviously we have people working all the time on finding out what happened to Sophie.'

'Aren't you bothered by walking that way by yourself?' inquired Jude. Tessa didn't know who he was and Ashleigh hadn't introduced him, so his question might seem innocent rather than pointed. That being the case, he thought she'd be more likely to answer it.

'I...well, I didn't really think.' She looked past them, up the hill to the Ullswater Falls, frowning. A car turned into its drive and crawled up the hill. 'I mean, I do walk this way from time to time myself, and it's never bothered me before. We didn't have any customers booked in this evening, though I think I would have cancelled them if we did. But I went down to look the place over, so I was on the path anyway.'

'You didn't think of driving?'

'No. We leave the car park for customers, even if there aren't any booked in. You know we can get three cars in there. There's a storage space underneath I suppose you could just about squeeze a car into if you had a mini but I was always too lazy to bother manoeuvring my car in there and if I did it's such a tight space I probably wouldn't be able to get out of the car.'

'Aren't you at all worried?' he asked.

'No, not really. Leo offered to pick me up but I said I'd meet him here rather than have him come up to the spa or the house. That back road gets a bit treacherous when it's icy.' She drifted past them. 'I'd better go. I said I'd see him at the bus stop.'

Ice or no ice — and the temperature was still well above freezing — Leo Pascoe could easily have gone down that back road, so maybe there were other reasons why Tessa didn't want him to.

'At least we know there'll be no-one at the spa,' he said, when she was out of earshot.

'None of the Walshes, at least.'

He led the way along the path. It was smooth enough under foot, even in the darkness, but once they were round the first bend and screened from the lights of the village and the surface began to break up under their feet, he was forced to get out his torch.

'There are certainly plenty of places for people to hide,' said Ashleigh in a low voice, but that was all. Neither of them was going to discuss the case where there was no certainty that they could do so in silence.

'Why don't we walk up to the hotel through the grounds? We'd go past the Three Sisters that way. You never know what might shine a light, so to speak.'

It took them fifteen minutes, in which time they met no-one, heard nothing but the startled rattle of a pheasant disturbed in its roost, to reach the Three Sisters. The spa crouched across the boundary between land and water, in darkness except for a dim, low energy fitment inside. Broken moonlight glittered on the lake and beyond it, on the far shore lights gleamed in homes, barns, hotels, and cars, but the path and the spa were still and silent.

'Let's have a closer look,' said Jude. 'I'd like to see how easy it would be to identify Sophie when she was leaving work. I'm going to wait here, just by the hedge. You go up to the steps and then come down.'

'Using my phone torch?'

'Yes, I think so. She'd dropped her phone and it was on the ground rather than in her bag, so I'm guessing she'd have had it in her hand if she didn't have it switched on. I'd like to see how easy it was for someone to be sure it was her.'

He watched as Ashleigh walked up the broad steps to the front door of the Three Sisters. The ghostly flow from the lights showed her silhouette but not her face. When she flicked on the torch the beam shone downwards and there was nothing distinctive but her shoes as she came down the steps and walked quickly across to him.

'Could you see me?' he asked.

'Just about, but I knew you were there. If I'd been distracted, or thinking of something else, I probably wouldn't have noticed you.'

'Right. And obviously I could see you but I couldn't tell it was you. You could have been anyone of broadly your height and build. I wouldn't have mistaken you for Aditi, for example, because she's noticeably smaller than you are, but that's about it.' And her shoes. Sophie's shoes had been flat, black and sensible. 'Did you notice what the Walshes were wearing on their feet?'

'Flip-flops. I imagine that's something to do with not marking the floors and so they would have worn something else outdoors. But Tessa was wearing trainers back there, even though she was going out.'

'She might have had another pair of shoes in her bag. But that was the only thing I could see that would have marked you out in any way.'

'I can always ask them about the shoes.' Ashleigh shivered. 'It's a bleak spot, isn't it?'

'It's okay in summer. Let's get up to the hotel. The gate's just along here. It'll be much quicker and I'd like to know how easy it is for someone to get away through the grounds.'

The old, narrow gate hung on one rusty hinge and

creaked when Jude lifted it to ease it open. A churned puddle of mud had gathered beneath it; another bunch of flowers was propped against the fence. When Jude shone his light on it he revealed a bouquet of lilies in a rosette of gold tissue paper — an altogether more sophisticated offering than those in the car park, though the petals were blackened and the wrapping had disintegrated into a soggy mess. A stiff square of card the size of a business card was stuck in among the flowers and though its hand-written message had run away to oblivion its origin was clear from the embossed heading.

'Look,' he said, 'it's from the Ullswater Falls.'

'I have a feeling that's a very Tony thing to do,' said Ashleigh. 'All for show. I hope he's on duty. I'd love to see him in action, so to speak.'

The path led through a broken belt of rhododendrons that ran along the fence and protected the grounds from prying eyes, then dived into a small but dense shrubbery, and finally emerged at the bottom of the slope where it filtered through lumpy, rough-cut grass and finally petered out in wide lawns. A jumble of dark outbuildings, boarded up with plywood, was a reminder of the sad state to which the hotel had sunk but the main building had a vibrancy about it, lights shining from the bar and the dining room to spill irresistibly through picture windows and onto a blighted terrace whose cracked walls were under attack from a knotted mass of ivy.

'Very rustic,' said Ashleigh.

'The grounds aren't a priority, I imagine. That's handy if you want to make a quick getaway. There are plenty of places around here you can hunker down until you get a chance to follow the hedge back to the village, or even the other direction to the campsite and the public road back. Hop in a car you've left parked up there, and you're away.

Simple.' But the search of the grounds hadd found nothing.

'What do you reckon?' Ashleigh asked, staring up at the hotel with her hands in her pockets.

Jude thought about it. 'It would be really easy to mistake someone for someone else in those conditions outside the Three Sisters, at least as we replicated them. That makes me think Sophie may not have been the intended victim. But I'm not quite convinced.'

'Nor me. Because if you knew there was a murderer out there, you'd expect everybody to be really concerned, wouldn't you?'

Like Mikey had been. 'Exactly. But here's Tessa, cheerfully walking along in the dark without a care in the world. And she's coming to meet her boyfriend on her own, in the dark, not even asking him to come and meet her. And staying late at the place on her own.'

'Exactly. It doesn't look to me as if she's particularly bothered about her own safety.'

And there were two very good, and very incriminating, reasons for that. Either Tessa knew who the intended victim had been and was reassured that it wasn't herself... or she was the murderer.

SIXTEEN

'It'll be interesting to have a look at the place,' said Jude, as they approached the Ullswater Falls Hotel. 'It had been closed for a while before Tony Charles bought it, but it was pretty shabby before. I don't suppose you ever made it up here?'

Ashleigh shook her head. She'd been in Cumbria for over two years and when she'd moved from her previous post in Cheshire (under something of a cloud after a disastrous workplace affair) she'd promised herself that she'd spend a lot of her free time getting out and about and seeing the place, but somehow it hadn't happened. Too often what happened to her free time was exactly what had happened to it that afternoon and she ended up working, either at home or in the office.

'I only vaguely know of it,' she said, stopping to survey those huge picture windows that looked out from the bar onto the terrace. The hotel's heavy wooden doors stood open and welcoming, to reveal a glass door into an impressive hallway. 'Lisa's trying to introduce me to some of the more salubrious eating places around here, whenever the purse strings allow, but this place isn't on my list.'

'It wouldn't be on mine, either, normally. Not until recently, anyway. It had a reputation as a bit shabby. I don't think it's been redecorated since the 1970s and it had the original carpet. And by *original* I mean from back in the 1800s as a private house, and I don't even think it was a particularly good carpet back in the nineteenth century.'

They went up the broad but shallow steps to the main entrance and Jude held the door open for Ashleigh to go ahead. The entrance hall had both been redecorated and fitted with a new carpet, in thick pile and a blue so deep it was almost black. Against that, the deep red of leather-upholstered armchairs around tables with arrangements of dried flowers looked both dramatic and luxurious. 'I'd say this is a good start.'

'Yes, me too. Mr Charles looks like he knows what he's doing.' Jude wiped his feet on the thick coir mat. 'Let's head to the bar.'

Signs directed them straight on to reception (a little cubby hole unstaffed and behind the impressive staircase), to the right to the bedrooms (thirty of them, Ashleigh had read, just under half in the main building and the others in a more functional extension at the back) and to the left to the bar and restaurant. They headed left, where Tony Charles's approach was immediately obvious. On a stand by the bar a neat notice reminded guests that the hotel was under new management and asked for their forbearance *as we continue to improve and upgrade the Ullswater Falls over the coming months*. Phase one of the work must have been planned to make an immediate, positive impression; the blue carpet drew them in to the bar, which was cosy with comfortable armchairs scattered among older, solid tables. There was an open fire in a solid period fireplace with slouchy sofas on either side of it and a heavy sideboard equipped with local magazines and guidebooks set against the wall. A glimpse through into the restaurant showed that work hadn't made it that far; it had scuffed floors, dingy walls and shabby curtains.

'I hope the food's better than the decor,' said Ashleigh. 'I was reading up on it. He's engaged a new chef who worked with him in London. All the usual stuff — a new twist on traditional dishes, best of local ingredients and so on.'

'He seems to know what he's at, doesn't he? I was expecting something a little more beige. This feels so edgy it's almost dangerous, but I like it. I've certainly got a much better impression of the place than I was expecting. And it looks pretty good, I have to say.' Jude stepped forward into the bar and looked around, and Ashleigh sensed him stiffen. 'Ah. Too late, damn. She's seen us.'

A second later, she saw what he was looking at. In a high-backed armchair in a corner of the bar, almost as if she was deliberately tucked away so as not to be obvious, their boss, Detective Superintendent Faye Scanlon, looked at least as unimpressed at seeing them as they were at seeing her.

'Awkward,' sighed Jude, under his breath. 'I don't suppose we can ignore her. Let's say hello and then we'll go elsewhere.'

Faye was sitting at a low and fashionably distressed antique table, marked with the rings of a thousand spilt drinks. A second, empty chair opposite told them they'd walked in on a scene set for a cosy date and they weren't welcome to join her.

Not that either of them would have wanted to. Faye was an uncomfortable, uncompromising individual with plenty of emotional and professional baggage coupled with a strange lack of empathy. Her relationship with Jude had been rocky from the start and they'd taken a long time to reach some kind of accommodation. He, being more easy-going liked her but she, being unforgiving, failed to return the compliment. With Ashleigh the situation was both more awkward and altogether more complicated. Some years before, in a previous incarnation, they had briefly been lovers until Faye had unilaterally decided that it had been a mistake.

She had been right, though brutal in bringing the affair to a conclusion. Ashleigh still didn't know for certain why the then-married Faye had rushed so quickly into that unfortunate situation, though she guessed it was the same reason as she herself had done — a rebound to the breakup of her relationship, and the subconscious choice of a partner as different as possible from the previous one. With hindsight, Faye's subsequent behaviour towards her had verged on bullying, but at the time she'd been only too glad to put in for a transfer and start afresh. It had been both awkward and amusing when Faye had pitched up in Cumbria some months later.

A while back she might have been more unnerved by it. In the office Faye still made her feel uncomfortable, not only because she was still capable of wielding her rank and power to protect her own interests but also because her presence reminded Ashleigh of just how naive she herself had been. No-one liked to be reminded so persistently of their mistakes. It was lucky that Jude, always a man to stand up for his junior officers against their seniors when-ever it was required, was in full possession of Ashleigh's version of the relationship and in the face of Faye's in-office prickliness and sensitivity could always be relied on to make his feelings clear.

Out of work it was different. Ashleigh overthought her

relationship with Faye but was not intimidated by her. Seeing her, standing dressed for a night out and looking softer and much less severe than she ever allowed herself in the office, she nevertheless left it to Jude to take the lead.

He did so immediately, with that practiced, bland politeness which so obviously infuriated her. 'Hi, Faye. We weren't expecting to see you here.'

'Nor I you.' She looked quickly at him, at Ashleigh, then at the door behind them. 'I had rather thought the two of you might be…' She glanced meaningfully at the clock.

'At work?' he supplied, cheerfully. 'Technically we're both on a rest day today, although we've both been in the office today. When you look at the costs for this job you'll have a nervous breakdown when you see how much overtime we'll be paying out to Ashleigh and her colleagues.'

Budgets were Faye's weak point, and all three of them knew it, but if the point hit home she waved it away. 'I think it doesn't always look good if detectives working on a case are obviously out having a good time when the case remains unsolved. And this particular venue is a little close to the scene, in geographical terms. That's all.'

She had no self-awareness. She might only have a watching brief over the case but she was a much higher-profile officer than either of them, and more recognisable among the certain section of the community that was more likely to complain.

'We just thought we'd come for a drink,' said Ashleigh, cheerfully, and stepped away, in an attempt to bring this awkward confrontation to a close.

'Yes, of course. But time and place.' Faye jingled the heavy copper bracelets on her wrist in irritation.

Jude lingered on. She could see Faye's attitude had annoyed him. 'We were here on business, in a way. We were planning to get a feel for the place.' He lowered his voice, but there was no-one else within earshot. 'There's a historic relationship between this place and the Three Sisters. There's the possibility that the killer escaped through the hotel grounds, and I understand the girl who died was interested in applying for a job here.'

'I wasn't aware of that.' Faye, who could have worked at least some of that out for herself, looked uncertain.

'I haven't had much of a chance to speak to you in the office for the last couple of days and obviously you were off today, or I'd have talked it through with you. But on reflection, I think you're right. It's perhaps not a good idea to be in here, socially.'

Jude was playing games, now, and it was a risk. Faye wouldn't forget it. Ashleigh laid a restraining hand on his arm.

'I don't think I need you lecturing me on ethics, thank you.' To her obvious fury, Faye was checkmated. She flicked an anxious look at the door. 'I haven't been here before. I'm meeting someone here and this was his suggestion.'

So Faye had a date. No wonder she hadn't looked keen to see them. 'Jude, we can go somewhere else.'

'Probably wise. We'll leave you to enjoy your evening, Faye. See you next week.'

'One lime juice and soda.' Tony Charles, dressed in a tuxedo, whisked across the bar and placed a tall glass garnished with swirls of lime zest, sprigs of mint and clinking with ice and a dish of nuts, on the table in front of Faye. 'The chef roasted the peanuts himself, in some special concoction of spices only he knows. Let me know what you think.' Then he stepped back and looked at Jude and Ashleigh, measuring them up with a professional eye.

'Can I get you a drink? A table for dinner? Do you have a reservation?'

'No, thank you,' said Jude, politely. 'We were here for a drink but unfortunately something's come up and we have to leave.' He managed a sigh of regret.

'That's a shame.' Tony seemed unabashed by this rejection. 'Just to let you know, the dining room will be closed for couple of weeks in February for the next stage of the refurbishment, but we'll be doing a limited menu in the bar.'

Jude took three careful steps way from Faye and addressed himself to the hotelier. 'What a remarkable transformation you've made.'

'It was a sad old place when we took it on, for sure,' he said, with obvious pride. 'It's a long-term project and we're getting there, slowly but surely, but I'm not a miracle-worker.' He'd switched his attention from Jude to Ashleigh and not for the usual reasons that men did so. Although Jude had lived in the area all his life and was well-known locally Tony, as a recent arrival, would be unlikely to recognise him, but he must have seen Ashleigh down at the Three Sisters on the Thursday morning when Leo Pascoe had been so determined to goad Suzanne.

'We'll certainly be back,' said Jude, again.

'We'll make sure you have a very special evening when you do.' Tony beamed. 'If you'll excuse me...' He nodded once more and backed away from them, still smiling, still watching.

'I'll see you on Monday,' Jude said, to Faye.

'I'll call in to the office tomorrow.'

'Tomorrow, then.'

They headed out of the bar. Snatching a look back, Ashleigh saw Tony staring after them with a frown of perplexity on his face and Faye sitting typing furiously into her phone.

'Do you think he realised who we are?' she asked, as they strolled down the steps.

'I hope so. I particularly hope he realises Faye is a senior detective, and I do think he might have done by the expression on his face. I like it when suspects think we're onto them. If they've got anything on their consciences it makes them get nervous and then they make mistakes.'

They followed the pale glimmer of the solar lights down the drive, pausing to look across the lake to where the lights of the far shore sparkled on the water while the eerie glow from that low overnight light at the Three Sisters diffused through the leafless hedges.

'You get a good view of it from up here, don't you?' she said.

'You do. It makes me all the more intrigued as to why Tony was so keen to make sure the Walsh sisters could see him when all he had to do to keep an eye on the place was to sit in his office with a pair of binoculars and pretend to be looking for red squirrels.'

At the bottom of the drive, a car passed them on the way out and they had a glimpse of Faye, driving carefully but not acknowledging their presence. She'd either abandoned her lime juice and soda or bolted it very quickly indeed, and had presumably been in time to head her date off. 'I hope we didn't ruin her Saturday night out.'

'She's put a damper on ours, so it wouldn't bother me if we did.'

She laughed at him as they cut through to the car park and he flicked the Mercedes open. 'Surely it takes more than Faye to ruin an evening out.'

'No, you're right. let's go back into town and find some hearty pub grub and a pint. We can go back to my place afterwards. Fancy dining's all right, but I saw some of the plates they were taking through to the restaurant, and they wouldn't feed a sparrow. If we'd eaten I'd be up at the Angel Lane chippie for a portion of chips on my way home.'

They got into the car and he drove back into Penrith, parking in Wordsworth Street outside his house. From there there was a clear view of Adam Fleetwood, sitting with the telly on and watching golf. He didn't turn round.

'Maybe he's bored watching me,' said Jude, cheerful. 'I knew he'd get fed up of it before I did.' But Ashleigh noticed that he'd speeded up as they passed across Adam's line of sight. 'Now, lead me somewhere where I can have a pie and a pint.'

She laughed at him. 'You're particularly crotchety these days.'

'God, don't you start. I've had Doddsy and Mikey both telling me off for it.'

He rolled his eyes, and she reached up and ruffled his hair, affectionately. 'Maybe you're just working too hard.'

'There's not much option with poor Sophie dead in the mortuary and our boss on the case and coming in tomorrow to make sure we don't even get the chance of one of our two weekend days off, is there?'

It wasn't work that was troubling him. She was sure of that, but she rolled the thought over in her head until they reached the town centre, before she decided to say anything. 'I meant to ask you. Have you seen any more of Kirsty McKellen?'

'No. I got the distinct feeling I wasn't welcome so I won't waste any more of my goodwill on her.'

'Goodness me, you are out of sorts tonight!' she said, and laughed.

'With life in general, yes. But not with you.'

They'd reached one of their favourite pubs by then, and he held the door open for her. It was still relatively early and the place wasn't busy, so they took a table in the corner and ordered.

'You'll feel better when you've eaten,' she said, as the smell of hearty pub food drifted across the bar from a nearby table. 'Maybe you're just hangry, as the kids say these days.'

'Maybe.' His pint had arrived, and he immediately looked more cheerful, lifting it to his lips and drinking deeply. 'That's better. To hell with Kirsty.'

'I expect Becca will keep you informed,' she said, delicately.

'Don't you start. Mikey accused me of hanging around her place as if I was a teenager. It's more like she's always in lying in wait for me.'

'Maybe she still cares.' Because it was obvious what was really wrong with him — unfinished business.

'I've told him, I've told you. That's all in the past. I'm with you now.' He drank again, and remembered himself enough to pat her on the arm in a show of affection.

But he still cared for Becca. Ashleigh had always sensed that, and these days he occasionally admitted it. There was a poignancy about it, one that echoed with her; after all, she'd never get over her own real love, the feckless Scott Kirby.

She lifted her own drink, raising it in a gesture of salute. 'Now bring on the steak pie. Maybe that'll improve your mood.'

He laughed. 'I promise I'll be sweet and smiley as a fairytale prince from now on.'

'Please don't. I like a bit of grit in the oyster. And being grumpy really is a part of who you are.'

'Bloody cheek,' he grumbled, but he was smiling at her, and the smile redoubled when their meals appeared.

He'd know what was bothering him, as well as she did. Becca and her inability to let him go troubled him more than Adam's close and unwelcome attention. What remained to be seen was whether he'd sort it out and regain some of his previous equanimity or whether he'd continue to become as bitter and unsatisfied over his lost love as Suzanne Walsh seemed to be over hers.

SEVENTEEN

'I want the place sold.'

Tessa looked across at her middle sister in surprise. That wasn't what she'd expected — was anything but what she'd expected — but her immediate response, even through the emotional exhaustion that had dogged her over the preceding days, surprised her. It was optimism.

'Yes.' Hazel went over to the cupboard, reached into it, extracted bottles and a glass and poured a large gin and tonic. Then, remembering, she poured two more and placed them in front of her sisters with no grace. 'And I'm going to have a cigarette,' she said, and glared at them.

'You can go outside, then,' said Suzanne. She was sitting in their mother's rocking chair in the corner of the cramped living room with a closed expression on her face and her hands clasped on her lap.

'This is my home.' Hazel turned her back but Tessa could see her face, lip-read the obscenity she couldn't bring herself to speak. 'You chose to move out. You don't get a say in where I smoke.'

Their mother had been as strongly opposed to swearing as she had been to smoking, and so many other things. Tessa had felt her influence waning but Suzanne's reproving presence brought it back. She shivered.

'You tell her to stop, Tess.'

Tessa hated smoking at least as much as Suzanne did, but her sisters were spoiling for a fight. *Sorry mam*, she thought, suddenly irreverent, *I'm not taking sides*. She shook her head, felt the tension grow in the dingy living room as Hazel fiddled with the packet and lit herself a Marlboro from the fire. In a second, as she sat down in her second favourite armchair (Suzanne had appropriated the rocking chair) the room filled with the scent of nicotine.

Suzanne, coughing, rocked the chair furiously with her foot.

'So,' said Hazel, clutching the gin in one hand and the cigarette in the other, 'I told you. I'm out. I hate the bloody place and I want to sell it.'

Suzanne rocked even more furiously. Tessa, who was generally more observant and emotionally aware than either of her sisters, recognised an internal struggle. She had a small bet with herself that Sue wanted to sell as well and was furious that Hazel had beaten her to it.

'Well, indeed,' said Suzanne, after a while. 'And who is going to buy it?'

'Someone will buy my stake, I'm sure.'

Tessa put down her glass and picked up her knitting. It would smell of smoke, which was a pain, but it gave her something to do with her hands while the other two fought, slowly as always but then on a rising crescendo of bad temper and accusations until she had to intervene and try and keep the peace.

She hoped that wouldn't happen but the conflict raging

between her sisters found an echo in her soul. She'd loved the Three Sisters once, still did, but the moments when she hated it had grown more frequent and increasingly intrusive.

'Don't be ridiculous,' snapped Suzanne. 'You can't sell it without our agreement.'

'Who says?' Hazel breathed out a long, braided stream of smoke and the firelight, catching it, translated it into a glowing orange tongue as if she were a dragon, poised to bring devastation upon them.

'Mum said. She wanted us to run it together.'

'What she wanted isn't legally enforceable. And anyway, you can't prove she wanted it to be the three of us. It could just be she wanted the business to continue, and it will. It'll continue without me, that's all.'

There was another moment's silence while Hazel smoked and sipped, Suzanne rocked and Tessa knitted. If you didn't know any better, looking at the three of them sitting round the fire in that cosy though crumbling old cottage you might think they were close, that you were looking on a scene from a contemporary version of Little Women, the three remaining March sisters grown old and grey with cynicism.

'Why?' challenged Suzanne.

Hazel pushed her long hair, loose on her shoulders now she wasn't working, away from her face with the hand that held the cigarette. She wore no make-up and looked ten years older than she was but nevertheless in the dim lights she seemed suddenly sophisticated, a bad-ass matriarch from a film noir. How deceptive looks were. She was as scared and torn and desperate as her sisters. Their mother had always warned them to be paint-smart the whole time, just in case anyone should call by and think it reflected badly on the business if they were in any way untidy, but no-one ever did call and the business might be beyond saving. 'I'm spooked.'

'You'll get over it.'

'No I won't. Every time I go down to the spa I'll think of poor Sophie and every time I step out of there on my own at night I'll be in fear of my life.'

'Then we'll get better lighting.'

'All along the path?'

'You usually drive anyway.'

'It isn't just this.' Hazel took a deep breath. Arguing with Sue was futile but nevertheless you had to give her credit. She was going to try. 'What happened to Sophie is the final straw. I'm tired, I'm old. My knees have gone from all that standing and my shoulders ache all the time. I'm getting arthritis.' She spread out the hand that held the cigarette, keeping it clenched between two misshapen fingers. 'I don't want to do this job any more. That place will be my grave. I want out and I want us to sell the business.'

'I won't allow it.'

If only Suzanne hadn't come. Tessa's heart had sunk when she'd heard her sister's car outside but it had been her home and she still owned a stake in it. When she'd rolled up saying she was tired and wanted some company, neither Hazel nor Tessa had had the heart to turn her away. Cursing her weakness, Tessa sipped her gin. She'd planned to spend the evening with Leo but he'd had something else on and they'd had to content themselves with a quick drink in Pooley Bridge. If she'd brought him back to the cottage, as she'd hoped, Suzanne would have turned up on the doorstep, taken one look and then stormed back out without a word.

Regrets, Tessa hummed to herself, too quietly for either

of the others to hear, but she stopped right there. There had been too many to mention.

'You could use the money, too,' pointed out Hazel. 'You've got the extra expense of living in that one-roomed hovel you call a flat.'

'It's better than living here with your constant whining and Tess flaunting herself at that playboy she thinks loves her,' said Sue, contemptuously.

If only it had been Sue who had landed in the water. Immediately, Tessa regretted the thought, but she couldn't help it. Sue was getting older and more bitter and less tolerant, harder to deal with and belligerently obstinate about any decisions that might have improved the business. She was like their mother, doing everything the way it had always been done with no acknowledgement that change might sometimes be improvement, but at least their mother had realised the commercial necessity of keeping in touch with what her clients wanted. These days, and with every week that passed, the Three Sisters lost contact with its customers as they died off and no new ones came to replace them, and was cut further adrift.

If it hadn't been for Sophie, whose presence had a calming influence and whose youth had somehow kept them relevant in a fast-moving market, they would have gone under. 'It's such a shame about poor Sophie,' she said, watching under her eyelids.

'Yes, you listened to her rather than us, didn't you?' Hazel shook her long hair again and scowled at her sister. 'Why was, that, eh? Were the two of you getting a bit too close?'

A psychiatrist would have a field day with Hazel's deliberate and inaccurate taunting, because it was clear as day that the attraction between Sophie and Suzanne had never been sexual. It wasn't just that Sophie had that endless run of boyfriends, or that Suzanne had never forgiven her parents for separating her from the man she had, presumably, loved (though Tessa always thought he could have made more of an effort to keep her). There had never been anything remotely touchy-feely between them and in her more charitable moments Tessa saw the relationship for exactly what it was — a friendship rooted in genuine affection, understanding and shared interests. Sue could have had that with her sisters if she wanted, but she always seemed to regard them as part of the burden their parents had imposed upon them.

'Were you jealous?' Suzanne asked, mockingly, taking on the challenge. 'You were always supposed to be the good-looking one, weren't you, but let's be honest. No man's ever looked at you.'

'That you know of,' snapped Hazel, but with a lack of confidence that suggested Sue was right and that the barb had struck home. She tossed the last third of her cigarette onto the fire and stared at it as it smouldered.

'And did you fancy Sophie? I would say that's a very unprofessional approach to a young woman to whom we have a duty of care,' mocked Suzanne.

She might be right, of course. Tessa was sure Hazel had wanted marriage and kids of her own and it had never happened. Her sexual frustration must be strong, so maybe she wouldn't care where she got satisfaction. She felt a pang for her middle sister. How in the world had they allowed their parents to bind them into this lifelong emotional contract? And how, after their mother's death, had Tessa herself been the only one with the strength to try and break it?

Perhaps for her sisters it was just too late. 'Sue,' she said, realising that it was up to her, as always, to play pacifist, 'that's not what we're talking about.' Her needles clicked.

'No,' said Hazel, rallying. 'It isn't. We're talking about selling the business. Whether it's the whole thing or just my part of it, it doesn't matter. I'm out of it.'

'And what are you going to do at your age? Start a new career? Stay in this place, live off what little capital you'll get for it, and then end up in penury on a state pension because your company pension won't get you very far?' Suzanne laughed. She sounded exactly like their mother on a bad day.

Laying her knitting down to reach for her gin, Tessa realised that she was shaking, and that the needles on her lap shivered and jolted, clicking like tiny castanets. 'I think,' she said, trying to be measured though she could feel her blood pressure rising, 'that if Hazel wants to sell up them we can't stop her.'

'We don't have to try. No-one's going to buy a stake in a failing business. Sorry, Hazel. You're stuck with us until you die in harness.'

But she wan't. None of them were. Maybe Tessa had been spending too much time with Leo, but his enthusiasm and entrepreneurialism had rubbed off on her. Her sexual awakening had been followed by a rebellious one. She was thinking for herself. She dared.

The gin gave her courage, but even so she was nervous. She cleared her throat. 'It's okay, Hazel. I'll buy you out.'

Her sisters turned and stared at her, Hazel with a light of hope in her eyes, Suzanne with a dark cast of suspicion. More and more they resembled something else, something portentous and literary. They were the three witches in Macbeth, the three daughters of Lear, both cursed and cursing.

'Okay,' said Suzanne, with what was almost a sneer, 'then let's hear how you plan to do it. Because unless you've been playing the stock market in secret, you're as poor as the rest of us. I know you don't have any money of your own. You can't have, or you'd have been gone long ago.'

In fact Tessa liked the the cottage. She even, as she'd told the detective sergeant, liked the Three Sisters, most of the time. It was living and working with her sisters in an occupation she'd grown to hate that was getting her down. 'No. But Leo has the money. He'd buy it.'

'I will not allow you to sell your stake to that man,' said Suzanne to Hazel, as if there was anything she could do to stop it.

'Then I'll borrow the money from him' said Tessa, sounding far more calm than she felt, 'and I'll buy it. There you go. Problem solved.'

'I don't have a problem with selling to him' said Hazel, eagerly. 'It wouldn't matter to you, Sue. He wouldn't interfere. He wouldn't be interested in running the business. In fact I've never thought he's interested in it at all. But if he's got money to invest why wouldn't he invest it here?'

This was true. Leo wasn't interested in the business, other than that he quite enjoyed the occasional massage, which Tessa always had to arrange in secret or with Hazel's connivance because of what Suzanne, who had fiercely resisted any suggestion that the business should expand into treatments for male clients and thus find a whole new market, would say if she knew. What made him different to anyone else was that he was always interested in investing in a new business proposition, and he loved Tessa.

'That's exactly it,' she said, cheerfully. She wished she'd thought of it before. There would be nothing Sue could do about it once she was outnumbered. 'He wouldn't interfere. He'd be a sleeping partner.'

Suzanne burst out laughing. 'He's that already, isn't he? And not showing any interest in marrying you either. Why would he, when he can get everything he wants from you without commitment?'

'Tess's relationship has lasted way longer than your marriage.' Hazel got up and went to fix herself another gin. She didn't offer one to either of her sisters. 'Credit where credit's due. I don't think you're in a position to bitch about either of us.'

'I'll buy you out, too, Sue, if you want.' Tessa's imagination began running away with her. They didn't have to keep the spa. She could easily persuade Leo how well the place would work as a gallery and an artists' retreat and he'd be delighted to indulge her. He loved her.

'Shut up.' Suzanne stopped rocking and turned to focus her fury on her younger sister. 'I won't sell, and anyway he won't do it. You think he loves you but he doesn't. Why would he?'

'Bitch,' said Hazel, in a long, low hiss.

'My relationship with Leo is none of your business,' said Tessa, but she was agitated. Leo did love her — just not exclusively. She liked it that way. He had a high sex drive and it would be far too exhausting to bear the sole responsibility for satisfying his desires. Nevertheless, what Suzanne said bothered her because she was saying it to hurt.

'You know he was sleeping with her, right?'

'Who?' said Tessa, before she could stop herself.

'Sophie. She told me. And let's face it, she's young, she's pretty, she's vibrant, she's fun. So why wouldn't he?'

Young pretty, vibrant, fun. All things that Tessa wasn't. 'I knew that,' she said, breathlessly, though she hadn't known for certain, only suspected. And maybe Sue was lying and she wasn't. She'd ask him and he'd tell her

147

because he was honest. 'So what if she was? I mean, he's Leo. He has a high sex drive. Yes, he sleeps with other women.' Some of them she knew about, because he admitted it, though only when directly asked. Others she suspected. 'But do you know what? He keeps coming back to me.'

'He comes back because you don't have the guts to stand up to him and send him packing.'

'He comes back because he loves me.'

'Did your husband do that Sue?' mocked Hazel from the sidelines. 'Did he love you? He didn't, did he? He buggered off the minute he realised what he'd done, and what kind of family he'd married into and what kind of cow he'd shackled himself to. Wherever he is I hope to God he's having the time of his life married to a better woman than you. But you don't know because he doesn't care. And do you know what? I bet he never even thinks about you.'

'Leo is a man,' snarled Sue at Tessa. 'That's why he treats you like that.'

'Right,' said Hazel, sinking the gin. 'But you know what, Sue? Just because a man made you unhappy it doesn't mean everyone else has to be unhappy too, and just because Mum and Dad wanted us a to do things a particular way, that doesn't mean we have to.'

'You just want his money, and so does she! He'll just be using you to get a foothold in the business.'

'The business you say he doesn't care about? I don't care if those are his motives. His money's as good as everyone else's and if he gives me money for my share of that dump we call a spa, that's not using me. It's a commercial proposition. And all I can say is that if you won't accept that proposition you'll have to find a buyer for the business yourself. Okay?'

The bottle clinked on the glass. Hazel flourished her third gin in a few minutes in her sister's direction and grinned triumphantly.

'This is your fault!' said Suzanne, staring accusingly at her youngest sister.

There were tears in her eyes but Tessa, who was usually kind-hearted, looked at her and felt no sympathy. Suzanne never cried and seeing her do so was strangely exhilarating. 'Too bad. I don't care.'

'You are a bitch,' whimpered Suzanne. 'And do you know what? I hope your so-called lover was shagging Sophie. I expect he was. He'd mount anything female wouldn't he, and for all I know anything male as well. He's not discriminating or he wouldn't be with you...you're just the only person who doesn't have enough self-respect to see him for what he is and tell him to sling his hook!'

It was too much. It always happened. Tessa bounced to her feet, sending the knitting flying on to the hearth where Hazel swooped unsteadily to rescue it before it caught fire and consumed them all. The glass was still in her hand as the red mist descended and she flung it with all her strength at her sister, heard it smash against the wall, heard Suzanne's squeal of shock and stormed out of the room, out of the cottage and into the cold night. She was shaking. She'd tried so hard to be reasonable and break free from her own nature and she'd failed.

She was just like the other two after all — a spiteful, middle-aged woman with a temper and a frightening hatred for the people she ought to have loved. That was what what their mother, and the Three Sisters, had done to her.

EIGHTEEN

Tony Charles had invited the three sisters up to meet him at the hotel.

As we're going to be neighbours, his breezy, Sunday-morning email had read, *I think it would be a good thing to meet and talk about how we might work together for our mutual benefit.*

Hazel, who had been the one to pick up this message, had immediately replied in the affirmative (out of sheer spite, thought Tessa with a sigh) only informing her sisters once she'd confirmed a time and they were committed to an awkward hour at the Ullswater Falls that afternoon. There had, of course, been an almighty row over it, as Hazel must surely have expected. Suzanne had initially refused to have anything to do with it and it had taken a blizzard of self-righteous WhatsApp messages and a monumental effort at mediation on Tessa's part before she had acquiesced, with extremely bad grace, and agreed to show face.

Curiosity could be the only thing that motivated her. Tessa sighed as she waited for Hazel to come down the stairs and for Suzanne to arrive at the cottage, where they had agreed to meet. She was just like their mother. Knowledge was power and if you let someone find out something you didn't know they would be able to use it against you, just as Hazel had done with her unprecedented reply to that email.

Suzanne arrived while Hazel was still primping and sighing at herself in the bathroom mirror, flouncing up to the front door and flinging it open. Her bad temper surged ahead of her into the hallway.

'Let's get on with it,' she said, tweaking the thick scarf that muffled half her face against the keen wind and made her look curiously shapeless. 'The sooner we go there, the sooner it's over.'

'It'll be fine.' Hazel came running down the stairs like a teenager, almost excited. It was clear to Tessa that, belatedly, Hazel was realising she could flex her muscles with their eldest sister. It had only taken five years since their mother's death. For a moment Tessa felt a pang of sympathy for Sue. Tessa herself taking a lover had outraged her enough and if Hazel decided to assert her independence and break free they would find themselves unable to hold on to the spa. What would she do then?

But the spa had to go. Tessa had reached that conclusion in the middle of the night, after hours of lying awake trying to reconcile her conflicting emotions. For all its comfortable familiarity it had become a toxic influence, a prison in which they had no need to be trapped. Her offer to buy her sister out, with Leo's help or without it, had been made on the spur of the moment but she would stand by it and if, for some reason, the offer fell through the Three Sisters would disappear anyway. If necessary she'd burn the place to the ground and take the consequences.

They walked up the path through the hotel grounds in

a chilled silence. Tessa lagged, enjoying the company of a flock of sparrows that fluttered through the shrubbery keeping pace with her and, when they had escorted her off their territory and returned home, taking pleasure in an unexpected burst of late-afternoon sunshine. Ahead of her, her sisters walked side by side without looking at one another; Hazel had an unusual spring in her step but Suzanne was clutching her shoulder bag as if she expected to be mugged. Clinging on to things. God, yes. That was exactly what she doing with the spa and it would end in tears.

But it would end. There would be no more Three Sisters.

Suzanne was still clutching her handbag as they made it on to the terrace and stood in front of the heavy doors. 'You can go first, Hazel, since you're the one who got us into this mess.'

It was an unusual abdication of responsibility and Hazel, who didn't appear to consider this a mess at all, took full advantage and bounced cheerfully up the steps and into reception. There was no-one in the lobby but she led the three of them to the reception desk and struck the brass bell that sat on its polished mahogany top next to a strikingly minimalist scarlet flower arrangement. Its ring was remarkably loud and brought an immediate response.

'Ah!' Yes, it was him, the man who'd been loitering about outside the Three Sisters on the day Sophie died, popping out of the bar like a genie from a lamp, sharp, keen and interested. His expression was underpinned with a curious excitement, so that Tessa felt a tug of foreboding. 'It's the ladies from the spa. What an absolute pleasure.'

At least he hadn't called them *the three sisters from the Three Sisters*, as too many people did, thought Tessa, taking her turn (age order, of course, despite Suzanne's reservations about the matter) to shake Tony Charles's hand.

She liked him. That was the first surprise. After that initial unguarded moment — and surely it wasn't unreasonable for him to be as nervous about the meeting as they were — his smile was honest and open, and why not? He was in business, they were in business, they were neighbours not competitors. There was nothing to be dishonest about.

He took their coats and hung them on an antique coat stand in the corner.

'I'll begin with my apologies,' he said, leading them through the bar, which was looking better than it had done in decades. 'The first is for the state of the place, though of course we're working on it. The second is to apologise in case I upset you the other day. I'd intended to introduce myself and make sure you weren't alarmed, knowing I was your neighbour and would be out and about on that path. It was clumsy of me, and ill-timed, and the police have ticked me off for it. Rightly so.'

He shot a nervous little glance at Suzanne at that point, turning to look around the bar.

'No, no,' said Hazel, who hadn't even seen him. 'It's fine!'

'That's a relief. This way.' He waved them to a table set for tea and pulled out the chairs before an approaching waiter, who looked barely old enough to be out of school and a little overawed at having to serve his boss, had the chance. 'And thirdly,' he said, after the briefest pause, 'I must apologise that my wife isn't here. She has to be in Keswick and won't be back until later. Though she did say to pass on her apologies and she'd love to book a facial at the Three Sisters and get to meet you. Tea? Coffee?'

Suzanne's thunderous expression at the idea clearly indicated that Mrs Charles needn't expect mates' rates. Even Hazel wasn't so overwhelmed the she fell into that trap. 'Yes, of course,' she said. 'I think we might have availability tomorrow afternoon. We'd love it if she could stay and have a cup of tea. As we're going to be neighbours.'

The waiter, gaining confidence, served them from a slightly dented silver tea set that looked as if it had been in a box in an outhouse for a century but which had, at least, been polished to within a minute of its long life, and then produced two cake stands, one with a delicate set of savouries and another with a selection of miniature cakes.

'I have a new chef,' explained Tony, shaking his napkin out into his lap, 'and he's experimenting. I've identified a gap in the market for high quality afternoon teas. I hope you don't mind him experimenting on you.'

'There are plenty of excellent providers locally,' said Suzanne, but her gaze lingered on the tantalising display.

'And all very busy. Demand is skyrocketing. In my view if you're going to do something you have to do it well and wisely. I don't mean I'll throw money at it. You'll know yourselves that if you price cheap people will undervalue whatever you have to offer. But nor can one overprice, or customers will go elsewhere. Do help yourselves and see what you think.'

Hazel nodded her agreement. Suzanne nibbled at the edge of a salmon and cucumber sandwich. Tessa sipped her tea and, of all of them, enjoyed the experience. It was a pleasant change to be waited on by someone, to be given good food that she hadn't prepared.

'And how is business?' inquired Tony, when the sandwiches and cakes were almost gone. As they'd eaten he'd done his best to draw the sisters into conversation and Tessa had tried to chat — and she thought Hazel had, too — but Suzanne's forbidding and relentless silence had somehow stopped them. Their oldest sister was behaving badly but neither of them seemed able to do anything about it. Tony, apparently oblivious, had chatted on about his experiences around the world — India, he'd said, had been the most wonderful experience, but he thought he preferred New York — and how he'd ended up deciding to run his own business.

'But why here?' asked Hazel. 'I mean, obviously we love it here. If you're brought up in Cumbria you almost always do, thought I admit sometimes we forget how lucky we are. But if you've been running all these splendid hotels all over the world, why here?'

He shrugged. 'Half a dozen reasons, personal and professional. I was ready for a change. My wife knows and loves the area. I thrived on working in high-end hotels but it's draining and I'm not getting any younger. I don't expect it to be any less tough here, in many ways, but I'm counting on a change of style and of pace. And, of course, there was opportunity. The place was up for sale.'

'All very fortuitous.' Suzanne finished the last of the tiny chocolate and raspberry eclairs that had come with the tea and discreetly wiped crème pâtissière from her fingers with a starched white napkin.

'Yes. There were a couple of other investment opportunities available, but this one seemed the best.' He'd been waving his teacup around as he spoke, but at this he placed it down on the saucer with a rattle and seemed to switch into a much sharper mode. 'I looked in Keswick and Windermere, and there were places with much more immediate earning potential. This building needs a lot of money spent on it, of course, but I think it's a gem.'

It was. It might be crumbling but it was beautiful. Tessa nodded.

'I see a visit to the resurrected Ullswater Falls as a very upmarket, yet informal, experience. I envisage it as somewhere people can come and feel they're very special guests indeed, almost as if they were staying in a private home owned by the rich friends we've all dreamed of having.' He smiled again. 'And of course, that means I want to look at expanding the facilities that are on offer.'

Suzanne put her teacup down, too, with even more purpose and at great risk to the china. 'I'll stop you right there, Mr Charles.'

'Tony. It's Tony.'

'Mr Charles. The Three Sisters is a family business and a proudly independent one. I'm sure I speak for Hazel and Tessa as well as myself when I say that we aren't interested in being subsumed into a business over which we have no control.'

'I thought you might say that.' He looked at Tessa, who nodded because Sue had phrased the answer correctly and she certainly wasn't interested in being employed by someone else at the Three Sisters, but only in seeing it develop into its own new incarnation with herself playing a key role.

Hazel nodded, too, but more cautiously. Perhaps her desire to sell up wasn't as total as she'd said, or as irrevocable, or perhaps she regretted her outspokenness of the previous evening and wasn't going to repeat it, but she was listening carefully. She'd ruled nothing out. She helped herself to a bijou chocolate muffin and split it open. Brandy chocolate cream oozed out onto the plate.

'And so,' Tony went on, 'I have an alternative proposal. I am prepared to buy you out, and I would make a very generous offer.'

'I'm afraid that's out of the question.' Suzanne again, inevitably.

Opposite her, Hazel looked dashed. 'It's only fair to listen to what Tony has to say, Sue.' She turned back to Tony. 'Did you have a price in mind?'

'I've given it some consideration, subject to a survey and so on.' He named a sum that surely was way in excess of what the place was worth, certainly exceeded the valuation on which their annual insurance was based, and that Tessa privately thought was ridiculously high. She drew in a sharp breath and regretted it immediately as Suzanne looked across at her with a scowl.

'Tempted?' said Tony, smiling. 'I know it sounds a lot, and it is. But I've explained my philosophy. I have the money available and you have to speculate to accumulate, as they say. You have a nice little business there already, but it would be a perfect fit for my hotel. That makes it worth a lot to me. That's all. Value is relative.'

'The Three Sisters isn't for sale.' Suzanne had had enough. 'It's been lovely to meet you, Tony.' At last she'd relaxed a little, switched into the more genial manner she kept for the clients. 'And it's been very generous of you to entertain us for tea like this, but I'm afraid we don't soften up that easily.'

'The tea was unrelated to the offer,' he said cheerfully. 'If you turn it down outright and continue to run the spa we'll be neighbours and there will be no hard feelings. But take your time. I don't need an answer immediately.'

'We've already given you our answer.' Suzanne folded her napkin neatly and laid it on the plate. 'I'm sorry, but we have a sentimental attachment to the place. Our father designed it and our mother set up the business. They made it what it is. It's part of us and we will always be part of it. Thank you, but I'm afraid the answer is no.'

'The offer remains open,' he said, as they stood up and he gestured to the waiter to bring their coats. 'And I'm happy to discuss any aspect of it with you. You might want to work with me as a subcontractor, even.'

'I think you realise that would be the least satisfactory

option.' Suzanne slid her arms into the coat the waiter held for her and smiled as he moved on to assist Hazel and then Tessa. 'Thank you so much. And what a fabulous afternoon tea that was. Especially those muffins.'

'I'll tell the chef,' said Tony, cheerfully, and guided them off the premises.

On the terrace they paused and a moment of stillness came over them as they waited to see which one of them would spark the inevitable row. The last rays of the dying sun settling in the west showed through skeletal trees. A few stray leaves swirled across the sodden January grass.

'*The Three Sisters isn't for sale*,' mimicked Hazel, cruelly, in a brutal impression of her older sister. 'It's not for you to say. My share of it definitely is up for sale. And if he doesn't want to buy a part of it someone else will. It's worth something, financially, and it's worth a whole lot more to me to be rid of it.'

Suzanne's face was still. 'Did I say it wasn't for sale?'

'You said it in so many words!'

'Maybe I wasn't exact. I'm open to selling after all, I think, but not to that man.'

Hope had leaped briefly in Hazel's face but was gone as quickly as that flash of winter warmth from the sun. 'We don't have any other offers.'

'No-one else will give us that kind of money.' Tessa pulled her coat around her, miserably. The joy of the day had gone with the last of the afternoon light and the brutal cold of a January evening was upon them. The birds had fallen silent, except for the chatter of crows in the woods on Dunmallard Hill. The sisters had always argued, as siblings always did, but these days there never seemed to be any moments when the three of them were in agreement and now they found themselves in an existential crisis and still they bickered and fought. *It's part of us and we are part of it*, Suzanne had said. Tessa shivered at the truth of it.

'Fine. Then if you can find a buyer we'll accept less and if you can't we won't sell.'

'I'm sick of you speaking for all of us just because you're the oldest. We're equal partners.'

'He's trying to take advantage of us.' Suzanne's lips narrowed.

'It's a bloody generous offer,' Hazel countered.

'Yes, and he said why. It's because it's worth a lot to him. But if we don't sell, and don't allow ourselves to get sucked into being a part of someone else's business, his guests will still come.'

But they wouldn't. Guests at a hotel that was as smart and luxurious as the Ullswater Falls was going to be wouldn't want to come for treatments at a spa that would surely be even more rundown by the time anyone was considering going there. It would be like a den at the bottom of someone's garden, and any self-respecting holidaymaker would turn their nose up at it. More than that; they could be sure that Tony, if asked, would recommend other, much more upmarket, places, in the short term at least.

'What if he establishes his own spa?' asked Tessa.

'Exactly' said Hazel, almost in triumph. 'It'll break us.'

The solar lights along the driveway flickered on, one by one, as the darkness closed in. 'I don't care.' Suzanne was as stubborn as their mother. 'I'd rather go under with my pride intact than be bought out by him.'

'For God's sake,' said Hazel, exasperated. 'What have you got against him?'

'I don't like his manner, I'm not having that man storm up and think he can bully us out of our business.'

'It was a reasonable offer!'

Sue hated men, that was the problem. The husband who'd run off and left her after just a few weeks of marriage had a lot to answer for. When Tessa stopped to think about it that was the obvious explanation. It must be why her older sister was so hostile to Leo, and why she was so reluctant to accept the spa's programme for the male facials and treatments that might have offered them a financial lifeline. 'It was better than reasonable. Can we afford to refuse it?'

'The answer's still no, and it's always going to be no.'

'You don't have any right to bully us like this. He can have may share. I'll sell.' Hazel pouted.

'He won't want your share. He wants to control the business. You didn't buy all that stuff about partnership, did you? He'll want to do everything his way and I'm too old for that now. I will *not* sell to him. That's final.' Suzanne turned and stalked off down the driveway.

'Go to hell!' Hazel shouted after her, like a fourteen-year-old rowing with her mother. 'I hate you! I never want to see you again!' She swung round. 'I'm going home. Come on Tess.'

Caught between the two, Tessa hesitated. It was dark and who knew who was lurking in the shadows of the rhododendrons that grew like a fortification near the main gate? If Suzanne went one way and Hazel the other, which way should Tessa go?

'I think we should go after her,' she said. 'Make sure she gets down to Pooley Bridge safely. Then we can walk back to the cottage together.'

'I don't care if she gets there or not. I hope she dies.'

'Hazel.' Tessa put her arms round her sister, felt her shaking. 'Oh, Hazel. Don't say that.'

'I'm sorry. I didn't mean it. You know I didn't. But she tries my patience so much. And God, I so want to get out of the Three Sisters while I still have a chance to do something else with my life, even if it's just a few years working somewhere else. On the Med perhaps, or in a city. Anywhere but here.' Hazel's voice rose to a wail.

'I know. I know. And something will come up.'

'It's all right for you. You're so much younger than I am. And at least you have Leo.'

You should be grateful for small mercies. Love wasn't a substitute for the fulfilled professional life that Tessa, too, had had to pass up on, but it was its own joy and it made life worth living.

'We'd better get back,' she said, watching Suzanne until she was out of sight around the bend. 'He's coming round later on.'

'Is he? Thanks for the warning. I'll stick in my AirPods and turn up the music and the two of you can get on with your horizontal jogging without disturbing me.' She took a step off the grass, towards the path down to the gate and the spa. 'Let's go, before it gets properly dark.'

They set off across the grounds and the lights of the hotel faded behind them.

'Tess?'

'What?'

'I didn't mean it about wanting her to die.'

'I know.' But Hazel had said it and Tessa had heard it, and it would always be between them and could never be taken back.

NINETEEN

Despite her promise to use AirPods, Hazel had turned up her music and Tessa and Leo, relieved of the obligation to make polite conversation with her, had gone up to Tessa's bedroom and made love. Now they lay curled up in her bed under the cramped eaves of the cottage in the void between the evening and the night, while the living room below them throbbed with Wagner and frustration. Even without Suzanne's glowering and increasingly malevolent presence, this was an altogether unsatisfactory arrangement.

Leo lay back and put his hands behind his head. The light from the bedside lamp pooled on his handsome face. 'Sorry, Tess, but I think I'm going back home tonight.'

She turned to him, looking through a soft wash of love at his bestubbled chin and the firm set of his jaw, laid a hand on his chest with the fingers splayed like a starfish. 'Must you?'

'I wasn't going to. But.' He jerked his head, in no direction in particular but meaning only one thing. 'There's a bit of an atmosphere.'

'God, yes. I'm sorry. It's just been so awful.' It would be so nice to spend these evenings — these nights — at his place. She'd been there a few times, but only at his suggestion. She didn't dare seem needy or possessive.

'Not awful. But it can't be any fun for you.'

She slid her hand up to his shoulder, drawing herself closer to him. She'd told him what had happened at the Ullswater Falls, whispering it in his ear as if it was the sweet nothings of pillow talk instead of a catalogue of her woes, because she didn't want Hazel to hear it and know they were discussing family business. Her sister would guess, but you had to pretend. And he'd been so understanding, listening, holding her, soothing her. 'I don't know what to do. About Sue.'

'I think your sister is losing her mind,' he said, robust and reassuring.

'I'm so glad she doesn't live here any more. It's like walking on eggshells all the time at work.'

'I wasn't joking. I honestly think she's unbalanced.'

'It sometimes feels like it.' Still she held on to him. Leo was like a lifeboat in a storm, and the only time she felt secure and safe was when she was with him. 'I wish I could move in with you,' she said, and cursed herself for having taken the conversation exactly where she hadn't intended — onto his territory.

'You could move in with me, for sure. I wouldn't mind, but you'd hate it. I'd be out all night like a tomcat. I wouldn't be faithful to you. If I thought I could be I'd have married you by now.'

Maybe Suzanne was right to be so cynical about men, but at least no-one could accuse Leo of being dishonest. *I've got a reputation as a bit of an old goat*, he'd said to Tessa, laughing, when it had become clear to her that she was going to end up in bed with him that first time, *and you'll never be the only one, but if you want to take that chance on me I'm here.*

He was still there after a year, and although as he'd warned her he wasn't faithful, at least he was more faithful to her than to any of the other women he saw, and as far as Tessa knew they came and went at a rapid rate. She was the only one he was serious about, the one who loved him selflessly and unconditionally. She couldn't complain about that. It was just that she wanted more than a lifeboat in a storm. She wanted a home in a port, a place of permanent comfort. So unsatisfactory. 'I hoped you'd stay. I'm sorry you thought Hazel was difficult. But—'

'You said. It sounds terrible. And it's not altogether her fault, is it? She gets stick from your older sister, too'

Suzanne had been bitter and provoking. There was what she'd said about Sophie. She should ask him, but why spoil the moment by asking for an unspoken truth? 'No, but I don't know what to do about the business.'

'Does Hazel really want out?'

'I think so.' There had been a steely determination about her that Tessa had never seen before, an echo of her mother's character that had appeared in time to help her throw off her mother's chains.

'And what about Suzanne?'

'I think she wants rid of it, too, deep down, but she won't admit it.' Sue had been their mother's favourite, the one who had started learning at her elbow and watched and worked, just as Sophie had done with Suzanne herself.

Sophie, niggling at her. She mustn't ask him.

'Because Hazel wants it?'

'They're quite close in age. They fight.'

'I can see that.' A pause. 'And what about you, Tess? What do you want?'

Neither of her sisters ever asked her that. 'I want rid of the business but not rid of the building. You know that. And so while I agree with Hazel at one level and think we should move on from it, I agree with Sue at another. I don't want to see it become part of the hotel. And so I can't agree to selling it to Tony Charles, but there's no-one else to buy it. Unless.' She bit her lip.

'Is this what we'd talked about before?'

People shared dreams as well as fantasies in bed. When she came to think about it, Leo was probably party to a lot of people's dreams, maybe even Sophie's. *Stop thinking about Sophie.* 'Yes. I was serious.' Lying there in the darkness, whispering about how they might extend their partnership from the bedroom to the boardroom — or rather, the small cubby-hole where she and her sisters had their weekly meetings and discussed the ever-more depressing matters of business. Talking about how she would make the Three Sisters the place where people came to buy local art and partake in drawing courses, how they could expand it and maybe provide teas and coffees and home-made cakes for the walkers on the Ullswater Way. That would be an asset for the whole of the local economy, too, surely? 'It's just a dream, though, isn't it?'

He turned his head and looked at the clock. It wasn't even ten o'clock, far too early to turn in for the night. He would get up and leave and she would have to decide whether to stay up in her room when she wasn't tired or to go down and face Hazel, who might not be as scornful of her as Suzanne would be but who was capable of being both amused and patronising. 'Is it?'

'I need money for the art centre and the only way to get it is to sell. But, obviously, if we sell I won't be able to build the centre.'

'You could set it up somewhere else.'

'But there's nowhere like the Three Sisters.' That view down to Helvellyn, different every day. That trembling light on the lake. Those fast-moving clouds, gambolling, boiling up, fading away. 'Let's be honest, it's a terrible place for a spa, but I do think it would be a perfect art facility. And I own a third of it already.'

'But your sister won't sell.'

'She won't sell to Tony Charles.'

He sat up, and Tess's hand slid away onto the duvet, the contact broken. 'I think I understand that. Old Tony can be a bit bumptious. He's got a high opinion of himself, with all that talk about the wonderful places he's been to and how important he was. He puts my back up, too, and I think I'm a lot more reasonable than your sister.'

This was undeniably true. 'Yes, but—'

'The solution is for you to get sole ownership.'

'I can't afford to buy them out.'

He swung his legs over the side of the bed, reached for his watch and strapped it on and then, in the half-light, began to stir around in the pile of discarded clothes they'd left on the floor. 'Do you think your sisters would sell to me?'

Tessa drew in a long, juddering breath. He was doing just what she'd told her sisters he would, and what she'd thought was wishful thinking was her dream come true.

'It's just a thought,' he went on. 'I know we've sort of talked about it before. I can't match Charles's price, of course. If you ask me it's a ridiculous one, far too high, and bound to come with strings attached. But I can make a reasonable offer for your sisters' share, and you could keep yours. You could be the creative director, I could run the business side. Do you think it's a goer?'

She lay there and stared at the ceiling and the dream

flickered tantalisingly within reach. The Three Sisters fulfilling its potential in a different sphere. A future in which she wouldn't be left working and fighting with Suzanne if Hazel carried out her threat and left. And maybe she and Leo could take their partnership further. They could be married…

No, she was getting way too far ahead of herself. Leo might be in his forties but he still had a lot of wild oats to sow before he was ready to settle down, if he ever was. 'That would be amazing.'

'I can make some inquiries, if you like. Planning permission might be an issue, because we're in the National Park, but it would be a valuable addition to the local amenities, and we'd make sure it was sensitively done. I can have a quiet word with a few people, and I'm sure I can get people to look on the proposal sympathetically. I know a few architects. And I'll see if we can make some discreet inquiries about how much a property of this nature might cost, and how much we'd need for the changes and renovations. It shouldn't be difficult.'

Hazel would certainly sell and even if Suzanne refused. the two of them would outvote her on every business decision. She might cling on through sheer stubbornness but she would be powerless. 'That sounds perfect.' But there was one other thing. She got out of bed and unhooked her dressing gown from behind the door, pulling the belt tightly around her. 'Can I ask you something?'

'You know you can.' He straightened up, shaking out his clothes item by item and dropping them on the bed before stepping into his boxers.

'It's about Sophie.' She thought she'd regret asking, but she'd regret it much more if she didn't. 'Were you sleeping with her?'

He yanked up his trousers and turned his back while he

fixed the buckle on his belt. 'You know me, Tess. I can't help myself.'

'I'm not angry,' she said, although deep down she thought she might be because this relationship was close to betrayal. Mostly he had the decency to keep his other women out of her sight, and if she knew about them they were never people she'd met. 'I just wanted to know.'

'I'm sorry.' He made no attempt to defend his behaviour. What was the point? And anyway she'd heard it all before. *I couldn't help myself. Such a pretty little thing. I know, Tess, I know, but I'm a man. It's not like it meant anything.* 'I came back to you, though. I always do.'

Perhaps only because Sophie had died. 'You're going to have to tell the police.'

'I expect they'll come after me soon enough.' He pulled his jumper over his head, then sat down on the bed to put on his shoes.

She hated him leaving. The other part of her dream was that he'd stay with her, change his ways, and who knew? Maybe an interview with the police might just shock him into changing his behaviour and settling down. 'It looks much better if you tell them. It would be awful if they thought you had anything to do with her dying.'

'It's much more likely they'd think you had something to do with it. That's why I didn't tell them.'

'But I'm not the jealous type.' Tessa was no idiot and she was fully aware the police must have considered whether she might have killed Sophie, but it was chilling to hear it from him. 'I put up with all the other women.'

'I know that.' He stood up, crossed the room and tilted her head up towards him, placing a sweet kiss on her lips. 'They don't. That was why I didn't say anything.'

For a moment she wavered. They could keep it a secret

after all. But her hesitation was short. She didn't want anything to jeopardise this new future she saw for them both. 'That's so good of you. But it's much better to be honest.'

'Can you prove you didn't kill her?'

'No.' The police had asked her, but in a much smarter, more roundabout way. She had answered all their questions but at the end of it she hadn't been able to prove where she was, had been unable to back up her claim that she'd left work and gone straight home. 'Can you?'

'No. So we'd just have to trust that they can find the person who did do it, and I'm not sure they're making a very good job of it so far.'

'She was killed outside, near the path. It will have been a stranger. We may not be able to prove we didn't do it, but that doesn't matter. They have to prove one of us did, and they won't be able to. I'd be much happier if you told them.'

'Then that's what I'll do.' He kissed her again, hugged her one final time and then tore himself away. 'I'll call you. And I'll make sure I get to see you soon.'

After he'd closed the door behind him, she sat on the bed and listened to him heading downstairs through the kitchen. His good mood was obvious; she could hear him joking with Hazel, who had relaxed sufficiently to turn down the Wagner. 'Book me in for a massage with Tess this week, would you?'

'You've got very brave all of a sudden,' Hazel responded. She knew, if Suzanne didn't, that the blank appointments blocked out in the diary at the end of the day when Tessa was in on her own were always with him. 'But don't worry. I'll put your name in. I might even book you in with Sue, for a laugh.'

'Something tells me she wouldn't find it funny.'

The front door snapped shut behind him and Tessa, unable to resist, lifted the curtain and watched his long strides taking him back down the path towards Pooley Bridge.

TWENTY

'Jude. There's a gentleman on the phone wanting to talk to the detective in charge.'

Jude had dropped in to the incident room at what turned out to be the opportune moment; Chris Marshall, having scanned the room, had spotted him and waved him over.

'Yes, he's just coming,' Chris was saying as Jude threaded his way through the desks and chairs to the phone. 'What was the name? Right. Okay. Here he is. Jude, that's Leo Pascoe for you.'

Well, well. Jude took the phone and settled himself into the nearest seat, yanking the long lead of the phone base free and repositioning it. 'Good afternoon, Mr Pascoe. It's Jude Satterthwaite speaking, senior investigating officer for this case. How can I help you?'

'I'm hoping I can be the one who can help you.' The voice bubbled with confidence — or was it bravado? 'It's about the girl who died at the Three Sisters.'

A confession? Probably, though not to the murder. Jude had had his suspicions. 'Go on.'

'I knew Sophie. A smart young woman, quite the delight. She and I were very close,' said Leo Pascoe, sounding almost smug about it, as if it was a badge of honour. 'I don't know how your forensics work, of course. I'm a businessman not a scientist and I've never been in trouble with the law.' He sounded as if the very idea shocked him. 'But it did occur to me that, given time, you might be able to identify things of an intimate nature.'

Jude shook his head. That was a new take on it. 'Correct me if I'm wrong, Mr Pascoe, but aren't you in a relationship with Tessa Walsh?' *My girl*, he'd called her, when he'd come charging down the path like a caricature of a white knight in his apparent determination to rescue her.

'Well, yes, but we're not exclusive, as the young people say.'

'Okay.' Jude sat back. 'Let's get this straight. Are you telling me you were having a sexual relationship with Ms Hayes as well as with Ms Walsh?'

'Yes, but not the same kind of relationship. Not a permanent one. I mean, Sophie was so very much younger than me.'

Sophie had been young enough to be his daughter, and though that was neither something legally relevant nor something Jude was judgemental about he sensed that Leo's problem was that the age gap made him feel briefly young and, in the long term, aware of his own mortality. 'Okay. I'm sure you know that this is highly significant to the inquiry, so I need to ask you some more questions. Beginning with the last time you and Sophie—?'

'We slept together on the night she died,' he said in a rush. 'I thought I'd better tell you. I went down to the Three Sisters just as it was closing and waited until I saw Tessa leave.'

'And was this by arrangement, or on the off-chance?'

There were plenty of people whose morals were flexible, but Leo's attitude to Tessa was one that left a lot to be desired, by any standard.

'No,' said Leo, without any apparent shame. 'Sophie and I had arranged it when we knew the rota. When Tess had gone I went into the spa. After we'd finished, I left. That would have been about half an hour later. I didn't check the time. Eight, maybe.'

'Okay. And did you and Sophie leave together?'

'No. She stayed behind to tidy the place up. Obviously I didn't want to hang around any longer than I had to. In case someone came along. One of the sisters might have seen a light on or something.'

'I can imagine Tessa Walsh wouldn't have been too pleased,' said Jude, dryly. He'd known about Leo Pascoe but had formed no real impression of him from the scene that Ashleigh had described. Even this short call was putting flesh on the bones; Leo was a man who had hoped he would slip under the radar and now, realising he hadn't, was trying to cover his back, but he wasn't showing himself up well. If one of the sisters had come back after he'd left, it would have been Sophie who had to explain why she was still there and Leo would have been well away from the scene.

'No,' said Leo, with the faintest trace of melancholy, 'I'm sure she wouldn't. But it's all right. She knows now.'

'You told her?' How long had Tessa known?

'She asked me and I'm always honest with her, so of course I told her. I think a relationship needs honesty.'

'After the fact?' asked Jude, dryly.

'It's the way I am.' He could imagine the shrug, the air of injured innocence. 'Tess knows that, and she's forgiven me, but I thought I'd better tell you before…'

Before the net closed in. 'Thank you. And since what

you've told me places you very close to the time and place of her death, as I imagine you'll be fully aware, can I ask you if you saw anything on your way away?'

'No,' said Leo, mournfully. 'I went back along the road to Pooley Bridge, and home from there. I was in a bit of a hurry, because I didn't want to risk running into anyone who might tell Tessa I'd been there.'

'You thought Ms Walsh might be angry?'

'Hurt, rather than angry. I've never been a one-woman man, you see. It isn't in my nature. Tess knows that, but I can't help myself and I've never pretended otherwise. I like to be discreet because I don't like it when she's upset, and I think she would have felt that particular relationship was a bit close to home. I didn't want to make things uncomfortable for either Sophie or herself. That was all.'

'Thanks, Mr Pascoe. I'm going to send a detective down to take DNA samples from you, if that's all right. I'd also like to ask you to repeat what you've told me in a formal witness statement, and perhaps give some further details.'

'It'll be a relief,' said Leo, and sounded almost almost as if he meant it. 'And I expect you'll want to know about the business side of the Three Sisters, too.'

'We're looking into that.'

'You might not know everything. Tessa told me Tony Charles has made an informal offer for the business. I suspected he would. I said it to your detective at the time. It's a very generous offer, but Tessa says they've turned it down. That makes him a person of interest in the investigation, wouldn't you say?'

'Thanks, Mr Pascoe.' It was impossible to read Leo Pascoe over the phone. His sheepish pretence at innocence and his casual assumption that his own bad behaviour was somehow appealing were one thing but this enthusiasm for helping the police was something else. This wasn't about clearing his name but about implicating someone else. He'd done exactly the same thing at the Three Sisters on the day Sophie's body had been discovered. 'That's very helpful. We'll certainly follow that up.'

'It's a bonkers price he's offering,' supplemented Leo. 'That's what made me sit up and take notice. There's no way the place is worth anything like what he's offered.'

'Fascinating. Thank you. We'll be in touch.' Jude ended the call and drifted back to the table under the whiteboard where Doddsy was sitting staring at his laptop with a frown.

'Did he have anything interesting to say?' asked Chris, appearing next to them.

'I think so.' What a fascinating man Leo Pascoe was. 'Let's get Ashleigh over to join in and have a chat about it.'

While Chris went to fetch her from the other side of the room, Jude scrawled an asterisk next to Leo Pascoe's name on the whiteboard. In that conversation Leo had emerged from the paper impression of a classic womaniser to someone more complex and, Jude thought, more than a little anxious. 'Aditi's out of the office or I'd send her down to speak to Pascoe, but having said that, I wonder if this interview might be better done by a man. Not because I don't trust a woman, but I think by the sound of it he's probably quite good at deceiving people and I suspect he might be a little less comfortable with a man and more likely to slip up, if he tries to lie. But I might be wrong.'

Chris and Ashleigh came back and sat down and Jude ran them through his phone call with Leo. 'I wanted to bounce a few things around. I'd wondered about Pascoe as a possible suspect earlier, purely because he was so keen to get down to the scene the day after Sophie died and so reluctant to leave when Charlie asked him to. But up until now there was no suggestion that he'd been down at the spa.'

'He's properly put himself in the frame with that call,' said Doddsy, 'hasn't he?'

'He has, and he said as much. But I'd be more willing to believe him if he'd come forward straight away, rather than waiting until now.'

'It's obvious, now, why he was down there on Thursday morning.' Ashleigh frowned. 'Not in Tessa's best interests, either. His own.'

Yes; the white knight charging to the rescue when all danger had passed. 'I think he likes his heroism risk-free.'

'I bet. At the time it was odd, because there was never any suggestion that he'd been down there on Wednesday night, but now I think know why he was there. Tessa must have told him they'd found Sophie. Either he did it and was desperately anxious to see if we'd clocked it was murder at that point, or he didn't do it and he was getting worried he might find himself in the frame for it and wanted to see if we pounced on him.'

'Either works. And I have to say, from what he told us it does seem he might have a very good motive for having killed the girl, if he thought she was going to tell Tessa.' Doddsy sighed.

But he'd told her himself, and maybe she already knew. 'What else do we know about him?' Jude asked Chris.

'Not a lot,' said Chris, promptly. 'I had a dig around about him because he'd turned up there and because of his association with Tessa, but I didn't go too deep. I didn't have time. We were all focussing much more closely on Sophie's background, and the Walsh sisters themselves, but what I know of him caught my interest. He's well-known locally and has a finger in a lot of pies. He has a significant amount of inherited wealth but is also successful in business, though the second might not have been achieved without investment from the first. He's been in a relationship with Tessa Walsh for about a year.'

'Interesting that he was open about his relationships but didn't tell Tessa about Sophie,' said Jude.

'Yes, but I think I take his point on that one,' said Ashleigh. 'It would have made her life more difficult and he may just have been keen to make things simpler for himself, as well. Remember Suzanne certainly didn't like him, though Hazel's view is a little more ambiguous. He might genuinely have Tessa's interests at heart.'

'Okay, that's a fair point. But let's suppose that, having decided to keep it from Tessa, and having agreed that much with Sophie, she got stroppy with him and threatened to tell Suzanne?' Because Tessa might be compliant but Suzanne was anything but.

'I'd been wondering that,' said Chris, meditatively, 'just then, as you were talking to him. But is it really a big enough deal to kill someone for?'

Jude shrugged. On the face of it it wasn't, but he'd known murders committed for more slender reasons than that. 'It depends. We don't know what Sophie cut up rough about, if she did.'

'She might have wanted money,' said Chris promptly. 'She might have wanted commitment.'

'I can't see either of those things causing him a moment's stress. He's bound to have a good deal of skill in easing himself out of awkward relationships. Womanisers always do. But I grant you, he might have lost his temper and done it on the spur of the moment.'

'He might,' Ashleigh said, 'or it might be opportunistic with him set up as the fall guy. If someone knew he was going to be there, knew what was happening, it's conceivable that they picked their time, waited for him to leave and then did away with Sophie immediately afterwards. It would be an extremely elegant way to dispose of her and shift the blame neatly onto him. Because it is neat and tidy, isn't it? He's the perfect suspect. So much so that I struggle to believe it.'

'Right.' Jude frowned. 'I like a suspect. I like a neat and tidy suspect. I like a suspect with means, motive and opportunity, just like Pascoe has, but I never assume that just because someone has all three they necessarily did it. And actually what intrigues me most in this case is that I think we already had three people who could have done it and had reason to do it, and now Mr Pascoe has not only presented himself to us on a plate, so to speak, but he's also strengthened the case against another person.'

'Tony Charles,' said Doddsy, with a nod. 'Yes.'

'Let's talk about the sisters.' Any of whom could have done it. 'We'll do them in age order. Let's start with Suzanne.'

Her picture was on the whiteboard, along with the others — a studio portrait, taken from the website, in which she was smiling, neat and efficient. Maybe the smile had once been real but it didn't look as if it had been for some time.

'Bitter,' said Ashleigh, ticking things off on her fingers. 'She's committed to the business but having spoken to her I'm not sure she likes it. I think it's the only thing she knows and is confident about, and she's scared of letting it go. She has all sorts of emotional baggage stemming from being abandoned by her husband and is almost certainly sexually frustrated. She's jealous of her younger sister for having snagged an apparently desirable man, even if the relationship isn't permanent and he certainly isn't the knight in shining armour he'd like to be — or, indeed, that Tessa would probably like him to be.'

'Suzanne was emotionally highly invested in Sophie, too, it would appear,' said Jude. 'It may well be that she knew about Leo and Sophie and was jealous. She could easily have waited until after he'd left and then killed Sophie out of fury, but I find that difficult to believe because she seems to have viewed Sophie as the future of the business. By killing her she would have set up a whole load of problems for herself on that front. So that's a reason for her not to.' But Suzanne could have done it. She claimed to have gone to her house after leaving work on the Wednesday night but no-one had seen her arrive. 'What about Hazel?'

'Hazel was keen to sell the business,' said Ashleigh, promptly, 'so that she had some cash and could get out of it. Aditi had the impression she felt trapped and frustrated and had been looking for a way out since their mother died. She had hopes for making something of her retirement and she needed cash to do that. Her only chance of getting that, she might have felt, was to force both Suzanne and Tessa into agreeing to sell and as far as she, at least, was concerned, Sophie's appearance and influence was a significant obstacle to that.'

'There's nothing to stop her selling her own share in the business,' objected Chris.

'It's not easy to sell a one-third stake in a family business that's a going concern. And, exactly like Suzanne, we only have her word for it about where she was at the time that Sophie was probably killed.'

That applied to Tessa, too. Both sisters claimed to have been in the cottage after work, both in their rooms, neither seeing or speaking to the other. Tessa claimed to have been getting ready to go out and see Leo. Hazel said she had been asleep. The radio had been on, loudly, and neither woman had seen or heard the other until much later on in the evening, when Tessa had left and they had exchanged a quick word. Living in the same house without knowing where the other was seemed odd to Jude, but it was apparently normal to Tessa and Hazel.

'Tessa probably had the best reason to want Sophie out of the way of all of them,' said Ashleigh, thoughtfully.

'I think so. Jealousy is a very powerful emotion. I know Leo says he told her he wasn't faithful and was very open about his shortcomings, but the fact remains. He concealed the relationship from her and the reason he did that was because he knew she wouldn't like it.'

'She strikes me as the most sensible of the three of them. The other two were pretty highly strung, although under the circumstances that's perhaps not so surprising, and I wouldn't be surprised to find she's emotionally volatile, too. It may well be that she saw him as her last chance at snagging a lifelong partner. Sophie would have been a direct threat to her.'

'And, like the others, she could have done it. Her movements can't be verified and all three of them would have been physically capable of doing the deed.'

Doddsy rubbed his chin. 'Aye. And now we have Tony Charles.'

'I fancy him as a dark horse,' said Chris, cheerfully. 'Fast coming up on the outside. Look at what Leo just said. Before that call I would have thought of him as interesting, but not a real contender. Yes, he could have slipped down from the hotel under cover of darkness, done the deed and nipped back again through the grounds and been reasonably certain that no-one would see him. If anyone did he'd just tell them what he told us — that he always takes a walk around the grounds of an evening, and perhaps he'd say he thought he saw someone and gone down to investigate and found nothing. But any one of his guests might have gone down there and we'd have ruled them out for a very good reason. They'd no motive.'

'Leo's given us a good one, hasn't he?' said Ashleigh. 'Tony Charles wants to buy the business. I can see why. It would be an asset to him, and with a bit of marketing flair and investment he could make quite a thing of it, and it would contribute to making the place a bit special, which is what he's trying to do.'

'I wondered about him,' said Jude, 'when we discovered that he lied about knowing Sophie.'

'Remember, he said he might be mistaken.'

'Do you honestly believe a man who's run prestigious hotels in cities across the world overlooks the slightest detail? I don't. His work here will be much less frenetic than it will have been in the past. I don't believe he forgot that his wife mentioned Sophie Hayes to him, even if she didn't mention the name, and I don't believe that he won't have seen the email she sent with her CV.' It had been specific. Aditi had obtained a copy from the Ullswater Falls; Sophie had been absolutely clear about who she was and where she worked, in both the CV and the covering email. 'If he knew that Suzanne was considering bringing Sophie into the business as a long-term prospect he might have seen her as a threat to him.'

'Then why did she approach him about a job?'

'Hedging her bets, perhaps. It was common knowledge that the Three Sisters was struggling and she'd have known that if she had anything to do with the finances. She maybe thought there'd be nothing for her to take on, and wanted to see if there were any other options.'

'Tony really wants the business, doesn't he?' Chris was shaking his head. 'I wonder why. That amount of money he's supposed to have offered for it is way more than it's worth.'

'Yes. And remember, Mrs Charles says she told Sophie there wasn't anything currently available so she may have gone back and decided, after all, that the Three Sisters was her future.'

'They've left us a real headache, haven't they?' Doddsy shook his head.

Five possible suspects, all of them capable of the murder, all of them with a good reason to want Sophie out of the way either in the cold light of day or in a hot moment of passion — and all of them with their movements unaccounted for at the time of her death. Jude shook his head. It would be interesting to see if they got anything more from Leo Pascoe.

On his way back from the incident room to his desk, he took a moment to pop into Faye Scanlon's office. It struck him, as he did so, that it was most unusual for Faye, who was a control freak, not to have been in and out of the incident room on her own behalf, making sure she was up to date on everything and taking apparent pleasure in letting everyone think he couldn't do his job without her input. On the Sophie Hayes case, Faye had been notable for her absence.

Whatever the reason, he wasn't going to lay himself open to any future accusations of not keeping her up to date. He tapped on her door. 'Faye, hi. Do you have a minute?'

'As it happens, no.' She looked up from her computer screen. 'Is it important?'

'Not especially. I just wanted to let you know where we are with the Sophie Hayes case. I can come back later, if you prefer.'

She seemed to hesitate. 'No, there's no need. Could you just drop me a briefing note about it?'

It would be much quicker to update her in person but Faye was never shy of making work for other people. 'I'll do that. I just wanted to know if you've come across a Tony Charles before.'

'I know the name.' She turned back down to her computer again.

'And Leo Pascoe.'

'Oh, I've met Leo. Charming man. He sponsors some good citizenship award in the area. I was at his table at a dinner a couple of weeks ago. Very charming. Don't tell me he's a suspect?'

'I have so many perfect suspects for this case, you wouldn't believe it. Take your pick out of five.' Six, if you included a potential stranger on the path, who had struck for no reason and disappeared without trace.

'Excellent. So perhaps now concentrate on narrowing it down to which one it was, and let me have the details then?'

'I will do.' He hesitated for a moment. 'Pascoe has only recently emerged as a person of interest. We've only just discovered he was in the area around the time Sophie was killed. I'm going down to have a chat with him.'

'You are?' That irritated her. 'That's really not your job. You're a manager. God knows you have enough to do.'

'I like to keep my hand in talking to real people,' he said, 'from time to time. It makes the job interesting. And I think there's a lot about him that I'd like to know about.'

'If you find office work boring, you should probably have thought it through before you applied for promotion,' she said, scowling. 'I'm sorry, Jude, but I really am very busy right now and I don't have time to discuss it.' And she turned her back on him.

TWENTY-ONE

Philippa Charles headed down to the Three Sisters for her Monday afternoon appointment with a considerable degree of trepidation. There was a breath of frost in the crisp air as she followed the path down through the hotel grounds in the direction of the setting sun.

Halfway down the slope she paused for a moment. The distant fells sparkled with snow; the blue sky shivered under the thinnest veil of mile-high cloud; the lake, drowning the low-level summertime path, was choppy and angry. Beneath her the slate roof of the Three Sisters jutted out over the water. She stared at it for a while, then forged on towards the gate and the path. She and Tony had taken a turn down the place swiftly after their arrival, to suss it out and she'd both liked and disliked what she'd seen. She'd avoided the lakeside path since then.

It was cold enough for hat and gloves on the short walk down to the lake and even then she shivered in the knife-like wind. The lights were on in the spa and she could see one of the sisters sitting at the desk, but the woman had her back turned and was staring at a computer screen, so Philippa couldn't see which one of them it was. She paused for another moment, amazed at herself for showing such uncharacteristic hesitation, but she pressed on. Through the shrubbery, down to the gate, onto the path, through the gap in that screening holly hedge and up the steps. Through the first set of double doors, and the second...

It was Tessa on the desk. 'Good afternoon. Mrs Charles?'

'Yes. Tessa?'

Tessa's face flickered into disbelief. 'Yes.'

Philippa turned her back, pulled off her hat, shook out her hair and turned back again. By now Hazel had appeared from some back room. Her expression mirrored Tessa's.

'Sue!' called Hazel. 'Come here!'

'What is it?' Suzanne appeared in the doorway behind her, nudging her out of the way.

'Mrs Charles is here,' said Hazel, flatly, and stood aside.

Too late to back out now. The three of them were staring at her. 'So this is the Three Sisters,' said Philippa, and caught hold of her courage. 'Or perhaps we should call it the Four Sisters, now?'

'Pip!' said Tessa, in tones of utter shock. 'I thought I must be mistaken. It is you. Oh, my God!'

'What the hell are you doing here?' demanded Suzanne, elbowing Hazel out of the way and charging forward, only to stop at the desk. God, she hadn't changed. Or rather, she had. Her shortcomings had intensified.

'I've come for my manicure. Tony booked it for me. Tony Charles. My husband.' With steady hands, Philippa unbuttoned her coat and took a look round. All that pink. It must have been her mother's idea. So bland. It could be so much more modern. 'It's been a long time.'

'I—' stuttered Hazel.

'Am I dead to you?' inquired Philippa, sweetly. It had, after all, been twenty years. 'I thought you might be pleased to see me.' But they weren't. Her heart hammered.

Her sisters had different silences; they were such different people. Tess might be speechless with joy and Hazel with confusion, but there was no mistaking why Suzanne said nothing. She was furious.

Philippa took off her coat, walked across to the chairs arranged with the view over Ullswater and draped it over the back of one of them, then sat down. 'Which one of you is doing my mani?'

'Me,' said Tessa. She got up and walked across to the table then sat down. 'Oh Pip. I can hardly believe it's you!' There was warmth in her voice.

It would be all right. Philippa's spirits rose. Her gut instinct had been correct and Tessa, the one who was closest to her in age, the one she'd kept in touch with for a short while after the big bust-up that had seen her parents cut her out of the family business after she'd headed abroad to learn something about life, still cared. After all, there had been nothing to fear.

But there was much to forgive. Even Tess had stopped replying to her in the end.

'You're looking wonderful,' said Tessa, almost in envy, still looking at her as if she wasn't real, as if she wanted to reach out to touch her. 'How do you look so young? And now you're going to live at the Ullswater Falls? This is fantastic. I can't believe it.'

Philippa shot a quick look at the other two. Suzanne's expression had switched to neutral and Hazel, looking from one to the other as if she was trying to work out whose lead she should follow, opted for Tessa's. That was a surprise; once upon a time Hazel and Sue had been as close as Tessa and Philippa and the thought of them doing anything independent of one another was surreal. But here was Hazel, sweeping in for a hug, smelling of lavender and grapefruit and with a tear in her eye.

'Pip. I've missed you so much.' And a whisper, so quiet Philippa almost missed it. 'You're so lucky to have got away.'

'I'll get coffee.' Suzanne turned to the machine, as if to give herself a chance to think, and it was only when its buzzing and whirring were done and they were all round the table, together for the first time in more than twenty years, that Philippa managed to relax.

'I have so much to tell you!' she said, and beamed.

'We've nothing to say,' said Hazel, with a sigh. 'You see us as we are. As we always are. As we have been since God made heaven and earth.'

'But you're all right. All of you?'

'Our parents are dead,' said Suzanne, flatly.

'I know.' Philippa had found out by accident. 'I'm so sorry I didn't find out in time to come home.' It was always better to get your excuses in first, and this truly wasn't her fault. 'I would have done.'

'I wanted to tell you,' said Tessa, 'but I didn't know where you were.'

'Let's not sugar the pill. They didn't want to see you,' said Suzanne, brutally.

Their parents — their mother particularly — had been unforgiving and a deathbed reconciliation would never have been on the cards. In her own way Philippa was as ruthless as the rest of them. Why waste emotion regretting things that couldn't have happened any other way? 'I can't wait to tell you everything. I've had such a wonderful time, a wonderful life. I've been so lucky.' Luckier than her sisters, for sure.

'Why here?' asked Hazel, eagerly. 'Not that I— I mean, I'm so happy. But why here? Why now?'

'Because I love it here. Cumbria's my home. I said to Tony when we married that I wanted to come back here to live one day and now the time is right. Here I am. And here you all are, too.'

'I want to know everything,' said Tessa, beaming. 'I've missed you so much.'

Tessa and Hazel, so open, so enthusiastic. Suzanne nervous. As she should be. *What the hell. Why not now?* 'Have you told them, Sue?'

Suzanne shook her head and looked away. She must have known her secret would come out one day.

'Told us what?' demanded Hazel, agog.

'The truth about what happened when you came out to visit me in America.' Philippa sipped at her coffee and left a lipstick stain on the rim of the cup.

'America?' said Tessa. 'Sue, but that was when you got married.'

That was the thing about Tess. She wasn't the smartest of them but she always got there in the end. 'Yes, where I was working when Sue came out and tried her great escape.' By any means possible. Yes, ruthlessness ran in all their veins. 'She came to see me. Getting married was the perfect solution, wasn't it?' She smiled. Revenge was so, so sweet. 'You didn't have to marry my boyfriend, Sue, though, did you?' She flexed her hand out in front of her and looked at the wedding ring on it, nestled under the large solitaire engagement ring. It had been there so long now she didn't think she could take it off.

'I don't remember it being like that,' said Suzanne, flatly.

'It doesn't matter. I've forgiven you. Karma bit you on the backside, and deservedly so, but it all fell out fine for me. I have Tony.' She, not Suzanne, had earned her happy ever after.

'Shall I do your mani?' Tessa's eagerness to get away from Suzanne and get all the gossip was obvious. 'We can talk. Bring your coffee through here and I'll show you round. You'll love the pods.'

'I'm going home,' said Suzanne. 'We aren't busy and I have things to do. You two can clean up and lock up.' She turned away and went for her coat.

Philippa followed Tessa into the treatment area. It was nice enough as a space — but oh, the views from the three pods! 'These are stunning, Tess.'

'You mean the pods. Yes. they're great. The rest of it is a bit shabby, I know.' Tessa made a face.

'The building is amazing. It has such soul.' And it did, even though it had been forced into the wrong use, like Cinderella in the kitchen.

'Except for the pink and gold.' Tess waved her to a seat in the middle pod.

'Yes. It's ghastly.'

'I've never said how much I hate it, because it it was Mum's colour scheme and Sue really is turning into her. Here, have a look at these colours and see what you like.'

Philippa stopped laughing when she thought of her mother and turned her attention instead to the sheaf of coloured cards her sister presented her to, each one bright with a different shade of nail polish. 'What about this one?'

'Maybe a bit Christmassy?' said Tessa, doubtfully, looking at the green Philippa had selected, so dark it hinted at witchcraft and madness.

'Do you think so? I really like it.'

'Then go for it. It's a gorgeous colour at any time of year. And you always were a bit way-out,' said Tessa, admiringly, as she took her sister's hand in hers and began

189

to tidy up the cuticles. 'I'm so glad to see you. And I'm so sorry we lost touch, but everything was difficult. You know how it is.'

Their parents were toxic, but Philippa had no regrets and so could afford to be forgiving. 'I know you tried.'

'Somehow they knew I was still in touch with you and they made it intolerable. I was still quite young and impressionable. And now I understand. Sue meeting her husband when she was visiting you makes it somehow your fault, too, in their eyes.'

Philippa extended her hand for Tessa to apply the base coat. 'Yes. But it ended okay. I'm back.'

'Is it true what you said about Sue?'

'That she ran off with my boyfriend? Yes. We'd had a huge row and he ran off and had a fling with her out of sheer spite, I think. I could cope with that, but I didn't think he'd marry her and I think even he realised that he'd gone too far.' She managed a wry smile. 'I expect when Dad came over to sort him out, he was only too glad of the opt-out.'

'I'm really sorry she did that to you.'

'She's changed, hasn't she?' Philippa felt her lips narrow in judgement. 'Never mind her. What about you? Tell me all about this place. I knew where you were, you know.' The Three Sisters had come into being after she'd left and she'd kept an eye on it from a distance. From the outside, at least, it seemed so striking. Tony, whose optimism and good nature were as far removed as possible from the grim single-mindedness of Philippa's upbringing, had laughed when she'd told him about it but a couple of months later he'd come up with the suggestion that they buy up the Ullswater Falls. What a sweet moment that had been.

As she worked, Tessa chatted on and on about her life

— about how Suzanne had come back with crushing disappointment after the disaster of her marriage and how their parents had tightened the ropes, financial and emotional, to keep them there. About how they had lived together like three old women after their parents' deaths. About her lover, and how he wouldn't commit or give up the other women. About how Sue had moved out and grown more and more sour. About how Hazel was so suddenly determined to break free. About how much she wanted to buy over the building and remould it.

She grew more wistful as she talked, bending her head over her sister's hand and working away, while Philippa gazed out across the grey water and marvelled at how beautiful the lake was even in January, until the manicure was done.

'You sound as though you hate it here,' said Philippa as Tessa's voice tailed away into silence.

'I think I do.' Tessa released her sister's hand. 'There. That's you done.'

'I thought you might be happy.' It had been a long shot. 'I hoped you were.'

'I could be happy, if it weren't for…well, the way we all are. I don't want to be a beauty therapist. I want to do something that fulfils the creative side of me. All I do is make other women look adorable and attractive for their dates or their weddings or just for a special night in with the husband who loves them. I'm just dull and drab. And invisible.'

'Except to Leo.' It wasn't the homecoming Philippa had hoped for. She sighed. 'Is everything all right?'

'Not really.'

'I thought you'd be glad to see me.'

'I am. I am, really. But it's just—' Tessa put the brush

back in the bottle of the nail polish. The last steamer chugged past on it way to the port for the night.

'That's me off, Tess,' called Hazel, through the door. 'See you, Pip.' And that was it.

'What have I done to upset you, Tess?'

'Nothing.' But Tess said it too quickly.

'Tess,' said Philippa, warningly.

'No, I mean it. I really do. But it's like I said. I'm so dull and plain and you're so beautiful. I just know when Leo meets you he'll—'

'Nonsense,' said Philippa, robustly. 'I'm not a marriage wrecker.' There was only one of those in the family. 'I'm happily married and I'll take no nonsense from anyone, certainly not your man. Don't worry about me.'

'I do hope you're right.' Tessa stood up. 'Sue's changed so much. She used to want other people to be happy. I don't think she does any more.' She took a deep breath. 'Sometimes I hate her.'

Hate was such a strong word. In the dim evening Philippa sensed malice, as if it was woven into the fabric of the building like a curse. She wanted to go home, not be left here on her own at the mercy of her sisters. Sue hated her for what had happened in the past. Hazel, she could sense, resented her for escaping the present. And even Tessa — dear lovely Tessa — didn't really want her back. 'Do you want me to stay and help clear up?'

'No, I'll be fine.'

'I can wait. I can walk you home.'

'And how would you get home?'

A fair point. Philippa turned her hand in the light, admiring it. There were gold flecks in the green, something more festive than was fitting for the post-Christmas grave-yard of January, but she didn't care. 'Can we meet up again? Go somewhere away from here, maybe? For a walk or a coffee or to an art exhibition.' She'd hoped she could walk straight back into Tess's life but that had been folly. They would need to spend time to get to know one another again.

'Yes. I'll call you,' said Tess, and began to tidy away the paraphernalia.

Philippa retrieved her coat and hat and put them on. Her homecoming had been bittersweet, on so many levels, and the only thing that had panned out as she'd expected was Suzanne's horror. 'Bye, darling Tess.'

'Goodbye, Pip.'

She loitered at the top of the steps, scanning what she could see of the car park and the path, aware of her vulnerability. Perhaps she should call Tony and get him to come and fetch her. But he would be busy, and in any case she was being stupid.

Gathering her courage, she walked briskly across the car park, through the lane to the gate. Something stirred behind her, or she thought it did, and she sprinted up the hill as fast as she could, reaching the lights with gratitude.

'Phil! Is that you? What's happened?'

She stopped. 'Tony! Yes, fine. I just—'

'I was on my way down to find you and saw you running. Are you all right? How did it go?'

'Yes, fine. Just a bit unnerved. It didn't happen quite the way I thought it would.'

'No? Tell you what,' he said, slipping his hand in hers, 'why don't we head up to the bar and I'll fix you a G&T and you can tell me all about it.'

TWENTY-TWO

Jude went down to Leo Pascoe's office, a small suite of rooms above a tea shop in Glenridding, on the Tuesday afternoon. As he scaled the flight of uneven stairs to the first floor, he shook his head, thinking about what Faye had said and reluctantly acknowledging she had a point. Seniority had its drawbacks and he didn't even have the luxury of delegating the paperwork that would still be there when he got back, but he'd found it impossible to resist a rare opportunity to step out of the office and back into the field. As he paused outside the door with its bright brass plate — *Pascoe Enterprises*, an indication of Leo's high opinion of himself — he justified his actions to himself as he might one day have to justify them to Faye. It was good to get out and about, be seen by the local community, and when you spent time in the office it was too easy to lose the knack of listening to witnesses, only seeing what they'd said through the transcript of the interview, not being able to read their body language and pick up the subtext of what they said and — more crucially — what they didn't say.

Leo answered the door himself, looking mightily cheerful and not at all like someone who was about to be interviewed by the police in relation to a murder.

'Come on in,' he said, waving Jude through. 'My secretary's just popped out to the post but if you don't mind waiting while I try and fight the coffee machine we can have a cuppa to see us through the afternoon.'

Jude declined the coffee. 'It's strictly business, Mr Pascoe.'

'Oh, I'd have thought a coffee wouldn't hurt.' Leo Pascoe looked faintly bewildered by that. 'I understand, though. I know all the emergency services are hard-pushed. Can't say I've ever come across a copper I didn't like.'

Yes, he was turning on the charm, putting across a bluff sense that they were on the same side, that honesty was speaking to honesty, the good guys to the good.

'Glad to hear it.' Jude took the seat that Leo waved him towards, in the tiny, bright and overcrowded office crammed with papers and boxes of brightly-coloured marketing brochures, a dusty Swiss cheese plant struggling towards the thin winter light, a mug half full of cold coffee. The walls were covered with framed pictures of Leo at this event or that, with royalty at the opening of something or other, in tweeds with a shotgun broken over his arm.

'I don't really understand how these things work, I mean. Police investigations and so on. So you'll have to keep me right.' Leo looked soulful, but the pictures reinforced the outline of his life that Chris had dug up and which Jude himself had taken the time to flesh out before his visit. It was a story of privilege and achievement — a minor public school and Durham University, where he'd studied French and economics, followed by an internship in the City. His career had progressed via readily-available investment, a small estate that was way more grand than this tiny office (perhaps chosen deliberately to seem unassuming) would suggest and where, he had told a newspaper interview, he dabbled in breeding Herdwick sheep.

It felt, like Leo himself, more than a little fake. 'Can you tell me a bit about yourself, Mr Pascoe? Not your full life story, perhaps.'

'I expect you can find that out for yourselves,' said Leo, with puppyish cheerfulness.

'Indeed. But I'd like to know a little about you and your role in the community, perhaps. You're very much part of it.'

Leo needed no encouragement. 'I'm a big supporter of the tourism industry locally. Not just for the direct economic benefits that it brings, but for wider recognition of the area.' He indicated the picture on the wall. 'HRH over there was delighted to support some of the work we do in conservation, for example.'

Jude allowed Leo five minutes to lull himself into a sense of security, buttressed with endless notable names dropped — royalty, international sports stars, actors and other celebrities — and noted down every single one of them, dutifully, nodding. There was, it seemed, no-one Leo didn't know. He even tried out a few names of colleagues from other departments in the police, and Jude knew some of them. So much the better; he could see if they had a view on Leo Pascoe.

'You're obviously highly regarded locally, Mr Pascoe.' It wasn't going to be difficult to appeal to the man's vanity.

'I do like to think so.' There was an underlying cockiness to him, though Jude thought he was trying to cover it with a semblance of humility, but that was the interesting thing. Leo thought he was in control.

'Okay. I'd like to ask you some more specific questions.

You've told us you had a liaison with Sophie on Wednesday night. By late morning on Thursday you knew she was dead. So, perhaps you can tell me why it took you so long to come forward and tell us about it.'

'Ah.' Leo leaned back in his chair and stared past Jude, out of the window. 'I know, I know. I told you, and I get why you don't believe me. I deserve a slapped wrist for that, though I hope you don't think it's anything too serious.' He looked convincingly regretful. 'It really was Tess, though. As I told you I didn't want to hurt her feelings by telling her about the silly fling I had with Sophie.'

'Were having,' corrected Jude, 'from what I understand.'

'I mean, yes, technically, though it was never going to last.'

'Did Sophie know that?'

'Oh God, yes. It's no secret that I like the ladies, Chief Inspector, but I'm not a cad. I never pretend there's anything serious when there isn't. As far as Sophie was concerned, it was just a bit of fun and she was very much up for it.'

'You didn't think it was potentially awkward, having a relationship with your partner's employee, in their workplace?'

'When you put it like that it sounds seedy.' Leo looked almost penitent. 'I hadn't thought of it that way. When the sap rises, you can't help yourself. You're a man. You understand.'

Every cliché in the book. 'I've always found the vast majority of men are capable of exercising a considerable amount of judgement and self-restraint.' Jude knew he sounded po-faced, but it was worth it for the look on Leo's face. 'But I'll accept you at your word. You have a lot of relationships with women, I believe.'

'Yes. They seem to find me appealing.'

'Okay. But you don't seem to have charmed either of Ms Walsh's sisters.'

'They were both jealous of Tess. Because neither of them managed to find themselves a man, and I tell you, it's not natural for a woman to be on her own. It troubled me that they don't like me. Such a bloody shame. The last thing I ever wanted was to introduce any discord to the household or the business, but I do love Tessa.'

Maybe he did. Jude had come across stranger matches in his time. 'You'd been with her for some time, I think.'

'Longer with her than with anyone else.'

'And she didn't know you were seeing Sophie until…when?'

'Sunday.'

'Are you sure?'

Leo sat back, elbows on the arms of his chair, fingertips together, flexing, flexing. 'This is why I didn't tell you,' he said, quietly. 'You'll think it was her, but it wasn't. She isn't the jealous type. If she was we'd have split up long ago.'

'It's why it's so important that you should have told us, Mr Pascoe. Someone murdered Sophie shortly after she left the Three Sisters on Wednesday evening. You were there with her. You told me on the phone that you left her to walk home on her own—'

'I can't tell you how bitterly I regret that.'

'I'm sure. But I need to be clear. You were there with her and she must have died shortly after you parted.'

'I didn't kill her,' said Leo, 'and you can't prove I did.'

Yet. 'How long had you been seeing Sophie?'

'Off and on, for some time, but I told you. It was a casual thing. When opportunity knocked. If she was working late and I was in the area.' He looked sheepish.

'Now you've made me feel guilty about it.' As if guilt were alien to him; and maybe it was.

'Are you sure Tessa didn't suspect?'

'I thought she knew. I mean, there was one occasion when I turned up to see Sophie and Tessa was still there.'

'That must have been very awkward for you,' said Jude, dryly.

'Oh, not at all. I'm quite quick at thinking on my feet, so to speak, and I hadn't said anything incriminating or anything. I just told Tess I'd called by on the off-chance that she could give me a massage.'

'Is that a euphemism?'

Leo roared with laughter. 'I like your sense of humour, Chief Inspector. No, it wasn't. It's good for the shoulders and Tess says everyone who spends too long at a desk should get one, regardless of our age or sex.' He shook his head.

Becca had said pretty much the same thing. Jude ran a hand over his own shoulder. 'Sports massages are a real thing, aren't they?'

'Not at the Three Sisters. Suzanne wouldn't have any of that. I'd said to Tess that they should branch out into that, and I think she and Hazel had both suggested they expand their services and offer a range of massages for people doing outdoor activities, to pick up on the walkers and so on. Relaxing your shoulders after a day carrying your rucksack around and the like. A plodder's pedicure. Some of the ideas they came up with were quite creative. But no. Suzanne wanted it to be a safe space for women and as far as I know I'm the only bloke who's ever had a massage at the Three Sisters.'

Jude could tell that particular distinction appealed to Leo's vanity. 'You had regular massages?'

'Every couple of weeks, although we did do it on the

QT to save hassle. Sophie knew. Hazel knew. I think for some time she was really pushing to expand into other areas to do something to keep the business going but Suzanne was pretty much strangling it. Hazel had a fairly recent change of heart, Tess said. Very sudden, as if she'd given up on the place.'

'You think she wanted to sell?'

'I know she did. Hazel wanted out. She'd recently come to the conclusion that the business wasn't going to prosper without major changes her sister wasn't prepared to make. There was a lot of tension there, and I think Hazel might have taken it upon herself to move things forward, one way or another, rather than have the place atrophy and herself with it.'

'You said Tony Charles wanted to buy the spa.'

'Tess mentioned it, but to be honest I don't know whether anything would come of it. It's too small to have the facilities he'd need. Even if it wasn't, it seems Suzanne has taken against him and won't sell, even at the crazy price he's offering. If you ask me, Hazel was ready to blow.'

It had been Tessa, not Hazel, who had been on duty on the night that Sophie had died, but that counted for little on that lonely path with so many places to hide. They couldn't know who was close by. They only knew that both Suzanne and Hazel — as well as Tessa — had left and that they could have come back. And so could plenty of others — including Tony Charles, and probably some of the hotel guests and staff. Any of them could, in theory, have killed Sophie either knowing who she was or thinking she was someone else. 'Thank you, Mr Pascoe. That's been most enlightening.'

'You say that as if I've incriminated myself.' Leo sounded hurt.

'Not at all. I just think you've given me a lot of useful background information.'

'I didn't do it. And Tess didn't, either.'

'Thank you again, Mr Pascoe.' Jude got to his feet. 'We may have some further questions for you.'

'Of course. Of course. any time.' Shaking his hand vigorously, Leo saw Jude to the door. 'Any messages, Sarah?'

In the outer office his secretary — who, Jude noticed, gazed at her boss adoringly the minute he emerged — snapped to attention. 'One from the Three Sisters about your massage. Is there any chance you could pop down this evening instead of tomorrow?'

'I think I can make that,' he said, as Jude exited the door. 'Let me have a look in the diary.'

'You have Faye in for this evening. Shall I call her and cancel?'

'No, no need. If I run down to the Three Sisters now I should still be in time.'

The door swung closed. Jude ran lightly down the steps and out into the chill afternoon. Faye, eh? It wasn't that common a name and surely Faye — if it was the same person — had too much common sense to get involved with someone who was part of a criminal investigation, if only at its margins.

But with Faye — touchy, needy and lacking in self-awareness — you could never be sure. He picked up his phone and put it back in his pocket. Some things, especially the tricky issue of challenging a senior officer on her ethical standards, were best dealt with face to face.

TWENTY-THREE

'Has Leo Pascoe called you?'

Jude didn't even knock on the office door and Faye, whose ego was frail enough to make her insist on the formalities where most other people were relaxed about rank, looked up, outraged. 'Do you mind?'

'I've just been down to see him.' He remembered himself just in time. Faye was his boss not his junior officer, and would cut him no slack.

'You've been down? I thought we'd agreed that you were supposed to be spending more time in the office rather than running around doing something we pay other people to do.'

'Faye.' A rookie error. He'd put her back up. He dialled it down. 'Sorry to barge in, but this might be important.'

'I don't see what your interview with Pascoe has to do with me.'

Did she think he buttoned up the back? Someone needed to remind her of her responsibilities but it wasn't his job. Rank was no respecter of right. 'As I was leaving his secretary asked if he wanted her to call someone called Faye about this evening. I wondered if it might be you.'

'Is that any of your business?'

They stared at one another, she daring him to go on. He took up the challenge. 'I think it might be. I didn't get the impression it was a business call. Not about a meeting. Not about some shindig for the great and the good. Not about a charity evening for the Police Benevolent Fund. And he stopped her pretty quick. I wondered what that might be about.'

'I hope,' she said, playing for time, 'that you aren't suggesting I've done anything improper.'

'No, of course not.' But the pieces were falling into place. There had been that time he and Ashleigh met her, so obviously waiting for her date, so obviously uncomfortable at seeing them, at the Ullswater Falls of all places. There was Leo's propensity for making contacts that he thought could benefit him in some way. There was his inability to resist an enthusiastic woman and a whole of host of women inexplicably unable to resist him. And there was Faye's unusual reluctance to keep on top of every detail in a homicide case. *Send me a briefing note* had been her washing her hands of it, a red flag if ever there had been one. He should have spotted it earlier.

'It's for information,' he said, as she tried to stare him down. 'Leo Pascoe isn't just an innocent witness in the Three Sisters case. He's a person of interest, right in the middle of it, with no alibi and a bloody good reason to kill Sophie Hayes.'

'Is that right?'

When Mikey was a child he would shut his eyes and stick his fingers in his ears when his mother tried to tell him something he didn't want to hear. Faye, it seemed, had been doing the same, metaphorically speaking, for the past week, but she couldn't avoid reality any longer. 'Yes. He was sleeping with Sophie, and Tessa Walsh, who was his partner didn't know about it.'

Faye motioned him to a chair. 'I wasn't aware of that.'

Not aware? How could someone so senior be capable of so great a degree of self-delusion? 'Do you know him?' he asked, calming down a little. 'You said you'd met him.'

'Yes,' said Faye, squaring her shoulders, 'at some charity do. He asked me out for a drink, purely socially.' Astonishingly, a flush of pink rose on her cheeks.

'You were waiting for him at the Ullswater Falls, weren't you?'

If she'd been in uniform she'd have tapped the pips on her shoulder. 'Please don't interrogate me — and may I remind you to show some respect. I had arranged to meet Leo for a drink at the Ullswater Falls, yes, but that arrangement was made long before the incident at the Three Sisters, and long before any suggestion that Tony Charles might have had an involvement.'

So she had read the briefings. That she'd chosen to keep so clear a distance and pretend at disinterest said something. For a moment he felt a flutter of sympathy. Was it possible that touchy, over-sensitive, divorced Faye was as fallible to Leo's charm as so many others seemed to be? But why not? She lived alone among the wreckage of a broken marriage and he knew from Ashleigh's experiences that a single life wasn't her natural state.

But the sympathy was gone before he spoke again. 'We've been looking into his background. Pascoe's a clever man. He's a networker with an eye for the main chance.'

'I found him very charming, and he told me he was single.'

'Theoretically, yes, but it's more accurate to say he's uncommitted.' Faye was tough and not always appealing, the very opposite of the type of woman who seemed to attract Leo Pascoe, but she was a senior police officer and for a certain segment of society that meant she could be very useful to have on your side. 'I'm afraid he might have been stringing you along,' he said, and shrugged.

'I hope you think I'm not that naive—'

'As far as I'm concerned he's a suspect in this investigation.' There was no pretending she hadn't read the briefing now, no pleading an arrangement that pre-empted Sophie's death. She couldn't have anything to do with Leo Pascoe.

'Thank you for bringing me up to date,' she said coldly. 'Naturally, now that I know that I shall obviously cut my ties with him completely and recuse myself. I'll be stepping back from the investigation.'

Even further back, he thought, though he didn't dare say it. 'Did I deduce correctly? Are you supposed to be seeing him tonight?'

'We had an arrangement to meet for a drink, yes.' She said it primly, as if it was a business meeting. Who knew? For Leo, that might have been exactly what it was.

'He hasn't called you?'

Her irritation was obvious. 'Not yet.'

He checked his watch. Leo would have gone straight from his office to the Three Sisters. A massage would take him no more than half an hour. It was half past four.

'I'll call him.' Having taken the decision, Faye had no choice but to act. She got out her phone and dialled, only to lay the phone down again after a moment, shaking her head. 'It's ringing out. I'll try his office.'

This time she got an answer. 'No,' said his secretary, wearily, 'I don't know where he is. I've just had Miss Walsh on the phone — Tessa Walsh, that is, looking for him. He isn't answering her calls either.'

Faye hung up, and looked at Jude with narrowed eyes. 'I don't like the sound of that.'

'Neither do I.' He turned to the door. 'Let's get down to the Three Sisters, shall we, and see what's going on.'

The lights were on full at the Three Sisters, and there were two cars parked in front of it. As Jude squeezed the Mercedes in next to them, Faye got out her work phone and quickly checked the registration number of the second. 'The BMW is Leo's, of course. I recognise it. And the other is registered to Hazel Walsh.'

The fact that it was registered to Hazel didn't, of course, mean she had been driving it. Jude's brows puckered into a frown. 'Let's go and see what's what.'

He led the way up the steps and into the building. The reception area shimmered with warmth from a portable gas heater, whose blue flames roared merrily in the background. Whale music played through the speakers, a primeval sound whose thrumming, throbbing bass notes seemed to dominate the entire building, but that was all. The rest of the place was still. There was a man's overcoat hanging on a rack on the wall and a cup of coffee overturned on one of the tables; a screensaver wobbled across the screen of the elderly computer monitor on the desk. Otherwise, nothing.

'Hello!' called Faye.

No-one, nothing moved. 'This is like the *Marie Celeste*,' she said in an undertone, as if it unnerved her.

Jude took a look at the staff noticeboard behind the desk. Sophie's name and photo had been hastily removed but photos of the other three smiled out. *Duty Manager: Hazel*, said the board next to the photographs.

'Hazel!' he called, as if being more specific might get a response, but there was nothing. 'Let's try the pods.'

With a troubled look to Faye, who followed, he made his cautious way across to the door which led through to the pods. He'd never been inside the place but its layout was familiar to him through the sketches and photographs on the whiteboard in the incident room, and from the photographs on the website. The treatment area was lit and the screens which protected the pod on the left were open, showing everything in all its neat, startling pinkness; in the centre, the picture windows of the middle pod looked out over the dark water and the stream of moonlight that fretted on the lake surface. A rainbow of nail polish jars was set neatly out on a table by the window under the bright spotlight of a table lamp. The third pod, on the right, was closed off.

He strode over and pulled the screen aside. On the couch, face down with his head over the hole in the floor looking down to the glass panel, lay a male figure. A towel had been placed across his backside but his legs and upper body were naked. His hands lay limply down beside the sides of the couch.

Jude walked the few steps to the couch and reached for a wrist. Under his fingers it was chilly and still.

'Sorry, Faye,' he said, and lifted the towel over the man's head briefly, letting it drop again as soon as he'd seen who it was. 'Too late.'

'So I see.' Whatever Faye had thought of Leo — possibly not much, Jude now thought, judging by the way she looked at his corpse with a total lack of emotion, and certainly not with any real fondness — she was quick into work mode, digging out her phone and calling for back up. 'Yes. Detective Superintendent Scanlon here. We came down to the Three Sisters Spa looking for Leo Pascoe. He's dead. No, I don't know.'

Jude took a long look around. The door to the walk-in cupboard was ajar and he pushed it. A foot, clad in a leather flip flop. Hazel Walsh, face down on the floor, her body crumpled at a helpless, inhuman angle, as if she'd been clutched at the door for support. Her face was cherry red.

He moved to wrench one of the windows open, but he knew it was too late.

TWENTY-FOUR

'I t was a hell of an afternoon at all sorts of levels,' said Jude to Ashleigh, 'and the worst thing is that I can't make sense of it.'

'I thought you said it was carbon monoxide.' Ashleigh got up and began to clear the table. She'd been in a meeting for the latter part of the afternoon and had managed to miss the drama at the Three Sisters. 'Okay, it's a bit too close to Sophie, time-wise, but these things do happen way more often than they should. Shall I leave you the rest of this lasagne for your tea tomorrow?'

He inspected the dish, reviewed the chances of him actually getting to sit down and eat a proper meal the next day and fell prey to an unusual optimism. 'Yes, why not?' He took the lasagne through to the kitchen and covered it in foil while Ashleigh loaded the dishwasher and set the coffee machine humming.

'Right,' she said. 'Now we've got a choice. We can sit and see if we can find something on the telly we can agree to watch, or you can tell me what it is about this tragic but straightforward incident that's bugging you.'

He grinned. She knew he never thought anything was straightforward. 'I can't be bothered to look out for old compilations of Top of the Pops, so I'll talk. But I warn you, I'll be thinking out loud.'

'That's fine. I might be able to help.'

'Right. I expect you'll have picked up the order of events. Faye and I were worried about Leo Pascoe because no-one was able to get hold of him, so we went down to the Three Sisters, where he was booked in for a massage.'

'Faye went out of the office?' Ashleigh lifted a cynical eyebrow. Faye was notorious for not having the time or the interest for the general public. 'I thought anyone above your rank turned to stone if they went out in the daylight.'

'Wonders never cease.' It wouldn't be wise to share the full details of his conversation with Faye about Leo Pascoe. She wouldn't value his silence and she'd never forgive his indiscretion; even if that wasn't the case Ashleigh, who possibly understood her too well, wasn't the person to discuss it with. 'We went down. We went in. The reception was empty.' He outlined the scene that he and Faye had discovered and as he ran over it, he frowned. There was definitely something not right about it.

'Chris said it was carbon monoxide poisoning, according to the paramedics. Is that right?'

'It certainly looked like it.' Hazel's face had been the giveaway, the scarlet flush being the classic symptom. 'But that's the thing, you know. I think Faye and I made a huge mistake.'

'What do you mean?' Ashleigh closed the dishwasher and went to wipe the table, stifling a discreet yawn. He sensed she wouldn't stay long, that the real reason for her accepting his offer of supper was exactly the one he'd had in his own mind — to talk things out of the office.

'I think we rushed things.'

'What do you mean? If you thought there was carbon monoxide in the air you had to get out of there, didn't you?'

She was right. When he'd mentioned the gas Faye had exercised her duty of care, ordered him out of the building as soon as they'd established there was nothing they could do for either Hazel or Leo. 'I'd like to have stayed a bit longer.' Probably wrongly. 'I wish I'd had a look around. But Faye and I charged through the place and opened all the windows. Turned the gas fire off.' The paramedics had done the same with even less care, swiftly followed by the arrival of a team from the Health and Safety Executive. Now the Three Sisters was sealed off and in the care of the accident investigators, yet there was something in his mind that said it wasn't an accident. 'And do you know what? I wish I'd left that gas fire on.'

'Why?' She helped herself to her coffee and made another for him. 'It's the obvious source of the carbon monoxide and it could have been dangerous.'

'It looked a pretty healthy flame to me.'

'That's hardly conclusive evidence.'

'I know.' He followed her through and sat down in the armchair. Already there were a dozen questions in his mind. 'I'm not an engineer but I always thought carbon monoxide is produced when the appliance isn't working properly and that looked pretty healthy to me.'

'The health and safety people will be able to tell you that.'

But if it was fine, where had the gas come from? 'The place felt okay to me.'

'Carbon monoxide is colourless and odourless,' she reminded him.

'But I think I'd have noticed. I think the air would have been stale.' When he and Becca had been together she'd gone to visit a patient and had arrived just in time to save him from Hazel and Leo's fate. It had been a faulty heater then, too, and he remembered her saying that the minute she'd walked in she'd known something wasn't right. *The air felt wrong*, she'd said.

But the air in the Three Sisters hadn't felt wrong, just heavy with essential oils and scented candles, and the treatment area had been well-ventilated though the reception hadn't seemed to be. That was another thing. He and Faye had no choice but to let air in and by the time the health and safety team had got round to measuring the level of contamination, if they were able to, it would bear no relation to the level it must have been when they arrived. 'The carbon monoxide alarm wasn't working. I should have told them to leave it, but they'll have taken it away to check it. And the heater.'

'They'll be able to tell you if someone's tampered with it, surely?'

They would, but if it had been removed and replaced, or if it had been switched on and off, they would have lost valuable forensic information which would be less significant to an accident investigation than it would be for a criminal one. 'I feel we missed a trick. I should have ignored Faye and stayed in for better look.'

'You couldn't. And nor should you. She was right. If she'd let you go in there and you'd been overcome by fumes it would be her backside on the bacon slicer, not yours.'

'For a change,' he said, moodily.

'There's nothing we can do about it tonight, though, is there? And probably not for much of tomorrow.'

They would need to wait for the PM reports, and then they would have to wait to see what the accident investigators had to say. That probably wouldn't be for the next couple of days, and even then there might be nothing conclusive. Maybe, after all, it was an accident, and the heater was to blame.

But there was that whale music, that deep, disturbing rhythm that was probably intended to appeal to his subconscious. That and the spilt cup of coffee and the bright, blue flame of the gas heater. Three things that didn't sit quite right in his head.

But there was no point in dwelling on things. 'Okay,' he said, with a sigh, 'you're right. Pass me the remote. Let's see if we can find some rubbish telly.'

When Ashleigh had (with some reluctance, he thought) looked at her watch and said she thought it was time to go, and when he had walked her home for the sake of some fresh air and the pleasure of her company, kissed her on her doorstep and then made his way back across town, his thoughts returned to the Three Sisters.

It was a missed trick, that was the problem. Would he have acted differently if Faye hadn't been there and he had been — subconsciously — trying not to be too aggressive and too challenging of her authority? And should they, with hindsight, have treated these deaths as murder from the start rather than erring on the side of accident?

They had had no option but to open the windows and turn off the fire, he reminded himself, for their own sake. Carbon monoxide was dangerous, but people survived it. He remembered Becca describing her own experience, and how after the incident in which she'd found her patient unresponsive she'd been given strict guidance about what to do in such an event in the future. Which was not only what she'd done, but also what Jude and Faye had done.

And yet, and yet. The whale music that had throbbed like a drumbeat of doom. The spilt coffee. The bright blue flame. The silent carbon monoxide alarm. He shook his head as he strode up Wordsworth Street, past Adam Fleetwood's house and in through his front door. There would be answers, no doubt, when they got the results of the accident investigation but how long would that take?

He went into the living room and flicked the telly on to a replay of a Premier League football match, twenty years on. Arsenal. That reminded him. He hesitated for second and then he called Becca.

'Jude,' she said, and sounded a little apprehensive. These days when he called her it was never from an inconsequential desire just to hear her voice; there was always a reason for it, and so she would never answer without a concern. He could imagine her train of thought. What had gone wrong this time? What bad news did he have to break? What questions did he have to ask her? 'Hi.'

There was a snuffling and a meowing on the other end of the phone and an exasperated: 'Holmes! Go away!' from Becca. 'Sorry,' she said when she was back on the phone. 'It's that cat of yours. I swear he recognises your voice and wants to talk to you.'

He chuckled. Holmes wasn't his cat but he might as well have been. Jude was the animal's clear favourite human, much to Becca's annoyance. 'Give him my best.'

'I'm sure he hears and understands every word you say.'

'I'm sorry if I'm interrupting.' He racked his brains for a reason why, other than that fleeting glance of a football match. Becca was an Arsenal fan. 'It's just a heads up. I expect you'll hear soon but there's been another incident at the Three Sisters. An accident, this time, by the look of it.' There was no point in spreading fear and alarm. 'But I thought you might want to tell Kirsty before she sees it somewhere else.'

'Good idea. That's very thoughtful. I'll tell her. What happened?'

'It looks like it might have been a faulty heater.'

'Oh. Oh, right. Nasty. I remember when I found—'

'I remember.'

'But that was overnight, that poor patient of mine. I remember what the accident investigator said. He said it can take a couple of hours, depending on the individuals involved. But the heater was downstairs and my patient was upstairs, so it would probably have taken longer.'

Leo Pascoe had been fit and healthy, as far as Jude knew, and so had Hazel. It would be stretching things to imagine that both of them had hidden health conditions that would doom them immediately. It was another to add to his list of things that didn't make sense. 'Is that so?'

'I'm sure you know that,' said Becca, crisply. 'Don't you do health and safety training?'

He smiled. 'I expect it'll turn out to be a bit more complex than that. Those women do work long shifts. And I imagine it can get pretty hot and stuffy in there. They might not have realised there was a problem.'

'Those heaters can be lethal, too. Oh, dear.'

'Anyway,' he said when the subsequent pause had become awkward, 'I just thought I'd tell you.' And hung up.

A call he needn't have made. He'd tell Ashleigh about it the next day but he knew what she'd say. She'd say *you could just have Googled carbon monoxide, you know.* And then she'd smile.

TWENTY-FIVE

'This is your fault.'

It had always been like this. There always had to be someone to blame. Philippa sat on the tired old sofa in the cottage's dingy living room, holding Tessa's hand and stroking her forearm as if by so doing she could calm her down. Ensconced in their mother's place, Suzanne sat rocking the rocking chair with tight, short movements while the two of them traded insults and accusations across the room. Never had Philippa been so glad she'd made that break as a young woman, never thought she'd be so happy to be the outsider.

'It's nobody's fault,' she said, for the umpteenth time. And indeed, neither Tessa nor Suzanne had come up with any real reason why the other was to blame. 'It was an accident.'

'Accidents have causes.'

'I expect we'll find out what caused it when the accident report comes in.' Philippa stroked Tess's hand again. The room was cold and her sister's hand was as pale and chilly as that of a corpse.

'Yes,' Suzanne said, breathlessly, 'and they'll find out there was a problem with the heater and didn't I say to you that we needed a new one and you said we didn't?'

Tessa looked agonised. 'I didn't say that. I said we should probably get a new one but I didn't think there was anything wrong with it, and anyway there was the alarm. I don't know why the alarm didn't go off. We're supposed to get it serviced every year. It's on a contract. Why didn't we get it serviced, Sue? You deal with that sort of thing.'

'You know why it wasn't serviced. There wasn't enough money.'

Philippa stared from one sister to the other. 'But that's —' She stopped herself. What was the point in joining in this game? If the alarm should have been serviced and hadn't been, and wasn't working, then that took them out of the realm of accident and into the realms of negligence — a new world of lawyers and charges and convictions and massive fines Suzanne and Tessa couldn't afford, maybe even prison. Tony, who was never a man to cut corners, was always big on safety and even when money was tight he never skimped on this kind of maintenance. 'Oh dear.'

'Don't you dare start! If you hadn't been here this would never have happened.'

'This is nothing to do with Pip.' Tessa jumped up and strode to the window. 'Leave her out of it.'

The living room looked out on a small square of garden surrounded by a high brick wall which had been built in an attempt to preserve privacy and ended up making it look like a prison. Even in the summer, thought Philippa, getting up and going to stand next to her in a display of solidarity, it must be deeply shaded, its flowerbeds dry and its thin grass brown and gasping. 'It's okay, Tess.'

'It's not okay,' she said, softly. 'And it isn't your fault. It's hers. It's her fault we always argued and her fault we haven't sold the place and her fault that Hazel's dead. And Leo.'

'You're well rid of him at least,' said Suzanne, callously.

Tessa drew in an outraged breath and Philippa moved to position herself between her sisters. 'No, Sue. Don't ever say that. Just because you—' She stopped.

'Just because I what?'

Philippa had never met Leo and Tony, who had, hadn't liked him. His reputation as a womaniser had blazed a trail so that she would have mistrusted him even if Tessa hadn't told her about his fling with Sophie, but that wasn't the point. Tessa had loved him and Tessa had lost him. She was the one who needed comfort. There was Hazel, too, from whom Philippa had been so unwillingly estranged and with whom she now had no chance to rebuild the affection that had once been between them. Mentally, Philippa drew a line down the room and positioned herself firmly on Tess's side of it. Tess was right to be angry. Sue was not.

'I think you'd better go.' She walked forward and stood in front of the rocking chair.

'This is my house and you have no right to tell me to leave it.'

'You moved out,' said Tessa, almost breathless with anger. 'It's not your home. Go away. I never want to see you again.'

For a moment Philippa thought Suzanne would brazen it out, and then she would have to be the one to go because she didn't trust herself in the same room. God knew what would happen then. Her two surviving sisters might come to blows, as if they weren't already hurt beyond endurance.

But it didn't come to that. After a moment's more of that intense rocking, Suzanne got to her feet. For a second the two sisters occupied the same square metre of ground, closer than they had been for years. Close enough for Philippa to smell the lingering scent of lavender and patchouli that clung to her sister even when she wasn't on duty, for her to see the ageing skin on the hands she held up as if in defence, the greying hair she must try so hard to hide.

'I'm going.' Failing to meet Philippa's eye Suzanne turned to Tessa. 'But I warn you, it'll be your fault. That bloody heater.'

'It's not my fault!' Tessa shouted. 'Get out! I'll never forgive you!'

'Tess!' said Philippa, agonised.

'Don't worry.' Suzanne strode out into the hallway, grabbing her coat, which she'd dropped in the armchair and thrusting her arms into the sleeves as she went. 'I won't be back.' The door slammed behind her.

'What am I going to do?' Tessa said, her anger ebbing away into distress. 'What am I going to do without Hazel? We fought all the time but I did love her. And Leo. I know he wasn't perfect but we were so right together and I was so happy with him. That's what she hated. She hated me being happy.' She collapsed into the rocking chair with a strangled sob.

She was right, too. These days, now that she was married to Tony and their early fights and fallouts had settled into contented marriage and shared ambitions, Philippa had no need to dwell on the bitter argument she herself had had with her oldest sister all those years before but Tess had put her finger on it. Suzanne's nature, bequeathed to her by her mother like a curse from an evil fairy godmother, was antagonistic and unsympathetic; she was incapable of being happy. If that wasn't bad enough, she'd done her best to make sure no-one else was happy either.

'You've got me now.' There was no point in telling Tess that forty-three wasn't old, that if she left the Three Sisters and started again somewhere else or even changed career completely, there would be plenty of chances for her to find someone else and be happy. There was no point in joining in with her complaints and blaming Suzanne for everything. They must move on. 'I'll help you. I promise you'll never be on your own. You can come and live up at the hotel if you want.'

'I don't know.' Tessa passed a hand over her tired forehead. Like Philippa she couldn't have slept much the night before.

'I think you need to get away from here.' There would be so many memories and, if she knew Suzanne — and her parents — very few of them would be good.

'I know but I don't have anything else left of...of this life.' Tessa spoke as if it was already done.

'I'm going to make some tea.'

'Good idea.'

They went through to the dark kitchen and Philippa put the kettle on. 'Did the police come to see you?'

'Yes. God, it was awful. They asked me so many questions, but they were very kind. They wanted to know about Hazel and Leo and whether she often gave him massages.'

'And did she?'

'No.' Tessa's mouth crumpled into a quivering, tearful line. 'Or maybe she did. I didn't know. But she and I used to go to all sorts of lengths to try and make sure Sue didn't know he was coming so why wouldn't Leo and her do the same to me?'

You wouldn't put anything past Leo, that was the thing.

He'd slept with Sophie. Tessa had feared he might have made a move on Philippa herself...but Hazel? Was it believable? 'Do you think he did?'

'He was supposed to be...I mean,' burst out Tessa, 'it's nonsense! There's nothing wrong with a man having a massage. It was bloody Sue and her hang-ups about men. She had to punish people for having something she didn't. I never suspected Hazel might be...but why not? I know she was lonely. I know she was frustrated. I wouldn't blame her. But why did it have to be Leo?'

Why indeed? Now Tess would be left with a residual hatred of Hazel that embittered everything she did. 'Maybe it was a mistake.'

'But he was supposed to be having a massage with me. It would have been today.' She looked at the clock. It was four o'clock. 'About now.' She bit her lip.

'Don't stay here, Tess,' urged Philippa. 'Come back with me. This house is so full of memories. You'll never escape.'

'But I like the memories,' Tess said, simply.

The kettle hissed. Philippa made tea, went to the fridge and found only a dribble of milk. It didn't matter; she would take hers black. She made the tea too quickly, swirling the pot so that the tea bags steeped too quickly and poured out a thick, foul-looking brew. 'Here. Drink this. Are you sure about staying here?'

'Yes. I like it.' Tessa took the mug and curled her hands around it. 'Not the spa, though. I'm done with the Three Sisters.'

Philippa sipped her tea, regardless of the fact that it was too hot. 'Yes.'

'It's my whole life. You know that?'

'I know.'

'But it's toxic. When I first saw it I fell in love with it.

221

It's such a beautiful building. And Dad did it for Mum because he loved her so much, and it meant so much, and I loved being part of the family business instead of that grim place I used to work at in Kendal. But then it all went sour.'

'I know.' Tessa had told her about her dream for the building and how it had flickered in front of her with Leo's offer of financial investment, and now it had been snatched away again. 'But perhaps now you can—'

'Sue will never sell. Not to you. Probably not to anyone, now, because she'd die rather than see you there with it. And that means I'm stuck with it. I hate the place, Pip. I really hate it.'

It should have been so beautiful, but it wasn't fit for purpose. It wasn't just the lack of money. It was that it had never been suitable for a spa, too small and badly laid out. It was no wonder those pods had filled up so quickly with carbon monoxide.

It could so easily have been Tess. Thank God it hadn't been. And Philippa felt guilty at the thought, as though her second favourite sister was a suitable sacrifice to preserve her favourite. When she got home the guilt would grow and the memories would flood back, and the stress she was trying so hard to divert from Tessa would accumulate in her heart and on her soul. But at least she had Tony. Tessa — poor, poor Tessa — had no-one.

'Oh, darling!' she said. I understand. I really do.'

They looked at one another. They might have been apart for over twenty years but even that period of time couldn't erase their closeness. There was little more than a year between them, and when Philippa looked at Tessa she saw in her sister's eyes thoughts that mirrored her own.

'I wish,' Tessa said, and faltered. 'I wish I dared—'

'But you do dare,' said Philippa, reading the unspoken

word. 'You do. I'm here with you and when the time is right—'

'Can we?' Tess's voice was barely a whisper, even thought there was no-one to hear her. 'Will we do it?'

'Yes,' said Philippa, robustly. 'We will.'

TWENTY-SIX

J ude had been out of the office for a couple of days leaving Doddsy in charge both of the investigation into Sophie's death and of keeping a watching brief on the accident that had claimed Hazel and Leo. During that time he checked his messages far more frequently than he needed to, to no avail. The post mortem results had shown that both had died from excessive amounts of carbon monoxide and there was as yet no news from the accident investigators.

Nothing about this was in any way out of the ordinary, but still it bothered him. Time was the enemy. Even while he'd been occupied on other things he'd had the incident at the Three Sisters on his mind. It wasn't enough to act on a feeling; you had to have proof, and while he was pretty sure in his own mind that the two deaths were murder and in some ways connected to Sophie's death, there was little he could do just then.

If he was right then the pool of of potential killers had narrowed considerably with the loss of two of his potential suspects. He was never good at waiting for things to come up when he could do something to ferret them out. Arriving back in his office after a morning at a meeting in Carlisle, he poked his head around the door of the incident room even before he got back to his office.

'What have you got for me on the Three Sisters, Doddsy?' he asked, dropping his briefcase on the floor by the desk where his friend was deep in conversation with Ashleigh.

'Glad someone cares,' said Doddsy, with a broad grin. 'It's been quiet here, with neither you nor Faye popping in every five minutes to see what's going on.'

'Faye's recused herself.' Jude pulled up a chair and sat down. Doddsy and Ashleigh did likewise. 'I thought you knew. She knows Leo Pascoe, socially. Not well, I believe, but well enough for her not to want to get involved.'

'I thought she was looking a bit cross.' Doddsy laughed. Faye's micromanagement and her need to know everything were a running joke.

Faye's fury had been less about having to step back from the investigation than it had been about Jude's intervention in the matter, but he kept quiet. She should be grateful to him for keeping her out of trouble, but instead she'd add it to the column of things she held against him. 'So it's just left to you kids. What have you got?'

'Ashleigh was telling me you don't like the idea of an accident,' he said, nodding towards her.

'Do you?'

'I normally trust your judgment but the PM results were pretty clear.'

'They only tell us what killed them. Fine. I get that. But that doesn't explain how it happened.'

'I know that. You know that. That's where the accident

investigators come in. I called them yesterday morning. I called them this morning. No joy. They haven't finished doing whatever they have to do and you know yourself, they've as much of a backlog as us.'

'I've tried, too,' said Ashleigh, with what he thought was a fractious sigh that indicated she was increasingly in line with his own views about a malicious cause for this apparent accident. 'No joy.'

'Right. We'll just have to wait.' Jude picked up his briefcase. As he went out, Doddsy was humming *You Can't Hurry Love* under his breath. And fine, Jude thought as he made it back into his office, maybe you couldn't hurry accident investigations either, but you could at least remind them of why it was so important.

He took off his coat and dropped it on the chair, then sat down at his desk. His to-do list had a dozen or more things on it but he could spend a few more minutes mulling over the issue. It was all very well to talk murder but there were far too many things that didn't make sense. In his own mind he was certain that Hazel and Leo hadn't died by accident — but who had done it, and how? Was it planned, or had they seized an opportunity?

Opportunity. That was the word Tony had used to Aditi, with relation to his purchase of the Ullswater Falls, but a look back at his career suggested that might be a key characteristic of his. He was a quick thinker, for sure, and maybe he acted as quickly as he thought. And then there was Philippa, whose relationship to Suzanne, Hazel and Tessa had been the most surprising revelation to emerge from the incident, and her two bitter surviving sisters.

The full results of the accident investigation could take weeks. In these cases he tried to control his impatience but it was eating away at them, this idea that whoever it was —

Tessa, Philippa, Suzanne, or Tony — might be sitting there congratulating themselves on a crime cleanly committed. Or would they? Some people deluded themselves, especially those who were particularly arrogant and thought themselves much cleverer than the police, and he had been careful to make sure that the two deaths were treated by the local media as if they were a tragic accident rather than the crime he believed them to be.

Gathering the evidence and putting together the proof was another matter. He checked his messages once but there was nothing from the accident investigators. After five minutes his impatience got the better of him. He'd asked them to keep him informed, he'd stressed the urgency. It did no harm to follow up. He might as well call them.

'Jude Satterthwaite here. I'm calling about the incident at the Three Sisters spa. I know you're busy, but given there was that previous death I was hoping you'd be able to prioritise it for me.'

'I was about to call you,' said the woman at the other end of the phone. She sounded cheerful. Jude supposed her job was as interesting in its way as his own, and at least she was spared the direct impacts of physical violence. She might deal with incidents as messy as those the police saw, but at a step removed from the malice of human nature and connected, instead, with laziness, stupidity or just genuine error. 'I think you'll find it very interesting. I've taken that heater apart and looked at every bit of it, and I got a couple of my colleagues to do the same. There's nothing wrong with it.'

'Nothing?'

'Nothing at all. It's perfectly safe, fully functioning. You're always wise to have a bit of ventilation with these things of course, and from what my colleagues tell me some of the ventilation in that place was pretty poor, but even so. The heater wasn't capable of generating enough CO to kill those two, for sure.'

So he'd been right. That strong blue flame had been a healthy one, rather than the pale, guttering struggle of a dangerous appliance. If that set his mind at rest on one scare, it raised immediate issues elsewhere. 'I'm not an engineer, of course, but I can't see where the CO came from.'

'If you can find anywhere it might have come from I'll be most interested. Carbon monoxide comes from fossil fuels, as you'll know.'

The Three Sisters had no gas supply. 'There's a fireplace, but I'm pretty sure that's ornamental.'

'Let me check the report.' He waited for a moment until she came back on the line. 'No, the fireplace is blocked. Purely decorative. In fact I don't know if it ever worked.'

'Probably not. The place was never intended as a residential property.'

'Right. Well, this is going to be a proper puzzle for you, because I can't see how it was an accident. There was nothing at all wrong with the fire.'

'And the alarm?'

'The carbon monoxide alarm didn't work. That's something that's going to end up in court with someone dying from it, for sure. But if there was enough CO in that place to kill someone, it came in from outside.'

'You said it was badly vented?'

'Give me a second. I have a few initial thoughts here from my colleagues who looked at the layout of it, though it'll be a while before the full report comes in. The place was fairly shoddily built. There are four vents out of the reception area and four from the pods. Two of them go into the basement, which probably isn't allowed these days though it might have been when the place was built, and one of those was on the wrong way round. God knows how they got it past building standards people, but they must have done. That's all I can tell you right now.'

'Thanks. That's helpful.'

'I can tell you're going to have a long list of questions when we finally get this report done,' she said, and laughed.

He had a long list already, but most of those, in the first instance, would be for others and plenty of them were for him to think about himself. He thanked her again and rang off. Now, more than ever, he was sure that there was nothing accidental about those deaths. If the fire was blameless, then somehow the carbon monoxide had been introduced to the building and given the timescales involved it must have been done quickly.

He picked up the phone. 'Ash. Can you do me a favour?'

'Sure. Is this about Leo and Hazel?'

'Yes. Do you have five minutes? Doddsy's in a meeting and I need someone to think aloud to.'

'Of course,' she said, and a few moments later she appeared at the door. 'Are you still struggling with this? I am, too. I have things that don't make sense.'

'I know. I've just been onto the accident people. I need you to get on to the council planning department and see if you can get hold of the paperwork for the Three Sisters when it was built.'

'Am I looking for anything in particular?' She made a note.

'Yes. I want to know if the vents to the basement passed the inspection.' But they would, he was sure of it.

'I don't know how readily available the paperwork will be after twenty years, but I can ask. Were the accident people helpful?'

'Very. It wasn't the fire and there's no other source of the gas on the premises so it must have been introduced somehow. I'm sure it was murder, but I can't get my head around how it happened. That cup of coffee. It wasn't finished. As if Leo been waiting for Tessa and she'd arrived and then done the massage and they'd been overcome in the middle of it. I get that. But do you know what? Tessa wasn't there, or she says she wasn't, and we can't prove otherwise. But if she wasn't, why would Leo interrupt his coffee and go and get ready for a massage with Hazel? It doesn't make sense.'

'I know. I can see how he might have interrupted it if he'd been feeling a bit woozy, and maybe realised what was happening and that he would jump up and open a window. But not go and strip off for a massage.'

'No. And that's the other thing. Where did the carbon monoxide come from?'

'A car is the obvious thing.'

'I thought of that. But the garage is only big enough to get a very small car in, and I can't see how anyone could realistically have run a pipe from the exhaust into the building for long enough to fill it with a deadly quantity of carbon monoxide without someone noticing. Hazel would surely have spotted a car and wondered who it was.'

'You'd think so, wouldn't you? But I think that's easily answered. Those infernal pan pipes would drown it out.'

'Good point. But I still want to know where the gas came from.' And there was the timing. Becca had said it took hours, so for death to be so quick it must have been introduced quickly and in significant quantities. 'I don't think a car could produce enough to kill two people that quickly, so it must have come from elsewhere.'

'You can buy it by the canister,' said Ashleigh. 'When I was down in Cheshire on the beat there was a robbery and an industrial plant and one of the things that was stolen was a load of carbon monoxide canisters. There are companies that sell industrial gases. I can start by chasing up suppliers of industrial gases and trying to find how much gas we'd need and how portable it is.'

'Fascinating. And so. Two of the vents go into the storage area And one of them is fitted the wrong way round.' Jude slapped his hand on the table. 'I bet that's it. Someone would have had a canister of gas in there. Whoever it was — Tessa, or Suzanne, or someone else, because although it's kept locked it won't have been hard either to get the key from the spa if you know where it's kept, which we'll have to find out...'

'Or just to pick the lock if you know what you're doing.'

'Yes. But you haven't answered your central question. That storage area vents from the main reception area, not the pods, and Leo and Hazel would hardly leave the reception area and go to the pods if they thought there was something wrong.'

'Unless Tessa had somehow set it up and then stepped outside for some reason, leaving the two of them. Then Hazel could have gone in to see if Leo was okay and then also been overcome.'

Jude was still shaking his head over it. 'What about someone else? Could Tony Charles have done it?'

'I keep wondering that. I keep thinking of him, appearing outside the Three Sisters on the day Sophie died. Or his wife. She seems to have a reason to have a grudge against her sisters, but that isn't much of a reason to kill either Leo or Sophie.'

'Sophie by mistake and Leo as collateral damage perhaps?'

'That's a hell of a bad hit rate, if you have to kill two innocent people to get one you want to kill. And if it was her, who's next?'

TWENTY-SEVEN

'Okay.' Jude reached for a scrap of paper and began scribbling furiously. Normally his thoughts were a little more ordered. 'We've narrowed it down, haven't we? We had a good list of suspects for Sophie's murder and someone's taken two of them out. So that leaves us with Tessa and Suzanne and Tony Charles. It shouldn't be too difficult to find out which one.' It would need time and a painstaking reconstruction of evidence and a whole lot more, but they would get there.

'And Philippa Charles. The fourth sister.'

'Ah, of course. That's an interesting one.' It had been the most interesting nugget of information that Aditi had brought back after she'd been to break the news of Hazel's death to her sisters and discovered there were three survivors, rather than two. With other things on his mind, Jude hadn't been able to give Philippa the attention he now realised she deserved. He scribbled through the notes he'd written. They'd done the job and settled his mind. 'This is interesting. I'm desperate to know all about her, but let's do it methodically. I want to start with the basics. We're pretty sure it wasn't an accident. We don't know who did it but perhaps if we can work out how it was done we might have a clue.'

'I think I know.' Ashleigh looked sombre. 'I had a very interesting call this lunchtime, with a woman who works for an industrial gases supplier in Manchester. They supply carbon monoxide to a range of industries. It has uses in building, apparently, and there are no restrictions on its usage. She tells me that it would be fatal pretty much instantaneously at a level of about ten thousand parts per million.'

'That means nothing to me. I'm no chemist. Give it to me in terms I can understand.'

'In its simplest form.' said Ashleigh, slowly, 'in a building the size of the Three Sisters you could achieve that with one standard canister if you could introduce it into the place.'

'Which you can do through one of the vents if you blocked the others up and unblocked them later. And, handily enough, one of those vents, in the store where it wouldn't be seen, is on the wrong way round.'

'Yes, and on that note, the Building Standards people couldn't find the plans and reports for me but they were adamant they would never have let that past.'

'It makes sense,' said Doddsy. 'Someone could have reversed the vent and not had time to change it. You'd just hope it wouldn't be noticed. If they blocked up the other vents temporarily that would be easier to undo.'

'Yes. Because whoever our perpetrator was their priority would have been to get rid of the gas canister and hope the vent wouldn't be spotted.'

'Well now,' said Doddsy, meditatively. 'Just as well we've

got a thinker among us, eh? Because I wouldn't have picked that one up.' He winked.

Jude grinned at him, but his mind was moving on. The scenario in which Hazel and Leo had been murdered was finally taking shape. 'Those things must weigh a ton.'

'Twenty-two kilograms,' said Ashleigh 'I've done my homework on that. The gas is a small part of that weight but you could shift it over a fair distance with a barrow, or in a car, or even manually if you were strong enough.'

'I'll get on to some folk and see if any of our suspects has ordered any,' said Chris. 'Under a false name, I would imagine, but we'll find out. Unless they nicked it from somewhere.'

'Right. So now to think about who did it. I wondered for a while whether it might have been targeted on Hazel and Leo was just an inconvenience, but the fact someone called and changed his appointment rather gives the lie to that.'

'Hazel was on the rota that day,' said Doddsy, referring to his notes. 'There were no bookings. She was there on her own. No surprises there.'

'Okay. And where does Leo Pascoe fit in to this?'

'Easy,' said Ashleigh, promptly. 'He arrived at an inconvenient moment. An opportunist crime.'

Tony Charles prided himself on being an opportunist. 'I'd been thinking it would have to be someone closely connected to the spa, which would narrow it down pretty much to Suzanne or Tessa. Though of course neither of them admits to having been there at the time. Suzanne says she was on her own at home and Tessa claims to have been walking with Philippa around the hotel grounds.'

'And of course no-one saw them because they were, conveniently enough, not on a public road.' The grounds of the Ullswater Falls were extensive, and it might be plausible that the two sisters had spent a considerable time walking there. 'And, naturally enough, both sisters corroborate the other's story and it can't be independently verified.'

'I think you've done this job before,' said Doddsy, and laughed, without mirth.

'They should have had CCTV in that car park,' said Ashleigh. 'It would have made everybody's lives a lot easier.'

They wouldn't be sitting here now if they had, and perhaps Hazel and Leo, at least, would still have been alive. You could disable CCTV if you knew it was there, but even then it would have been another obstacle, another risk for a killer to take and so, very possibly, a deterrent. It would almost certainly have trapped a random intruder, had it been well enough concealed. 'It's a lonely spot. I'm surprised they didn't have anything.'

'Suzanne said the money wasn't there, and that seems to be true. They were going to have a look at doing it, but they would have had to cost it very carefully. It sounds like the place was in a serious state.'

'Or one of them wasn't too keen on having the CCTV there,' said Doddsy.

That was also a possibility, and something else that narrowed it down to one of the sisters. Or maybe they'd just thought that Sophie's death was a one-off and that there genuinely was no risk to anyone at the spa. 'Whatever. It's too late to do anything about it now. Except have a look and see what's going on.' And see if they can stop anyone else being killed. 'Ash, tell me what you learned from the sisters. All of them.'

'I spoke to them all. I'll tell you about Philippa first. She was the most interesting of them, I think, if only because she's lived a very different life.'

He listened intently as Ashleigh filled him in on the interview she'd had with Philippa — how she'd broken away from her family and then been cut off by them, how she'd lost her boyfriend to Suzanne, met Tony, made a life with him and finally come home to the Ullswater Falls, about the offer her husband had put in for the Three Sisters.

'Philippa also trained as a beauty therapist,' he said, nodding, 'and so would be perfectly capable of killing someone by putting pressure on the arteries.' They hadn't considered her as a suspect in Sophie's death, but maybe they should rethink it.

'Yes, but she hasn't worked in that line of business for years. She became much more involved on the management side and now, of course, she and Tony are running the hotel together.'

'And he wants to buy the spa for her. Interesting.'

'Very, and she was quite open about why. She said she wanted closure, that the rift with her family had hurt her very much and that for many years she'd been very lonely. With her parents dead it was the only way she could see to bring the saga to a close.'

Unimpressed, Jude shook his head. 'Right. I'm not sure I buy into that, not least because at least one of her sisters, Hazel, seems to have been more than happy to sell.'

'Yes,' said Ashleigh, 'and I don't think Tessa would have been hard to persuade.'

'Right. And so here we are. We have a newcomer on the scene with what has to be a massive grudge against Suzanne for what she did, arriving back to buy up the spa and allegedly give herself some peace and once again it's Suzanne who's in the way. And yet it isn't Suzanne who's dead. It's Hazel, and there's no sign of any mistake about her identity.' He doodled fiercely on the piece of paper. 'What about Tessa?'

'I struggled to get much out of her, apart from the fact that she and Philippa — Pip, they call her — had spent that afternoon walking in the hotel grounds. She was open about the fact that she didn't want anyone to see them, and when pressed it turned out that by *anyone* she meant Suzanne. They didn't go to the hotel because someone would have been bound to need Philippa for something. So we only have their word for it.'

'Tessa didn't know her sister was coming back?'

'No. Pip staged a grand reveal and Tessa was as shocked as anyone else, though much more pleased. She and Philippa had been very close when they were younger, and the fallout had been very hard on her. They had a lot of catching up to do, she said.'

'What about Leo?' Jude looked towards Doddsy. 'What about the message from the Three Sisters? Who sent it? Because I don't think his presence there at the precise time that Hazel was overcome by carbon monoxide was an accident.'

Doddsy shrugged. 'God knows. It came from the spa's online booking system and it was an automatic notification of a change of appointment. The computer has been packed off to our friends in the tech department and they reckon they can find out whether it was inputted directly from the computer, in which case we can pin whoever sent it down to a time and a place, or from a phone or tablet, in which case we it could have been sent from anywhere. If a phone, they should be able to identify it.'

This was too good to be true. 'And how long's that going to take?'

'Your guess is as good as mine. They're never in a hurry for the likes of us. Weeks, if we're lucky. I know we thought the accident investigators were slow but they're rapid reactors compared with the tech folk.'

The relationship between the tech team and their CID colleagues was strained to say the least. For the moment they would have to go by guesswork. An uneasy feeling crept over Jude. It was unlikely that any of the sisters, or Tony Charles, would try to make their escape, but the thing that worried him was what any of them might try in the meantime. 'I'm going to guess it wasn't Tessa.'

'Pretty obvious, I'd say.'

'You think? We don't know she wasn't at the spa that day. She may have changed the time purely because she knew she could take out Hazel and Leo at the same time and we would immediately assume it couldn't be her.' But it could have been.

'I'd swear she was in love with him,' said Ashleigh. 'And she's genuinely devastated.'

'Right. But people have killed the ones they love before now.' He'd never been great on literature but every now and again it came back to him, and the more he was confronted by murder the more he remembered Oscar Wilde and his *Ballad of Reading Gaol*.

'*The coward does it with a kiss*,' said Ashleigh, unexpectedly, but reading his mind in a way she did too often for comfort. '*The brave man with a sword.*'

She had studied English at university, he recalled. 'Exactly. And he hadn't exactly treated her well.' There had been Sophie, on their doorstep. There had been many others. There had even been that brief dalliance with Faye. 'I take it he hadn't been sleeping with Hazel?'

'Not recently,' said Doddsy, 'if at all. I think it's unlikely.'

'And Mrs Charles?' He looked to Ashleigh.

'I don't think they'd ever met, but I have to say she's

definitely the kind of woman you might make a pass at, if you were that way inclined. A very attractive woman I would say. And given his reputation I can see why Tessa might have had concerns.'

She flashed up a picture of Philippa Charles on her iPad and Jude looked at it. She looked very like her siblings, with the same square jaw and thoughtful eyes, but her face was younger and less troubled than any of theirs, even in the make-up masks they wore in the photos on the Three Sisters website. In fact, Philippa looked exactly as he imagined her sisters might have looked if they had lived less discontented lives.

'I grant you that Tessa might have found reason to kill Leo and Sophie.' Doddsy peered into his empty coffee mug. 'But not Hazel. That's a huge leap.'

'I think Hazel would have kept well clear if she knew Leo was going to be there, if only so she could tell Suzanne she didn't know anything about it with a clear conscience. And remember, Hazel was on the rota that day. She was always going to be on the premises. What about Suzanne? I understood she and Hazel were close.'

'I think Suzanne is experiencing a difficult time, emotionally, right now,' said Ashleigh, choosing her words with care. 'That's an observation, not an official opinion, and certainly not one with any kind of diagnosis behind it. I think she cared deeply for both her sisters. They wouldn't have been able to work together for so long for so many years if that wasn't the case and when I talked to her — and to Tessa, and to Hazel earlier on — I got the distinct impression that everything had been fine between them until their mother died. She was the life and soul of the place. Tessa seems to think she was very controlling but Suzanne herself said that it needed someone strong to hold the place together. I had wondered if the troubles they were experiencing in their relationship were in fact the result of trying to cope with their grief.'

That hadn't gone so well. 'And yet they gave the impression of fighting like rats in a sack.'

'Yes, but only after they lost their parents. I wonder if Hazel's move was just the first. Suzanne said in so many words that she'd hoped to carry the business on because it reminded her very much of her mother and she believed it was what her mother would have wanted. But she told me she was coming round to Hazel's point of view. She realised it was in the best interests of everyone to sell the business, either as a going concern or otherwise.'

'That might have been a bluff,' said Jude, 'because, let's face it, if Hazel was determined to sell and Suzanne wasn't, that might just give her enough reason to want to kill Hazel.'

'And Sophie?'

'That might have been a mistake. Or maybe she suddenly saw Sophie as an obstacle to them moving on.'

'I feel sorry for Suzanne.' Ashleigh gave him a sidelong look. They both knew this was her weakness, a tendency to empathise too much with women who seemed like victims but who might equally be killers. 'She seems lonely. She doesn't have much of a social life. As far as I can establish she lives between the spa and her flat, keeps herself to herself, has no friends. There's a bit of me can quite understand why she hates the idea of selling the business and retiring. She'd have literally nothing to do, and she doesn't seem even to have Tessa's friendship circle, limited though it is, or even Hazel's sudden realisation that there's another life out there and she'd be wise to grab it while she could.'

The Walsh girls' parents had a lot to answer for. For all Jude knew they'd intended to protect their daughters and give them a lifetime's security, but it had all gone horribly wrong. 'Timewise, I reckon — and I might be wrong — that Faye and I got there around half an hour or so after the event. That would easily give any of them time to get back home, even if they had to hide a canister of gas on the way.' It had been dark. Again. That was the curse of January, the dark evenings, the deep shadows, that lonely path. 'We'll need to talk to Tony Charles as well, but again I have a problem. Hazel was ready to sell so why kill her? There's no way she could be mistaken for anyone else.'

He frowned. It was a puzzle that would keep, for a while at least. 'Let's take her at her word just now. And let's talk about Tony.' He doodled on his pad again. 'I find it interesting that he told a guest that Philippa had suffered a family bereavement. He couldn't have known that at the time. Maybe the idea came from Sophie's death.' But it was interesting, nonetheless. 'He's a bit of a handyman, I think. He said he does a lot of his own maintenance, though I got the impression he was talking about the smaller stuff. But he could probably have turned the vent round.'

'We could get some CSI folk down to go over the place,' suggested Chris.

'I don't reckon Tony's the type to pop in and get his nails done.' Doddsy laughed.

'He might have popped in to repeat his offer for the spa, I suppose. And if it was him he'll probably have left some traces behind him in the store.' Maybe it wasn't beyond the realms of possibility that Philippa might have been prevailed upon to act as a proxy for whatever murder her husband might wish committed. She could have called in and distracted Hazel from whatever she was doing, committed the killing, murdered Hazel...but it didn't make sense. 'And that's another thing I keep coming back to. I can't persuade myself, in any way or form, that Leo would have stripped himself down for a massage from Hazel.'

'It seems to me that Leo would pretty much strip off for any woman who asked him,' said Doddsy, with a disapproving sniff.

'I confess, I'm baffled. Unless whoever killed him…' Jude sat up. 'Maybe whoever killed him had already killed Hazel. Maybe they told him — if it was Suzanne — to go through and change and Tessa would be with him in a minute.' Would Leo have believed that? Possibly. 'Or else they left a message for him to that effect.'

'If that's the case, we'll find it,' said Doddsy.

'Unless whoever it was took it away with them.'

Jude sat for a moment, reflecting on whether he had any chance of tracking down the note, wherever it might be. Anyone with half an ounce of common sense would have destroyed it straight away, and he thought his chances of getting a warrant to search either Suzanne's flat or Hazel and Tessa's cottage — or, come to that, Tony Charles's quarters at the Ullswater Falls — were slim to say the least.

'I'm really interested in Tony and Philippa.' He rubbed his chin. 'I don't know why, but I've got a hunch about it. Call it a nasty suspicion but I'm intrigued as to why he wants to buy the place when he's already got planning permission in for a much better, purpose-built spa at the back of the building, and why he was prepared to offer so much money for it.'

'Surely that has something to do with Philippa?' said Chris. 'Remember that it wasn't until they came here that the business was named the Three Sisters, so we can assume Philippa had gone by then, or she'd have been part of it. She doesn't own it and doesn't have any say in it. None of her sisters mentioned her when talking about their family background so we can assume they thought she'd gone for good. And then suddenly here she is.' But not until after Sophie Hayes was dead. 'I think we're nearly there. See what you can come up with and we'll all have a catch up later on. And in the meantime I think I might go down and talk to Mr and Mrs Charles. Ash, do you fancy coming along? You've got the knack of making people talk.'

TWENTY-EIGHT

'One day,' Jude said, testily, 'we're going to have a crime that's committed in the summer and we'll be able to try and solve it in the daylight, when we can see what we're doing.'

'Don't be daft,' said Ashleigh, affectionately. 'It's just a cloudy day. Look, it's breaking up over there. It's going to be a beautiful evening.'

'Weather-wise, maybe.' It was half past three and although there was, in theory, a good hour's daylight left the sun had already disappeared behind Helvellyn at the far end of Ullswater, although the mass of cloud that filled the western sky made it difficult to tell. Sometimes it felt like never-ending twilight.

'Maybe it's the lack of sunlight that makes you so grumpy,' said Ashleigh, laughing at him. 'Aren't you going to drive up the hotel?'

'No.' He passed the sign for the Ullswater Falls and turned instead into the car park. 'There may not be any CCTV at Three Sisters, but there sure as hell will be at the Ullswater Falls.'

'That's a bit conspiratorial.' She unclipped her seatbelt.

'Maybe, but whether he's guilty or not, Tony Charles is slippery as anything and if I'm going to talk to someone like that I always like the advantage of surprise.' If Tony Charles — or, indeed, his wife, or the two of them together — was responsible for the three deaths it was exactly the kind of detail a man like him wouldn't overlook. A smart criminal would be expecting them, if only for a routine inquiry, and wouldn't want to be caught unawares. 'We'll go by the lake path. It gives us a chance to have another look around.'

'For anything particular?'

'I think so. Nobody searched the area because it looked like a tragic accident.' He was kicking himself every time he thought about it. 'If we don't find a canister of carbon monoxide, it'll be because someone's managed to shift it, but I'd lay a large amount of money on the fact that it's still around somewhere.' He locked the car and paid for the parking.

'I've been thinking about that. Could someone have dumped it in the lake?'

They strode into the tunnel of thick rhododendrons that led on to the lakeside path. 'They could, but just now the water's incredibly high. You wouldn't be able to get it very far out anywhere near the Three Sisters, and it would stay exactly where you dropped it. If you didn't want to get very wet, which would draw unnecessary attention to you, it would probably be visible from the shore and even if it wasn't, it only takes a few weeks of dry weather for the lake level to drop. It'll be visible by spring. So I don't think it's that.'

'Okay. And obviously it wasn't in the store at the Three Sisters or anywhere else on the property, so whoever it was, assuming they didn't have it in a car, will have had to take it manually. It weighs a ton.'

'Twenty-two kilos maybe isn't that heavy, but it's something you'd struggle to carry a long distance. All three of the sisters are masseuses,' Jude said.

'They look like proper Amazons, I grant you, or Suzanne and Tessa do, and I wouldn't want to get into a wrestling match with any of them. So yes, they'd probably have managed it for part of the distance at least, but they'd risk being seen if they carried it to Pooley Bridge. So it has to be near here.'

'For my money it'll be in the grounds of the hotel somewhere, then. For someone to come and get it later,' said Jude, thinking aloud. 'It's possible it was left there to incriminate someone at the Ullswater Falls, but that might not work. The one person who has the opportunity to be carting this kind of thing around in the hotel grounds is Tony himself, and you can bet he'd have a very good story ready about what it was used for if he was challenged. For all we know he'd made an attempt to disguise it as a fire extinguisher.'

'It would pass in the dark, I suppose.'

'Yes. And he'd have got rid of it by now.'

They found nothing alongside the path and Jude was shaking his head as they went up through the gate and the grounds. A few yards behind them there was laughter from the path as a group walked along from the campsite to the village.

'Let's have a quick look in the shrubbery.' He pushed aside the first few branches and peered into the dark, hollow heart of a rhododendron thicket. 'Damn. These things are lethal. They don't look it but this will take an eye out if we're not careful. And it's black as the Earl of Hell's waistcoat in there, as my mum would say. Not a lot to see.'

'Let's hope Tony doesn't mind us poking about in his precious shrubbery.' With rather more care, Ashleigh followed suit and lifted a few branches. 'Ah! Look.'

He flicked on the phone on his torch and swept the beam where she was pointed. 'Well, well.' Not a canister, but a definite dent in the soft ground as if something had been dragged in there and laid to rest. 'I think we're on the trail, don't you?'

'I do. Though whether it was left here on the way down or on the way back is something the CSI lot might be able to work out. But I bet that's what it is.'

'I'll get someone to come down and have a closer look tomorrow,' he said, snapping away at the marks with his phone. 'And maybe get someone to have a look at Suzanne's place, and Tessa's, too. It has to be somewhere. I think we're going to find it and when we do we'll know who it was. It shouldn't be difficult to get a warrant, and if they think they've got away with it they might be holding on to it until it's safe to dispose of it.'

'There's probably CCTV up at the dump at Flusco.'

'I'll get someone to check that, too.' He switched off the torch, stuck his phone in his pockets and stood staring at the mark in the grass. It was a breakthrough, for sure, but where would it take them?

'You don't think it's Tony, do you?' Ashleigh was looking at him with interest.

'I haven't ruled him out. But no. I don't think so.' He paused for a moment, as if sensing movement in the bushes, lifted a branch. A rabbit, thrown into startled still-ness by their presence, shared at them with glittering black eyes, then turned round and bolted back into a clump of rhododendrons.

'Poor little thing,' said Ashleigh. 'What a rotten time he must be having with all these people and noise and so on.'

'Rabbits round here are used to disturbance.' Jude strode on up the hill. 'Look, see all that building work round the side? What did you say you used carbon monoxide for?'

'All sorts of things. But in welding and in—' Ashleigh stopped. 'There's a hell of a lot of building work going on round the back, isn't there?'

'And a whole lot of serious kit to go with it.' Jude snatched a quick glance along the back of the building. A builder's van was creaking its way down the drive. 'That's a stroke of luck. It looks like they've knocked off early for the day. If we keep to this side, we can get up there without making ourselves look obvious to anyone inside. I wish I'd thought of getting a warrant, just on the off-chance, but if we see anything interesting we can get someone down tomorrow to have a proper look.'

Tony Charles's renovation of the Ullswater Falls had focussed on the public-facing areas. Apart from that tangle of ivy along the terrace the place looked smart; the doors and windows had been replaced or repainted and the crumbling mortar in the stonework around the porch had been replaced. Behind the building it was a different story. Pallets of brick and stone and slabs, piles of wood, a shed whose creaking, leaking windows gave on to an array of power tools, a cement mixer and, in the corner a tarpaulin whose corners were barely secured.

Jude tried the door of the shed, but it didn't shift. 'Locked. I wonder who has the key. I'd love to know what's under that tarpaulin, because the size and the shape of it suggest some of those canisters you were talking about.'

'Shall we ask him?' asked Ashleigh, craning at the window.

'Maybe not today, but I'll certainly be asking someone to match up how much of the stuff those builders have bought with how much of it they've used. There's every chance they won't know, but you never know. One canister missing is all it takes.' He tried the door again, briefly thought about calling someone to search immediately, but contented himself with snapping more photos through the window. There was no point in alerting Tony to trouble before they had to. 'But that's very interesting. Very interesting indeed. Shall we go in?'

'Not until you've smartened yourself up.' Ashleigh brushed a cobweb off the sleeve of his jacket. 'You're not doing a good job of being under cover, are you? Anyone taking one look at you will know exactly what you've been up to.' She gave him a critical once-over, then brushed herself down. 'I think we look presentable. Let's go in and talk to Mr Charles.'

TWENTY-NINE

Philippa was expecting visitors and she thought she was expecting the police. She wasn't quite sure. That was what came of a sleepless night on the back of drinking too much to deaden the pain. So briefly reunited with Hazel, only to have her snatched away with fences still to be mended. She didn't regret the drink, only that she'd had to stop, and now that Tony had told her to take the rest of the day off she'd started drinking again to see her through. And so the visitors, the shuffling of steps in the corridor, the ring on the bell of the tiny, cramped staff flat, the receptionist's anxious voice.

'Philippa? Are you there? Are you all right?'

She made it to the door, polished up her bright front-of-house smile. 'Sorry, Paula, I had the radio on and didn't hear the bell.' She was the boss. It didn't matter if the staff knew she was lying. 'Are you coping? Do you need me to come and help out?' Her voice quivered.

'It's all right,' the woman said, cheerfully. 'We're doing fine. Tony did say I wasn't to bother you but the police are here and want to talk to you.'

'Oh God. Yes, of course. Well, they'd better come in, hadn't they? If you need me though, Paula. Just let me know.'

'Don't worry about it,' said Paula and headed off down the corridor leaving the detective sergeant, Ashleigh O'Halloran, and a tall, serious man in a smart suit to stand at the door.

Philippa watched her go with dread, on the edge of calling her back. She didn't know what the police could want with her, but no good would come of it; it was nothing more than picking over old bones. She looked at the warrant cards they offered her without seeing them, but she took note of the man's name. Jude Satterthwaite, the officer in charge of Sophie's murder. That meant bad news, surely. 'Come in. Please.'

'Are you all right, Mrs Charles?' asked Ashleigh O'Halloran, as Philippa stepped back and waved them on into the tiny living room.

She must have seen the glass that stood on the side table, and the bottle of red that a sympathetic Tony had dug out from the cellar for her in lieu of his company for the afternoon. 'Yes.' And they would see she'd been crying. 'But I've been so stupid. So very, very stupid. I'm supposed to be front of house today and I can't do it and now I should go out and help but God, Tony would never let me out in front of the guests like this.' She sank down into a chair, reached out for the glass of wine, almost full. 'But it's too late now.'

'I'm sorry you're upset, Mrs Charles.' The female detective had been sympathetic, presumably in the hope of eliciting answers, but her colleague apparently preferred to be brisk and formal. It didn't matter; she was easy prey to either. 'We wanted to to talk to you about your sisters.'

She gave a long, gusty sigh. 'Right.'

'You didn't tell us about them.'

'Your detective didn't ask,' said Philippa, with an outburst of spirit. 'And Tess told you anyway, so I didn't need to. Although after that awful thing that happened to Hazel…well, I think I would have told you. When I was ready to talk about it.'

Jude Satterthwaite lapsed into silence but was watching her carefully when Ashleigh said, gently, 'I'm afraid what happened to Hazel wasn't an accident.'

Oh God. It was bad enough that they were playing good-cop-bad-cop like that so she had to keep looking from one to the other as if she was watching a strange game of tennis. She clenched her hand around the stem of the glass, almost wishing she could break it. They couldn't interview her if she was hurt, surely?

'So Tony was right, after all,' she said, and relaxed her grip on the glass.

'Was he?' said the sergeant.

'He said it was too much of a coincidence and ever since then I've been tormented by it. And I said to Tessa — imagine if she'd been down there, too, instead of here, and she was really shaken by it — and Tony said he didn't think it was an accident and if Tessa had been there instead of up here with me it might not have happened, but I didn't know—'

The two detectives exchanged glances. Did that mean she was talking nonsense or had she told them something they wanted to hear? 'Did you and Ms Walsh see anyone when you were out walking that afternoon?'

She'd been looking at Ashleigh but at this, from Jude Satterthwaite, she whipped around. 'You think we did it.'

'I'm asking you if you saw anyone. That's all.'

She thought of Tessa, sobbing her eyes out on the bench in the shrubbery, and how they'd scuttled away into a corner to avoid the guests. 'We did, actually. Tony saw us.'

DCI Satterthwaite's silence was more eloquent than any words. He didn't think that was good enough, wouldn't accept that it would clear her. They would consider the possibility that Tony was complicit, and then what?

'And I think one of the guests saw us,' she said, dredging her memory for something — anything — that could help. 'Tony said he was speaking to her and she said she wanted to ask me about who we get to do the flowers but Tony said I'd had a family bereavement and couldn't be disturbed.' He'd come bouncing over afterwards like a dog returning a stick and wanting praise. *Saved you there, darling. Some ghastly old woman wanting to talk to you about dahlias.* And maybe he had saved her. 'You can ask him. I remember exactly what he said, because it seemed so odd. He said it was the first thing that came into his head. We didn't know then that it was true.'

The police officers exchanged looks at that, as though it was significant when in fact it was just typically Tony. 'What time was that?'

'I wasn't thinking about the time. Tess and I had so much catching up to do.' That was true. She had been in such a daze that she couldn't say, to the hour, what time it had been, or how long she'd spent with Tessa, or even whether it had been sunny or overcast as they sat on that cold bench in the shrubbery for what might have been hours. 'You know there were four of us. Sometimes I think I was the lucky one. Sometimes I think I wasn't.' Self-pity clutched at her. Suzanne, had she seen it, would have recognised it as weakness and pounced. 'It isn't that I didn't love my parents. I loved them very much. And I never intended to be estranged from them, never wanted to hate them, or them to hate me. To begin with, it wasn't like that. I think I was their favourite.' The youngest, the feistiest, the prettiest. How quickly that had turned against her. 'We lived in Kendal. My mother was a success, wonderful at her job, so talented and engaged. Sue and Hazel went into the business, too, and they liked it, and we always talked about Tess and me joining when we were old enough. But I wasn't sure I wanted that.'

'You felt the decision had been taken for you?' asked Ashleigh O'Halloran.

'Exactly that.' Philippa nodded. 'So I said to my parents that I wanted to go abroad and get a bit of experience of life before I came back into the business, and rather to my surprise, they agreed.' She drank, deeply, spread her beautifully-manicured hand out in front of her. Dark green nail varnish with flecks of gold. It was such a terrible idea, drinking to take away the pain, but she'd never lost a sister to violence before so nothing was normal. *Do whatever gets you through the day*, Tony had said to her. *Don't worry. I've got your back.*

'When was this?' asked the woman. 'The Three Sisters has always been the Three Sisters, as far I was aware.'

'It was while I was away that they bought the property. It was going to be called the Four Sisters, and I was going to work there when I got back. But it all went wrong. I went to America to work in a country club in Kentucky and while I was out there I fell in love with a wonderful, wonderful man.' She smiled. 'We had a volatile relationship — not violent, but full of arguments and demands and making up. We really loved one another. But then I fell pregnant and had an abortion and he was furious that I'd done it without asking him. As if it was any of his business.' She sipped at the wine, rather more circumspectly this time. 'And that's when everything went wrong. Sue came over to visit. I thought it would help.'

She'd been so depressed. Her sister should have been the one to help her but it hadn't happened. 'She set her cap at him, good and proper.' She picked at the nail varnish. 'She was a beautiful woman back then, I suppose, and I was quite a lot younger than him, had a lot of maturing to do. She'd got herself into a rut and with the new business coming on it was her chance to see the world. She probably let all the excitement go to her head. I thought it would all blow over, but it didn't. She married him.'

Yes, the wine helped after all. She drank, heavily, as if the trauma had been only yesterday, and a little of the pain of rejection slipped away.

'What a shock for you,' said Ashleigh O'Halloran, helpfully. 'I expect coming home brought it all back.'

Philippa looked at her, gratefully. She'd expected this interview to be harder but the woman made it so easy to talk. 'Yes. It was horrible at the time, and got worse. When my father heard he came out but by then her husband had already realised what a mistake it was. Dad storming in like the cavalry was the excuse he needed to leave her. She went home because she had nowhere else to go and my father tried to insist that I should go too, but I'd seen the world and I liked it. I refused, he told me never to come home, and that's it. I never did.'

'Did your parents cut you off completely?' asked Ashleigh.

'Yes.' Brutally. She'd never realised how merciless people could be, even those who were supposed to love you. 'I wrote to them and they never replied. And I kept in touch with Tessa for a while but after a while even that dropped off. I suppose it was just too difficult for her. My sisters never even got in touch after my parents died. I'd have liked to see them and maybe make things right. Even if they wouldn't forgive me, I'd know that I'd tried.' She sniffed, dug in her pocket for a tissue and dabbed at her eyes.

'And yet,' said the detective, gently, 'you came back.'

'Yes.'

'Why?'

Philippa closed her eyes for a moment, agonised. 'I knew you'd ask me that.'

'Was it for revenge?'

'You think I killed Hazel, don't you? And the girl? And Tessa's boyfriend. But I had no reason to do that.' But there had been so many nights when she'd lain awake at night and fantasised about how she'd take her revenge on them all, even on Tessa, who had abandoned her, and most of all on Suzanne.

'It was dark when Sophie died,' said the sergeant, 'as I think you know.'

'Bloody January,' said Philippa, and began to cry. 'Perhaps whoever killed her didn't—' She whimpered. The wine, and the sergeant's empathy, were too much for her self-control. 'I went down there sometimes, just to see them. I thought I'd speak to them, but I couldn't. And sometimes I waited and watched but I was never brave enough.' It was so unlike her. If you wanted something in life you had to reach out for it. 'And yes, if I saw them come out when it was dark I couldn't be sure who it was, so I never stopped them to talk. But I wouldn't have killed — I didn't kill—'

'Was your husband faithful to you?'

'Yes, of course.' That question had come out of the blue. 'But he—'

'You said had a volatile relationship?'

There had been bad times. There always were. 'Yes,

but he isn't a violent man. We love one another. We really do.'

'And yet I sense you don't trust him. Maybe because one of your sisters had already stolen your husband from you and perhaps, even after all this time, you were concerned. He told us it was his idea to come back here, not yours. And he told us that he was very keen to buy the Three Sisters. What did you think of that?'

'I hated the idea.' She crushed the tissue up between her manicured fingers and managed a watery smile. Didn't they say you always married a man just like your father? Tony was so much more modern, so less dictatorial than her father had been but in some ways he was just the same. He thought he knew what his wife wanted better than she knew herself and he would move heaven and earth to give it to her. 'Tony thought it would be a really neat thing to do. He thought it would make everything right. He didn't understand how much he'd hurt me the first time and I don't think I ever thought he'd do it again, but still I couldn't forget how terrible it felt, that time when he left me for my sister.'

There was a pause, in which she focussed on her glass and the safety net of a good St Emilion, and tried not to notice how they were looking at each other, as if she'd given herself away.

'He left you for Suzanne? You mean he was her husband?'

'Yes. But we loved one another, which is why he came back, so full of regret. We fought a lot, the two of us, but we still love each other. I'd die for him and he would die for me.'

'Have you seen either of your sisters today, Mrs Charles?' asked the detective inspector.

'Suzanne asked me to meet her down at the Three

Sisters this afternoon,' she said, turning to the wine again for solace.

'Do you plan to go?'

She shook her head. 'I was thinking about it, but Tony said he didn't think that would be a good idea, and anyway I don't think I could have gone. If she wants to make things up with me then she knows where I am.'

'Where is your husband just now, Mrs Charles?' asked Ashleigh O'Halloran. 'We came her hoping to have a word with him, as well as yourself.'

'He's in the hotel somewhere, I think.'

'I'd like to speak to him.'

She sniffed. 'He'll confirm what I said. Maybe, or most of it. He'll probably spin you a line about how we trust each other completely, but that's not sinister. It's just that he thinks twenty years of marriage means I've forgotten about what he did and I haven't.' Forgiven, yes, but forgotten? Never.

THIRTY

essa went back down to the Three Sisters, not because she had anything to do there — all appointments had been cancelled for that week and there were few for the next — or because she wanted to, but because it was preferable to being in the cottage on her own. Until a few days before it had felt small and constricted. There had been Hazel, who spread herself and her things out and liked noise, who was always singing or had the radio on. Sometimes there had been Leo, who had been a tall man and who seemed to fill space with his loud jokes and his all-encompassing optimism. Until a few months earlier there had been the dominant figure of Suzanne and before that their parents, growing older and more frail as they faded but still consuming disproportionate amounts of time and space and energy.

Sometimes Tessa wondered how they'd managed, but with only herself there for the foreseeable future, she realised how big it actually was. What filled her life was people and their needs, and some people could fill the largest space. The cottage was bigger for their absence, echoing with memories both good and bad, and she didn't see how she could ever fill it as a single woman.

The weather, which had been dull and heavy all day, had cleared with a startling suddenness; the sky fizzed with a champagne brightness and remnants of ragged cloud hung in the sky like clothes on a washing line. It would be a stunning sunset and if she hurried she could trap it in a quick, if amateur, sketch. She quickened her step as she approached the spa, nodding at an elderly dog walker plodding along the path with an even more elderly collie in tow.

It felt strange going back. Hazel and Suzanne had filled it, too. And Leo. She shook her head as she approached the front door and unlocked it. The police and the accident investigators had finished and the reception area, without its heater, was cold and damp. She turned on all the lights against the rising dusk and switched on the whale music to put an end to the silence and hurried through to the treatment area to catch the end of the sunset.

In a small wall unit to one side she kept her sketch book and pastels, stored among the odds and ends — batteries, stationery and so on. She got them out and took them over to the middle pod, with its perfect view of the setting sun and its deepening shades of red and orange. Holding her hand over the box of pastels she didn't start drawing but sat instead with the pad on her lap, gazing out over the lake whose waters lapped at the perspex panel in the floor, grey and full of threat.

She shook her head. These days her mind was so mazed with grief and — yes — fear that she couldn't process everything that had happened. Sophie's death had been a shock but Sophie had been a self-centred young woman, who gave little of herself and expected little in return and so its impact had been limited, a stone dropped in a puddle, its ripples quickly spent. And though Tessa had loved Hazel, in a quarrelsome way, she'd never felt close to her, never thought she couldn't live without her.

Leo was different. For all his many faults she believed he'd genuinely loved her. If she hadn't, she wouldn't have put herself through the torment of loving him in return. Her future with him would have been incomplete; she would never have been everything to him as she yearned to be, and his outside interests would always exclude her. He was incapable of committing himself to one person, exclusively, but when she thought of how her parents had been so fiercely protective of their children until their love had turned corrosive and ended up leaving them tied so unhappily together, that didn't seem such a bad thing. She might never have been everything to him but she would have been happy to have been more to him than anyone else.

At the thought, the first tear came. It was too cruel, that an accident had taken both Hazel and Leo so soon after Sophie's murder, and the grief was compounded by her fury and her questions. Leo had been sexually insatiable and she could see how he couldn't resist Sophie, but she couldn't believe he'd be attracted to Hazel. What had possessed him to ask her sister for a massage and what had possessed Hazel to agree? In the long-lasting difference of opinion between the sisters about what constituted appropriate sessions to offer and to whom, Hazel had taken an intermediate line. She would accept a booking for a massage from a man but would not seek one, and she would know for sure that when Leo slid into the booking system with a metaphorical wink that he wanted his massage from Tessa and no-one else.

So, why? A mistake? A confusion with the booking? Whatever it was, it was unlikely she'd ever find out.

She'd miss Leo. She'd miss him so much. She sniffed.

'Suzanne?'

She jumped. They had no bookings and after what happened to Sophie it was prudent to take certain precautions but she hadn't locked the door behind her. Her heart surged. 'Hello?' she called, her voice full of apprehension.

A man's voice. A chill came over her and she clenched her hands over the pad.

The door to the treatment area opened, with the usual shuffle that meant the visitor was someone not used to the peculiarities of the building. Tony Charles. Well. That wasn't what she'd been expecting. She put the pad down and stood up.

'Mr Charles,' she said, though when she thought about it she remembered he was her brother-in-law and so she was probably entitled to be a bit less formal with him.

'Tony. Tony, please.' He looked around him, a little nervously. 'I was looking for Suzanne.'

'She won't be very pleased to see you,' she said, shaking her head at him. Pip had told her everything, in that first long session they'd spent drinking coffee and eating cake and sitting in the bay window of the Ullswater Falls Hotel, before tragedy had claimed Leo and her life had fallen apart. Sue had been bang out of order, then and now, and instrumental in cutting their youngest sister off from the family. Once upon a time Tessa had thought nothing was unforgivable but these days she wasn't so sure.

'I'm not looking forward to seeing her, either,' he said, with a cheeky grin. 'Isn't she here?'

'No. Had you arranged to see her?'

'Not exactly.'

He looked unnerved, as though there was something not quite right in his world.

'Why don't you come and sit down?' she invited, and resumed her seat. The colour in the sky was deepening and she'd squandered too much irreplaceable time. She reached for the pad, knowing the best of it was gone and hoping only to give her something to do with her hands.

He came across in a little less than his normal bouncy manner and sat down. 'Suzanne asked Philippa to come down and meet her here, but she wasn't up to coming so I said I'd come down and see what was what.'

Wasn't up to coming was probably code for *doesn't trust herself not to do something she'd regret*. Philippa had always had a temper, just like the rest of them, but was better at controlling it. 'She wants to give Pip a piece of her mind, I expect.' Suzanne's range of response to anything unexpected — surprise, unforeseen circumstances, even (as they'd discovered) tragedy — was limited. Her instinctive reaction was always the same, to seek someone to blame, lash out at whoever was nearest.

'She'll try that with me once and once only,' he said, pugnaciously. 'I'm not having any of that. I'll tell her. It was her that caused all this mess in the beginning. I'm not having her turn on my Philippa.'

'Tony,' said Tessa, surprised at her own patience, 'really? You were the one who married and dumped her, remember.'

'I thought Phil had explained that to you.'

'She didn't leave me thinking you were blameless.'

'I know.' He sighed. 'I can't explain why. I mean, I can, but you wouldn't believe me. We have such a passionate relationship, Phil and me.'

Tessa could well believe it. Every one of the four sisters and their parents was, when pushed, volatile. Admittedly, some took less pushing than others and she could see that Tony, who was full of ideas and energy and passion for everything, would embrace everything enthusiastically, to a fault. These days he might have learned the lessons of maturity and acquired a degree of caution along the way, but she could see how he might act on impulse. 'I'm sure.'

'I was an idiot. It was always Phil for me, the only one ever, but we had that massive fallout and I was so angry. She said she didn't want to have anything to do with me and I was so mad. I thought if I had a fling with Suzanne she'd get jealous, but I got carried away and…well. When I look back I don't feel very proud of myself. But it was a long time ago and I daresay I don't remember the details. Only that it wasn't ever going to work between me and Suzanne and if we'd stayed together one of us would have killed the other in no time.'

Tessa winced. There was too much killing for her to appreciate flippancy about it. 'Please don't say that.'

'No, I'm sorry.' He sat back, his face filling with regret as quickly as it had filled with irritation. 'That was clumsy of me. I didn't realise what a mess this would turn out to be when I came here. In my business I think everything through, but in my personal life I'm ruled by my heart.'

'That's not a good idea, around here.'

'I see that now. But I'm glad to bump into you anyway.'

'You're hardly bumping into me. I work here.' For the moment, at least.

'I wanted to have a word with you, and now it's opportune. It was about your share of the business.'

She ought to send him away, tell him it was too soon, chastise him for being precipitate and insensitive, but these things needed to be tackled at some point, and the future of the Three Sisters wouldn't cease to be a running sore just because Hazel was dead. 'Yes, I suppose it is opportune.'

'You know what I'm going to say, I think.'

'Yes.' She reached into the box of pastels and tried a different colour. The sky was changing so quickly. She laid a slash of crimson over the scarlet already there and was pleased with the result, though it bore no relation to what lay along the horizon. 'I expect you're going to offer to buy my share of the business. Which will be half of the business, in effect, because Hazel's will be split between Sue and me.'

'That was the plan, yes. And I will make you a very generous offer'

'And what do you think Sue would say to that?'

'Does she have any say in your life?' he countered.

She did — way too much — but Tessa had little option but to sell. Her dreams of doing something creative with the place had died with Leo and the only alternative future was a constant war with Sue, who would either work until she dropped or else would retire and continue to meddle from a distance, just as their mother had done. Neither of those options was palatable. 'I don't think she'll like it.'

'I understand.'

'And obviously, nothing can be sorted immediately because of…of the will and everything.'

'I understand that too.'

'But yes. I'll sell.' He would be bound to put it in Pip's name. Tessa allowed herself a wry smile at the thought that her oldest and youngest sisters would become joint owners of the Three Sisters, partners in the business that had gripped the family like a curse and facilitated by the man who had been married to both of them.

'Shake on it,' he said, and they shook hands and smiled at one another. Relief washed over her at how simply the decision had been taken and the problem solved, but it was short-lived. A sudden scraping noise caused her to turn.

There was someone else in the building.

She turned inquiringly. 'Sue?'

Suzanne wrenched the door open.

Oh God. Now there would be a row and more shouting. Tessa couldn't bear it. 'Sue, Tony just came by for a chat.' She placed a warning hand on his sleeve, as if he was the kind of man who could be restrained from a confrontation.

But there was no confrontation. Suzanne slammed the door and before either of them realised what she was doing there was the rattling sound of a bolt and a scraping as something — the desk, almost certainly — was dragged across it.

She ran across the room and tackled that quaint, cursed door that opened outwards instead of inwards because their father had failed to solve the practical problems that the building's quirky structure had posed, but it was in vain. The door remained firm and Tony and Tessa were trapped.

THIRTY-ONE

'Interesting,' said Jude, in a low voice, once they were out in that long, muffled corridor between the flat and the reception and he was sure they couldn't be overheard, 'didn't you think?'

'Definitely. I'd never really thought Philippa was in the frame—'

'We didn't know about her connections with the Walsh sisters, to be fair. If we had done I might have considered her more closely to begin with. But no. I don't think it was her.' Especially not if they could verify where she had been for at least part of the time frame in which Hazel and Leo had died.'

'No, if for no other reason than if she was going to kill anyone it would probably have been Suzanne or Tony, both of whom...' Ashleigh paused and took a quick look around as they emerged into the reception, but it was empty. Wherever Tony was, he wasn't lurking behind the flower arrangements and listening in. '...as far as I'm aware, are still very much with us. But Tony himself is a different matter.'

'Very.'

Things hadn't looked great for Tony beforehand and though Jude's natural instincts had warned him that the man wasn't guilty there was additional evidence against him now — not least, the high probability that he'd had access to the weapon that had killed Hazel and Leo. He shook his head. Something about it still felt wrong.

'Making himself obvious like that on the day Sophie died really troubles me.' They stepped out onto the front of the hotel. 'What was that about?'

'I'm going to guess,' said Ashleigh, 'that he wanted to make sure Suzanne knew not only that he was there but that he was married to her sister.'

It was the obvious explanation, and the impact on Suzanne was obvious, too: she'd been furious. 'And now she says she wants to talk to Philippa and he persuades his wife not to go but he goes down there instead.'

'Knowing Suzanne will be there on her own.'

'Jesus,' Ashleigh said. 'Do you think he's going to take it out on her? Do you think she was the ultimate target after all? Is it really possible that he went to the lengths of buying the Ullswater Falls, letting her know Philippa's there, taunting her with an offer she can't refuse but doesn't want to accept? Really?'

'Yes, it's good so far, isn't it?' They'd hesitated on the terrace for a second, knowing the quickest way back to the car was along the drive, but the Three Sisters was exerting a pull on him. The answer was there. He strode down the hill towards it, into the gathering gloom with Ashleigh hurrying to keep pace. 'But that was before people started dying. That raises the stakes. If he gets caught he doesn't get his revenge. He loses everything. If he can't afford to get caught then either he doesn't take that risky strategy, or he keeps killing to try and get ahead of it.' And yet somehow Tony, who described himself as opportunistic, was in no way reckless. His business career showed he knew when to gamble and when to stop. His relationship with Suzanne had showed he knew when to cut his losses.

'Slow down,' said Ashleigh, losing ground on him. 'I'd like to have enough breath to talk to him when we get there. If he's there.'

He slowed, to allow her to catch up with him. 'He had no reason to kill Sophie, but he might have mistaken her for Suzanne. Unlucky for her, and bad news for him when he found out.'

'It would answer the question of why he couldn't keep away. Like a dog returning to his vomit, as the good book says.'

If he had killed the wrong person, he would surely have been thrown into a state of heightened anxiety. 'Exactly. He'd have a murder on his conscience, if he has a conscience, and nothing positive to show for it. And at a stretch I can understand why he might have killed Hazel, if he thought Suzanne had leaned on her to stop her selling. The problem with that is that Hazel had said she'd sell. I could understand it if it was Tessa. She'd also refused. But Hazel was willing to sell. That's one of two things that makes me think it wasn't him.'

'He had access to the carbon monoxide.'

He glanced back up the hill. The builders had gone. The shed, at the back, was in darkness and not overlooked. 'Anybody had access to the carbon monoxide. The lock on that door just needs one blow of a hammer, and it won't even be locked during the day. And the other thing that gets me thinking is that the gas can only have been vented into the building from the storage area underneath. And it's locked. Tony wouldn't have the key.' And the vent had

270

been the wrong way round. 'Time to take action I think.' Because now he was sure who the killer was.

He got out his phone and stood while the fragile signal kicked in, while the phone rang, while the evening got ever darker and the last of the light disappeared. 'Doddsy, can you sort something for me?'

'Made a breakthrough, have you?' asked Doddsy, with interest.

'I think so.' Briefly he outlined what they'd learned from Philippa. 'I'll check with the hotel guest — whose name she doesn't know but Tony surely will, and if he doesn't we can find out. But if the timings aren't right then we can realistically rule her and Tessa and Tony out and that only leaves one possibility. Suzanne Walsh.'

'You'll want a warrant to search her flat, then?'

'I think so. Her car, too.'

'What am I looking for?'

'Anything that might be relevant. Specifically, you might want to look for a length of hosepipe or other flexible tubing that could be used to connect a canister of industrial carbon monoxide or equivalent to an outlet. Duct tape, too. That's probably what she'll have used. And I'd like you to get on to the dump and see if her car was picked up there on CCTV at any time since Hazel's death.'

'Want me to pull her in?'

'Not just now. She won't go anywhere, and Ashleigh and I are on our way down to the Three Sisters right now. If you don't find an empty canister of carbon monoxide at her flat or at the dump, I'm pretty certain you'll find one with her dabs on it among the builders' supplies up at the Ullswater Falls.' He rang off. 'I should have seen it straight away. Of course it had to be Suzanne. We just need to prove it.' The fact that the gas was readily available at the

Ullswater Falls and had almost certainly come from there didn't mean Tony had been the one to acquire it. Suzanne, who was good with her hands and did routine maintenance around the place, would have had plenty of opportunity. 'She'll have nipped up there and brought it down.'

'She was certainly strong enough. And if she did it at night then it didn't matter if it took her a while.' He lingered for a moment, tempted to poke around in the shrubbery and see if there were other marks that proved his theory, but that would wait. 'And I'll tell you the other thing I should have worked out?'

'I think I can tell you that.' Ashleigh walked on ahead of him. 'It's Leo, isn't it?'

'Yes. Who killed him and why? I get the impression that Tony and Leo disliked each other, in a testosterone-fuelled kind of way, but Leo wasn't a threat to him, as far as I'm aware, in any way. Why did Leo agree to have a massage with Hazel when he always had one with Tessa? Who changed the appointment? And how did whoever killed them know that Hazel would offer to do the massage and that Leo would agree, or that Leo would ask and Hazel agree? Tony couldn't have done it. That was the one thing that never made sense to me, and now I know the answer.'

They had reached the bottom of the hill by now, and he cast another look back at the shrubbery, but discretion prevailed. They paused, by mutual consent, at a discreet distance from the gate to allow a woman and a bouncy border collie to pass along the path and sneak a curious glance at the now-notorious Three Sisters as she did so.

'Well?' asked Ashleigh. 'What is it?'

'It never happened. Hazel didn't offer a massage. Leo didn't ask.' So many things had bothered him about that, but the key was in front of him, all the time — the spilled cup of coffee on the table. 'We know Leo got a message from the Three Sisters about changing the appointment time and we know it was a trick.' Something that could realistically only have been done by Tessa who wouldn't need to, Hazel who was dead, or Suzanne. 'He fell for it. It wasn't from Tessa. She'd have messaged him directly.'

'And she was with Pip.'

'Yes, though I suppose you might argue they could have been in it together, but in that case we have no motive, and Philippa was adamant that they have an independent witness for where they were.'

'Tessa might have a motive. She knew Leo was having an affair with Sophie,' objected Ashleigh.

The dog walker loitered, with half an eye on them. There had been too many dodgy goings-on at the Three Sisters. Jude allowed himself an ironic smile at the prospect of a member of the public mistaking them for suspicious characters. It wouldn't be the first time.

'She knew he had affairs,' he said. 'She didn't care. Suzanne sent the message. She claimed to have been off the premises but I bet she wasn't. I bet she was either in the store under the reception area, or waiting nearby. She'll have set up the carbon monoxide trap and there we have it. Hazel and Leo sitting in the reception area waiting for Tessa to arrive and give him his massage.' He could imagine them, sitting there laughing and chatting. 'The carbon monoxide kicks in pretty quickly, you said.'

'A matter of minutes. Yes.'

'It would be quicker if they were in reception and the door to the pods was sealed. They start to feel woozy. Maybe one of them realises what's happening, jumps up, runs to the door, knocking over the coffee…'

'And the door is locked,' said Ashleigh, soberly. 'Yes. I see. But surely they could open the windows?'

The windows in the reception area, Jude remembered, didn't open. 'The windows are stiff and they were locked. They could try and open them, of course, but by then it was probably too late. With the concentration of carbon monoxide pumped in from that canister, they would both have passed out within minutes. And at that point, when they were either dead or unconscious and in a fairly serious state, Suzanne would have opened up the doors to let some air in, waited until it was safe for her but too late for them and — this is the crucial bit — managed to manoeuvre both of them into the pod.' She was a strong woman and Hazel wasn't big. 'Leo might have been a bit more of a challenge, but she overcame it. Got him onto the bench, undressed him and folded his clothes, lit the aromatherapy candles, lit the gas heater in reception, closed the door and left. Taking her canister of gas and a length of hose with her.' He looked at her. 'How does that sound?'

'Plausible,' she said cautiously as the dog walker gave up and ambled slowly along the path, fading into darkness at the bend. 'But what about the motive?'

'For Sophie, I think we'd have to guess, but we know she'd approached Tony — or rather, Philippa — about a job. If Sophie had told Suzanne about that, I imagine she would have felt a strong sense of betrayal, on top of every-thing else. As for the other two, I'd say it was clear. Hazel wanted to sell, and Leo was prepared to give Tessa the money to buy her out.'

'Right.' Ashleigh lifted the rickety gate and stopped, suddenly. 'Look.'

He looked along towards the Three Sisters. A figure moved inside, emerged, muffled in coat and scarf, but he recognised Suzanne. She turned to lock the door and then hurried across the car park towards the path, head down.

'Ms Walsh!' he called, wrestling with the gate. 'Jude Satterthwaite here, from the police. We'd like a word.'

She broke into a run. He gave the gate a shove and ran after her.

'Stop!' he shouted at her. 'Police!'

She rounded the bend, out of sight and a good twenty yards ahead of them, but the path wasn't empty. A dog broke into frenzied barking.

'Watch where you're going!' yelled a woman's voice.

Jude and Ashleigh rounded the bend. On the narrow path, perilously close to tumbling six feet or so into the chilly waters of the lake, Suzanne, the dog walker and the collie sprawled in a tangled heap on the floor.

'Suzanne Walsh,' said Jude, tersely, leaning down and putting a firm hand on her shoulder. 'You're under arrest for the murders of Sophie Hayes, Hazel Walsh and Leo Pascoe.' He groped in his pocket for handcuffs, and with Ashleigh's help he cuffed Suzanne's hands behind her back.

'Blimey!' said the dog walker, agape.

Suzanne slumped down, her back against the spindly trunk of an alder that clung to the steep bank. He face was blank and white, as if all the life had gone out of it. 'I don't care. I did do it. They deserved it. Without the Three Sisters there was nothing left. I'd have nothing to live for and they wanted to take it away. It doesn't matter now. You think you're in time but you're not. It's too late.'

'Too late?' Jude's blood chilled.

'I've got them all. All except that bitch Pip, but she'll wish she was dead when she finds out about her husband.'

'What?' Jude said to her sharply. 'What have you done?'

'Tony was at the Three Sisters,' said Ashleigh, breathlessly. 'Wasn't he?'

Suzanne had locked the door, and he'd noticed that there were lights on. 'Where are your keys?'

Suzanne spat. Ashleigh reached down and grabbed her handbag, tipping it up on the path. A set of keys, labelled, skidded a yard away.

Jude snatched them up and sprinted back down the path back to the Three Sisters. He noticed the smell first — the thick, sickly smell of essential oils and white smoke seeped out under the door of the spa.

'Jude! For God's sake be careful!' said Ashleigh, behind him.

'Tony's in there.' They couldn't leave him. God knew what Suzanne had done to him but if she hadn't killed him he might still be saved.

He wrestled the door open and stood back in case a fireball came billowing out towards them, but nothing came. The inside of the spa was thick with smoke and, under the huge of fresh air, a line of flame licked across the floor.

'Help!' cried a choking voice. A woman's. Tessa. Taking a lungful of air and cramming his arm over his face, Jude crashed in through the reception. With his arm pressed against his nose and mouth he headed across to the door to the pods. The reception desk stood in front of it and from behind came a desperate pounding on the solid door.

Ashleigh had reached for the fire extinguisher that stood in the lobby and was advancing on the flames. A hiss of foam sent them flaring up but the smoke redoubled, catching at his throat. He turned to the door for a lungful of fresh air and redoubled his efforts on the desk, dragging it away and reaching for the door. 'Dammit. It's locked.'

'Here.' Ashleigh thrust the extinguisher toward him and he and crashed it again the lock. Once, twice, a third time.

The door broke open and Tony and Tessa, coughing and crying, came stumbling out and into the fresh air.

THIRTY-TWO

Two days later, when Suzanne had been charged and Tessa and Tony released from hospital into the care of an anxious Philippa, Jude went in search of Faye. There had been no impropriety on her part, at least as far as he could tell, but you couldn't be too careful in terms of the public's perception. She had absented herself from the office, or at least from the incident room, ever since Leo Pascoe had been found dead and he had omitted her from the briefing notes he sent out on the case.

But he found himself in the unusual position of feeling sorry for her. Her romantic and emotional baggage was, as far as he understood it, complicated and unsatisfactory, blighted by a divorce she bitterly regretted and a broken marriage she had been powerless to save. Knowing this he thought he understood her antagonism, not just towards him but towards everyone with whom she came into contact.

She wasn't so different, in some ways, to Suzanne, though Suzanne's response to her own unhappiness made

Faye's in-office chippiness seem a model of good humour and restraint. If nothing else he owed her an update on what was going on, and if she chose to interpret it as an olive branch of sorts, that was fine, and so he tapped at her door on the way past. 'Evening, Faye.'

She looked up from her computer, said nothing, but waved him in. Her face was set in her usual expression, ready for a scowl, but he sensed there was an element of anxiety behind it.

'I'm heading out off home for a pizza,' he said, as to reassure her that he'd no intention of lingering. Besides, he didn't dare. He was supposed to be meeting Mikey, and he couldn't risk letting him down again. 'But I thought I'd update you on the Three Sisters case on the way out.'

'It's done and dusted, I believe,' she said, looking him up and down, taking into account that he was already in his overcoat, and deciding she could afford to be generous. 'You'd better come in.'

'Yes. Suzanne Walsh has confessed. Three counts of murder, two of attempted murder and a host of other ancillary crimes. The motive, as far as I can understand it, is pretty straightforward. A lifetime of frustration finally got the better of her. Not that that's an excuse.'

'The parents sound a pair of charmers.' Keeping her distance or not, Faye had obviously read the case notes. There was unlikely to be anything he could tell her about it that she didn't already know, but he lingered anyway. Going through the motions, perhaps, but he sensed something about the case had troubled her more deeply than it ought to. Sometimes it happened. Detectives were human — even Faye.

'Yes. It takes a lot of courage to break away from that sort of family set-up. It's easy to get locked into it. Tessa said they'd all thought they were content until their parents died. It was only after they'd gone that they realised what they'd never had.' From there, the descent into blame and recrimination had been inevitable.

'The youngest Ms Walsh sounds the most perceptive of them.'

He nodded. 'I think Philippa Charles is quite smart, too.' Though neither sister was without hangups about the Three Sisters. 'Their parents never forgave Philippa for escaping them and doing her own thing, and Suzanne never forgave her for, as she saw it, stealing her husband.'

'I don't generally subscribe to the view that you can steal someone's affections,' observed Faye, not making eye contact. 'All's fair in love, to a degree. And the fact that he was her sister's partner beforehand makes me feel a little less sorry for Suzanne and not altogether admiring of Mr Charles.'

That was true enough. 'It's a love match between him and Philippa, I think. They still seem very happy together after twenty years. But that's not what seems to have tripped all this off. It was the spa.'

'I mean, really,' said Faye, with a degree of contempt. 'A building?'

'It's what the building represented, to all of them. After her parents died Suzanne felt she had to hold everything together. For their sake, she said although I think it was because she was terrified of what the future held for her when it was gone.' No partner, little money, no meaningful relationships other than the love-hate battle with two sisters who were increasingly desperate to get away. 'At the same time, Philippa really resented the fact that her family, with the honourable exception of Tessa, had cut her off completely. That was where it all started. Tony knew it and saw the opportunity to come back and buy the spa. It didn't matter whether it was part of the hotel, or whether she was the major shareholder. It didn't even matter that she might not have wanted to take an active part in running it. His grand gesture of love was to move heaven and earth to let her have it entirely at her disposal.' Although, as it had turned out, Philippa had never wanted it.

Faye pushed her chair back. Her face looked blank under the artificial lights. 'Bizarre.'

'I'm starting to suspect that there are a lot of suppressed passions in the Walsh family. And the people they attracted.'

She shifted a little in her seat. 'Where does Sophie fit into this?'

'Tony had worked out that Sophie was the one Suzanne was prepared to listen to.'

'He lied to us about it.' For Faye, that was inexcusable.

'It was a spur of the moment lie, I think, to cover his back regarding Sophie's death, but Philippa let the truth slip. He'd had quite the chat with Sophie when she came up to ask about a job. He asked her to sound out Suzanne about how prepared she was to sell the spa. Suzanne says that when she told Sophie she wasn't interested, even though at that time she didn't realise who the prospective buyer was, Sophie had told her Tony would probably be opening up a spa of his own and she'd be more than open to working for him.' Without knowing the history, Sophie had stepped onto dangerous ground and had paid the price.

'And then?'

'Tony decided to show his hand and appear at the Three Sisters. That's what he was doing when he appeared the day after Sophie died — letting Suzanne know that he was there and sending a clear message that he'd put the Three Sisters out of business.' Suzanne hadn't known about Philippa, then. 'Then he made them the offer for the business and Suzanne turned it down — as did Tessa, which may have saved her life. But Hazel wanted to sell and so Hazel had betrayed her sister and the family. And Hazel had to die, too.'

In a long pause, Faye adjusted the lamp on her desk. 'And what about Leo?'

'Suzanne disliked him, for a variety of reasons, but he was also an obstacle to the business. Tessa's offer to buy the place out was a threat to the Three Sisters, but it depended on Leo funding it. Without Leo, who Suzanne was happy to have out of the way anyway, Tessa would have to stay and the business would continue, albeit with just the two of them. And, ironically, it would probably have been more of a success, because there would only have been two salaries to pay and they might — just — have been able to keep it solvent.'

'Did she plan it?' she asked. 'I can see Sophie's murder might have been on the spur of the moment, but the business with the carbon monoxide can't have been.'

'She did, which isn't to say she didn't take her opportunities. She spotted the carbon monoxide up at the hotel and crept back up and managed to get it down to the hotel. She knew the alarm wasn't working and she'd told Tessa that she'd get it fixed. She's good with her hands; she managed to reverse the vent from the reception area into the store and seal up the other external vents, then set the place up as a death trap. Leo had a massage with Tessa every week, and Suzanne changed the time of it. Piped the stuff in and then after they were dead she unblocked the vents and set the place up to look as if there had been an accident.' They'd found the evidence to confirm both his theory and Suzanne's confession, and the empty canister had been discovered concealed in the depths of the shrubbery. 'To a degree she was unlucky. If there had been a fault in the gas heater we'd have struggled to prove the two deaths were anything other than an accident.'

'I see.' Faye pinched her lips together. 'So Leo was just collateral damage, then.'

'Effectively.' He paused. 'I'm sorry, Faye. I know you liked him.' As if he were talking to his teenage daughter, not his boss.

Her look flashed irritation at him, but it was momentary. 'Yes, I did like him. We had dinner once and drinks once. I didn't know he was a womaniser at that point, though I expect I would have found out soon enough.'

'I understand why you didn't want to get too close to the investigation,' he said, holding the olive branch out further.

'We all need love, Jude, don't we? Or an approximation of it.'

'Approximation is about as close as it gets, in many cases.'

There was a silence in which he thought, and she must surely have thought too, about the relationship Faye had had with Ashleigh some years before, in the wreckage of both their marriages. You could go looking for love all you wanted but you could never guarantee you'd find it. He spared a thought for Becca, too. When you did find love, as they had, it didn't always last.

'I'm sorry about him.' he said, again.

'Nothing we can do about it. The less said the better.' She pushed her chair back to her desk again. 'You can include me in all your full briefing notes from now on. I take it Tony and Tessa are all right?'

'Yes, they were fine. Suzanne had planned the previous murders but this was very much a spur of the moment thing. She'd intended to lure Philippa down and deal with her.'

'Is the woman mad?' said Faye with a sigh. 'As you say, she might have had a good chance of getting away with the others but there's no way she wouldn't have been caught for this.'

'I think she knew that, but she was beyond reason at that point. She'd killed three times and she didn't care how many more people died as long as she got revenge over her sister. Fortunately for Philippa Tony guessed there was something up and went down to see what was going on. It was pure chance Tessa had gone there.'

And by then, Suzanne's mind had truly unravelled. She hadn't given it a thought, and locking the two of them in and setting the fire had been a doomed attempt at ending everything. With only the contents of the Three Sisters at her disposal she hadn't been able to do more than create a smother that had been easily extinguished. 'The two of them didn't even suffer too much from the smoke. They managed to break a window. Scared as hell, of course, because they didn't know what was going on behind that door and they could see themselves trapped in there and going up in flames. But they were never in any real danger.'

'And you?'

'Ashleigh and I were fine, too.' He backed away. 'I'll see you.'

'Enjoy your evening.'

He might offer to pick Mikey up and take the opportunity to drop in and see Becca, to tell her how Kirsty's adventure at the Three Sisters had ended. Then a drink and a pizza; their mother could play taxi driver for Mikey and Jude himself was in with a chance of an early night. He allowed himself a smile.

'Jude! Is that where you got to?' Behind him, brisk foot-steps came down the corridor.

He turned. Ashleigh was half-running towards him.

'Is there a problem?' He knew there was. That was his quiet evening, going up in smoke.

'There sure is. I just had a call. The Three Sisters is on fire.'

'Arson,' said one of the firefighters who was standing in the car park taking charge while his colleagues pumped water from the lake into the burning roof of the Three Sisters, 'or I'm a Dutchman.'

'Was there anyone inside?' asked Jude, though he was sure of the answer. The spa had been locked up; Suzanne was in custody; Tony, Philippa and Tessa were safe at the Ullswater Falls. There was no-one associated with the Three Sisters who could be harmed by its destruction.

'I don't think so.' The man wiped a gauntleted hand across his brow, dripping with sweat in the heat from the fire. 'Looks like pure vandalism from where I'm standing. Someone knew the place was empty and couldn't resist the firework display, I suppose. I know kids get bored but they give us a hell of a lot of trouble.'

At least there was some good news. When he'd heard about the fire Jude had feared the worst, but now he was already turning to the next task, of finding the culprit. The place was well ablaze now, flames leaping through its roof and from the basement of the building. The cracked glass doors opened onto a backdrop of flame and from where he stood he could see that the glass had fallen from the black-ened windows of the pods. Heat seared his face. Whoever had torched it had done a far better job than Suzanne.

JO ALLEN

'Looks like a proper effort,' he said, turning to Ashleigh.

'Yes, and I think I know who did it.'

He did, too. 'Let's go and see if you're right. If you are, they won't be far away.'

The route along the lake shore was closed off, though a knot of interested onlookers had gathered at the point where Charlie Fry stood, arms firmly folded across his broad chest. Jude and Ashleigh had made it a few yards beyond him, but no further; the intense heat would have held them back if the fire brigade hadn't.

'We'll have to go round via the main entrance.' She nodded towards the path, where the obvious route, through the gate and up to the Ullswater Falls, was blocked.

'No need.' Beyond the onlookers, Jude saw a gap in the fence and squeezed through it, through a thicket of rhododendrons and into the shrubbery. He looked up the hill. Yes; up on the slope two figures stood huddled together looking down towards the lake.

With Ashleigh beside him, he made his way up the hill towards them. 'Ms Walsh? Mrs Charles?'

Philippa turned first; her face was blank. 'Yes?'

'Jude Satterthwaite' he said, to remind her. 'Police.'

'Yes, of course.' She nudged Tessa. 'You lot don't waste your time, I'll say that for you.'

She turned back to the fire, as if fascinated. A roar came up to them from the burning building, a deep, painful groan like the death throes of a wounded lion. A second later the roof caved in, sending a pillar of flame to scorch a dramatic stripe of light across Ullswater, a violent palette augmented by blue flashing lights.

'There,' said Tessa. Tears, grimy with soot, streamed down her face. 'It's gone.'

'You made a good job of it,' said Ashleigh, gently, 'didn't you?'

'It's not a crime,' said Tessa. 'I own it. Half of it, anyway. It's not like we're going to claim on the insurance. And if you do charge us I don't care, since I'm in trouble for that bloody carbon monoxide alarm anyway.' She dabbed at her eyes with the back of her hand.

Jude let that minor point go. If there was any justice the health and safety people would go softly on Tessa. Suzanne still owned half of the business and she was the one who'd deliberately failed to fix the alarm. 'Why did you do it? Why now?' But he knew. The Three Sisters was only a building but it was ill-omened and symbolic.

'It ruined us.' Tessa put her arm around Philippa. 'It killed three people. It kept us apart. It broke us all. Even Sue. She was all right once. No-one will use that place again, but at last it's all over.'

Jude's phone pinged. Mikey. *Where the hell are you?* He took a moment to snap a quick reply. *Running late. But I'll be there.*

When he turned back, Tessa and Philippa were clinging together like babes in the wood. He shifted a little closer to Ashleigh and the four of them stood on the winter hillside and watched as the toxic legacy of the Walsh family met its end and the Three Sisters imploded in a fizzing, roaring, dancing hell.

THE END

ALSO BY JO ALLEN

Death by Dark Waters
DCI Jude Satterthwaite #1
It's high summer, and the Lakes are in the midst of an
unrelenting heatwave. Uncontrollable fell fires are breaking
out across the moors faster than they can be extinguished.
When firefighters uncover the body of a dead child at the
heart of the latest blaze, Detective Chief Inspector Jude
Satterthwaite's arson investigation turns to one of murder.
Jude was born and bred in the Lake District. He knows
everyone — and everyone knows him. Except his
intriguing new Detective Sergeant, Ashleigh O'Halloran,
who is running from a dangerous past and has secrets of
her own to hide. Temperatures — and tensions — are
increasing, and with the body count rising Jude and his
team race against the clock to catch the killer before it's too
late…
The first in the gripping, Lake District-set, DCI Jude
Satterthwaite series.

Death at Eden's End

DCI Jude Satterthwaite #2

When one-hundred-year-old Violet Ross is found dead at Eden's End, a luxury care home hidden in a secluded nook of Cumbria's Eden Valley, it's not unexpected. Except for the instantly recognisable look in her lifeless eyes — that of pure terror. DCI Jude Satterthwaite heads up the investigation, but as the deaths start to mount up it's clear that he and DS Ashleigh O'Halloran need to uncover a long-buried secret before the killer strikes again...

The second in the unmissable, Lake District-set, DCI Jude Satterthwaite series.

Death on Coffin Lane
DCI Jude Satterthwaite #3

DCI Jude Satterthwaite doesn't get off to a great start with resentful Cody Wilder, who's visiting Grasmere to present her latest research on Wordsworth. With some of the villagers unhappy about her visit, it's up to DCI Satterthwaite to protect her — especially when her assistant is found hanging in the kitchen of their shared cottage.

With a constant flock of tourists and the local hippies welcoming in all who cross their paths, Jude's home in the Lake District isn't short of strangers. But with the ability to make enemies wherever she goes, the violence that follows in Cody's wake leads DCI Satterthwaite's investigation down the hidden paths of those he knows, and those he never knew even existed.

A third mystery for DCI Jude Satterthwaite to solve, in this gripping novel by best-seller Jo Allen.

Death at Rainbow Cottage
DCI Jude Satterthwaite #4

At the end of the rainbow, a man lies dead.

The apparently motiveless murder of a man outside the home of controversial equalities activist Claud Blackwell and his neurotic wife, Natalie, is shocking enough for a peaceful local community. When it's followed by another apparently random killing immediately outside Claud's office, DCI Jude Satterthwaite has his work cut out. Is Claud the killer, or the intended victim?

To add to Jude's problems, the arrival of a hostile new boss causes complications at work, and when a threatening note arrives at the police headquarters, he has real cause to fear for the safety of his friends and colleagues...

A traditional British detective novel set in Cumbria.

Death on the Lake
DCI Jude Satterthwaite #5

Three youngsters, out for a good time. Vodka and the wrong sort of coke. What could possibly go wrong? When a young woman, Summer Raine, is found drowned, apparently accidentally, after an afternoon spent drinking on a boat on Ullswater, DCI Jude Satterthwaite is deeply concerned — more so when his boss refuses to let him investigate the matter any further to avoid compromising a fraud case.

But a sinister shadow lingers over the dale and one accidental death is followed by another and then by a violent murder. Jude's life is complicated enough but the latest series of murders are personal to him as they involve his former partner, Becca Reid, who has family connections in the area. His determination to uncover the killer brings him into direct conflict with his boss — and ultimately places both him and his colleague and girlfriend, Ashleigh O'Halloran, in danger...

Death in the Woods

DCI Jude Satterthwaite #6

A series of copycat suicides, prompted by a mysterious online blogger, causes DCI Jude Satterthwaite more problems than usual, intensifying his concerns about his troublesome younger brother, Mikey. Along with his partner, Ashleigh O'Halloran, and a local psychiatrist, Vanessa Wood, Jude struggles to find the identity of the malicious troll gaslighting young people to their deaths. The investigation stirs grievances both old and new. What is the connection with the hippies camped near the Long Meg stone circle? Could these suicides have any connection with a decades-old cold case? And, for Jude, the most crucial question of all: is it personal, and could Mikey be the final target?

Death in the Mist
DCI Jude Satterthwaite #7

A drowned man. A missing teenager. A deadly secret. When Emmy Leach discovers the body of a drug addict, wrapped in a tent and submerged in the icy waters of a Cumbrian tarn, she causes more than one problem for investigating officer DCI Jude Satterthwaite. Not only does the discovery revive his first, unsolved, case, but the case reveals Emmy's complicated past and opens old wounds on the personal front, regarding Jude's relationship with his colleague and former partner, Ashleigh O'Halloran.

As Jude and his team unpick an old story, it becomes increasingly clear that Emmy is in danger. What secrets are she and her controlling husband hiding, from the police and from each other? What connection does the dead man have with a recently-busted network of drug dealers? And, as the net closes in on the killer, can Jude and Ashleigh solve a murder — and prevent another?

Death on a Monday Night
DCI Jude Satterthwaite #8
An ex-convict. A dead body. A Women's Institute meeting
like no other...
It's an unusually challenging meeting at the Wasby
Women's Institute, with local resident and former drug-
dealer Adam Fleetwood talking about his crimes and
subsequent rehabilitation...but events take a gruesome
turn when prospective member Grace Thoresby is
discovered murdered in the kitchen.
The case is particularly unwelcome for investigating officer
DCI Jude Satterthwaite. Adam was once his close friend
and now holds a bitter grudge, blaming Jude for landing
him in jail in the first place. To complicate things further,
the only thing keeping Adam from arrest is the testimony
of Jude's former girlfriend, Becca Reid, for whom he still
cares deeply.
As Jude and his colleague and current partner, Ashleigh
O'Halloran, try to pick apart the complicated tapestry of
Grace's life, they uncover a web of fantasy, bitterness and
deceit. Adam is deeply implicated, but is he guilty or is
someone determined to frame him for Grace's murder?
And as they close in on the truth, Jude falls foul of Adam's
desire for revenge, with near-fatal consequences...
A traditional detective mystery set in Cumbria.

Death on the Crags
DCI Jude Satterthwaite #9
Everybody loves Thomas Davies. Don't they?
When policeman Thomas falls from a crag on a visit to the
Lake District in full view of his partner, Mia, it looks for all
the world like a terrible but unfortunate accident — until a
second witness comes forward with a different story.
Alerted to the incident, DCI Jude Satterthwaite is inclined

to take it seriously — not least because of Mia's reluctance to speak to the police about the incident. As Jude and his colleagues, including his on-off partner DS Ashleigh O'Halloran, tackle the case, they're astonished by how many people seem to have a reason to want all-round good guy Thomas out of the way.

With the arrival of one of Thomas's colleagues to assist the local force, the investigation intensifies. As the team unpick the complicated lives of those who claim to care for Thomas but have good reasons to want him dead, they find themselves digging deeper and deeper into a web of blackmail and cruelty ... and investigating a second death.

A traditional British police procedural mystery set in Cumbria.

Written as Jennifer Young
Jo writes romance and romantic suspense under the name of Jennifer Young.

Blank Space
Dangerous Friends Book 1
He's made a lot of enemies. She has some dangerous friends.
Bronte O'Hara is trying to move on from her ex-boyfriend, Eden Mayhew, but when she finds an injured man in her kitchen in the run-up to an international political summit in Edinburgh, a world she thought she'd left behind catches up with her with a vengeance.

Eden's an anarchist, up to his neck in any trouble around — and he's missing. The police are keen to find him, certain that he'll come back, and that when he does, he'll have Bronte in his sights. What does he want from her — and does she dare trust a handsome stranger with her life? With danger and romance in equal measure, Blank Space

is a contemporary take on the romantic suspense tradition
pioneered by Mary Stewart.

After Eden
Dangerous Friends Book 2
In the aftermath of a violent G8 summit when she almost
lost her life, Bronte O'Hara finds herself fighting against
her feelings for Marcus Fleming, the policeman who saved
her. When Marcus is cleared of any wrongdoing over the
deaths of three people during the undercover police
operation, Bronte isn't the only one who struggles to come
to terms with the outcome. The friends and relatives of
those who died are determined not to let the matter rest,
whatever the cost. Some are looking for closure; some want
justice. And someone is determined to use Bronte in a bid
to gain revenge...

Storm Child
Dangerous Friends Book 3
Scotland can be a dangerous place.
When their car comes off the road in a blizzard, Bronte
O'Hara and her boyfriend, detective Marcus Fleming,
stumble across an unconscious teenager in the snow. After
he's rescued by two passing strangers, the boy simply
disappears, and even Marcus's police colleagues don't
believe their story — until the youth's body is found.
It looks like the accidental death of a young criminal, but
Bronte and Marcus are convinced that things aren't as
straightforward as they seem. Who was he? What was he
doing out in the storm? Who else might be in danger?

And who will stop at nothing to make sure that Bronte and
Marcus never find out?

Looking For Charlotte

Divorced and lonely, Flora Wilson is distraught when she hears news of the death of little Charlotte Anderson. Charlotte's father killed her and then himself, and although he left a letter with clues to the whereabouts of her grave, his three-year-old daughter still hasn't been found. Flora embarks on a quest to find Charlotte's body to give the child's mother closure, believing that by doing so she can somehow atone for her own failings as a mother. As she hunts in winter through the remote moors of the Scottish Highlands, her obsession comes to threaten everything that's important to her — her job, her friendship with her colleague Philip Metcalfe and her relationships with her three grown up children.

ACKNOWLEDGMENTS

An author doesn't work alone. In writing this series I have had help and support from too many people to name.

For this book, however, I would particularly like to thank Fiona Erskine, who came to my rescue with answers to my many questions about the technical requirements for murder by gas. And of course there are the usual suspects: Graham Bartlett, who kindly advised me on aspects of police procedure; Mary Jayne Baker delivered, as always, a stunning cover; and finally, as before, I owe a huge debt of gratitude to the eagle-eyed Keith Sutherland, for proof-reading.

Thank you to you all!